SCOTT'S CHOICE

SCOTT'S CHOICE

CA SOLE

Helifish Books

Published in 2019 by Helifish Books

ISBN: 978-1-9161108-0-9 (Paperback)
ISBN: 978-1-9161108-1-6 (eBook-ePub)
ISBN: 978-1-9161108-2-3 (eBook-mobi Kindle)

British Library Cataloguing in Publication Data
A CIP catalogue record for this book is available from the British Library

I am sincerely grateful to my wife and editors who have provided valuable input to make this a better book.

Author's Note

The Scott Trilogy is about choice and consequence.

This book should be read first. The two sequels can be read in any order, although it would be best to start with *Nature's Justice*. You will see why when you reach the end of the second sequel, *The Pilot*.

Cuthbert Jonathan Scott is a young man with a dominant adventurous spirit. He grew up being indoctrinated by his father into an approach to life that was completely at odds with his nature: take no risks, caution in everything, settle down while young, save your money, on and on. A random event results in a decisive moment. He is torn between two options: following his father's teaching or being himself.

Two personae emerge. One, Jonathan, begins a life following his natural instincts. His spirit of adventure predominates. His choice has consequences which bring several life-threatening events but also great rewards.

Jonathan's alter ego, Cuff, is the brainwashed youth who tries to adopt the more cautious approach. But his nature conflicts with this and leads him on a dangerous path to escape the mundane existence which was the consequence of his choice. It seems he cannot avoid risk. Indeed, danger appears to seek him out.

* * *

Two independent stories develop in *Scott's Choice*. The tales are linked only by his friends and enemies who continue to influence and react to events in Cuff's life in one way, and in Jonathan's life in another. However, certain events are common to both and fixed in the calendar.

Taking note of the title of each chapter will help the reader identify which of the two independent lives is being related.

1

OCTOBER

He was well built and tall, but for this evening he hunched his shoulders and took short steps. The hood of his jacket was pulled up to cover his distinctive hair. He gave it an extra tug to make sure. Toolbox in hand, he ambled along the row of little aeroplanes between the hedge and the machines. His idea was to present the image of a reluctant engineer who would rather be in the pub than fixing a small problem before the next flight.

It was ten to six one Friday evening in October, and the afternoon's rain had long since given way to a perfectly clear sky. A magnificent blue and orange sunset was reflected in the puddles in the parking area and cast its tint across the airfield. The daylight would last longer than it had in the past week, which served his purpose well.

All flying was over for the day, and the student pilots had secured their aeroplanes before making for the clubhouse. No one would be left outside.

At the far end of the row next to the single hangar was a blue and white Cessna 172, a popular four-seat trainer. When he reached it, the man confirmed he could not be seen from the building. To be more certain, he went round the far side of the aircraft before putting his toolbox down on the concrete. Inside the engine cowling a smell of warm machinery greeted him.

The complexity of pipes and components were just as he expected. He had never seen inside an aircraft engine bay before, and so had spent a great deal of time researching critical items and where they lay.

The aviation fuel in the high wing tanks was fed by gravity to the engine, so there was little pressure in it. He located the line and cut the tube, ignoring the small amount of fuel which escaped; it would evaporate overnight. He then rejoined the line with a piece of plastic tubing from his toolbox, mopped the joint dry with a rag and used a penlight to check for leaks. Taking a construction he had made himself and which he could almost enclose with his fingers, he secured it to the joint.

Someone came running his way with pounding steps. Torch switched off, he retreated a few paces to make his feet and legs less obvious behind the Cessna. There was a scrabbling of a key and the door of the adjacent aeroplane opened. The person was panting. The door thudded shut, the lock was turned and the steps thumped away towards the clubhouse. He relaxed and went back to work.

His next task was to connect his home-made unit to an electrical source with the two wires which came from one end. That done, he tried a variety of keys to open the pilot's door. Selecting the two largest instruments, he removed their securing screws, giving him access to the area behind the panel. He fed a similar, but narrower and shorter, home-made unit through one hole, made sure it was vertical and taped it in place before connecting its two wires to another electrical source.

The job had taken him thirty-five minutes, after which time it was getting dark. He had already set the timers; they only needed an electric current to start running.

A beer was calling him. He closed his toolbox and sauntered back the way he had come, unaware of the young boy watching from the corner of the hangar.

2

CJ Scott at 14

SCHOOL

The thing that caught CJ Scott's attention as he crossed the school courtyard was the new boy, the one who never seemed to stop sniffing. What was his name, Martin something? He was okay, kept to himself – probably a bit shy. He was sitting on a bench, ignoring the rain and staring at something by his feet. The youngster took a sandwich out of his jacket pocket and peeled back the wrapping without taking his eyes off whatever held his attention.

The reason CJ was watching was not because he couldn't see what Martin was absorbed with, but because Barry Castle was heading in the kid's direction followed by his two acolytes, Jeff and Larry. This spelt trouble.

The difference between Martin and Castle could not have been greater. Castle was big for his age, Martin was small. Castle had a great shock of almost-white hair, Martin was ginger with freckles. Castle led a small group of boys who worshipped him, Martin kept to himself. Castle always appeared to be healthy and tough, Martin was weedy and sniffed the whole time. He was harmless. Castle was not.

Castle stamped in the puddle at Martin's feet. The water shot up into the younger boy's face and over his sandwich. CJ's anger rose; he'd seen enough of Castle shoving other kids around this term. The big lad reached out and made to snatch the sandwich. Martin pulled it towards his chest. Thick fingers crushed Martin's slender digits and tore the food away. Castle peeled what was left of the bread apart.

'What's Mummy made for little Ginger Beale today? Ham and greens in healthy brown bread. Bloody pathetic.' He dropped the sandwich in the puddle, and the two hangers-on giggled.

'Leave him alone, Castle.'

'Oh, it's Cuffy Cuthbert.' The sneer was exaggerated. 'Sir Scott rides in to rescue the weed.' Keeping an eye on the new arrival, he stamped on the sandwich, sending another shower over Martin. 'What are you going to do about that, eh?'

Insanity.

No conscious thought drove him. CJ did the most stupid and dangerous thing he could. His body took two quick steps forward and punched up at Castle's face. His voice yelled, 'I'm bloody sick of you.'

The bully stumbled backwards, lost his footing and sat on the ground. The blow could not have hurt, but his eyes were wide, his mouth open.

'No one does that to me.' He was fingering a split lip and his front teeth as he got to his feet. His face tightened. He advanced with an intense glare. 'You little shit.'

CJ came back to earth and retreated. He swallowed, there was no way he could defeat Castle. He could run for it, but felt anchored to the ground. Still facing the bully, he stepped back again, waiting for it, for it was going to come. Larry, or was it Jeff, stuck out a foot. CJ fell backwards. Castle was on him, a great weight on his chest. The sky vanished. In its place, Castle's torso and grinning face. Behind him the smirks of Larry and Jeff, and one massive fist poised to strike.

It did. It landed on his cheekbone and bashed his head against the ground. Castle pulled it back and held it so CJ could anticipate the next blow. Larry's and Jeff's faces were closer, laughing and egging their idol on.

They chanted together. 'Smash 'im. Smash 'im. Smash 'im.'

The cacophony of other children playing, screaming and laughing died as they circled to watch the fight. A few joined in the chanting, but most kept quiet. They knew Castle and what he could do.

'Go on Barry, give it to 'im.'

'Crush his bloody head.'

CJ squirmed and threshed, desperate to free his arms. He forced them out from under Castle's knees to try and protect his face. The fist descended. Down it came in slow motion, down, down. He closed his eyes and turned away, his arms up to break the force. He failed. It hurt.

The fist was back up again, ready for the next one. It was going to come and more would follow, because that's what Castle did to boys who crossed him.

But it didn't come. Before the acolytes could stop him, little Ginger Beale jumped on Castle and pulled him back. He punched the bully, landing six quick, puny, harmless blows before Larry grabbed him by the collar and yanked him off. But CJ had rolled away out of reach.

Somewhere in the distance the end of break sounded, but that wasn't going to stop Castle finishing this off.

'Stop this now! Castle, Scott – get up. What's going on?'

CJ clambered to his feet and faced Mr Butler. 'Nothing, sir. We were just playing around.'

Castle stood next to him, a head taller. 'Scott pushed me into the puddle, and we were having words about it, sir. No harm done.'

Mr Butler's expression was cold. 'Go and clean your face up and get to class immediately. Both of you – quick.'

Castle glared at Martin. 'You are dead. And you,' he said to CJ, 'had better watch it. This isn't the end, nobody treats me like that.'

'Yeah,' echoed one of the others, 'you'd better watch it.'

CJ ignored him. His face hurt, and his voice sounded distorted. 'Stop playing the big shot, Castle. You only bully kids who are smaller than you. You're a coward. Live with it and leave Beale alone.'

CJ's own words and actions were surprising. All his life to this point, a fear of failure or of making a fool of himself had dictated his response to strangers until he was sure of his ground. Speak up in class unless asked? Never. Voice his opinion in a debate? Not a chance. Approach a person, let alone a group of people he didn't know? Incredibly difficult.

He had no such qualms over his physical abilities, though. That punch had come out of nowhere; no thought had gone into it, only anger. Boosted by that rush of adrenalin, he had been able to snarl his thoughts at the bully.

But the only reason he had got the better of Castle was because he caught him by surprise. The boy was a year older, bigger and stronger, and CJ would have to be careful never to be trapped in a situation he could not control.

Martin caught up with CJ after school. He had to run, and he was panting. 'Thanks, Cuthbert. You didn't have to help, I'm used to it.'

'First, don't call me Cuthbert. It's an awful name my dad insists on. It's stupid. Nobody's used Cuthbert since the Middle Ages, and I have to put up with crap from idiots like Castle. The name's only used in front of my parents, everywhere else I'm called CJ.'

'Thanks, CJ. It's easier than Cuthbert anyway.' Martin sneezed and sniffed.

'It was brave of you to get Castle off me – thanks. You could have been badly hurt.'

'Well, you stuck up for me.'

'Castle's not going to let this go. We'll have to be careful. Don't walk around alone.'

'Yeah.' Martin sniffed again.

'Have you got a permanent cold?'

'No. The doctor says I've got local allergic rhinitis. It makes my eyes itch as well.' He rubbed his nose. 'It's a curse.'

'What were you doing before Castle snatched your lunch? Head down, staring at your feet; it looked odd.'

Martin gave a short laugh. 'You'll think I'm daft, but I like to analyse and calculate things. I was watching the rain add to the puddle at my feet. The pool had expanded a centimetre over seven minutes and forty seconds, and I was busy calculating whether it would fill enough to merge with the one next door before the break ended, which, at that moment, was in three minutes and forty-five seconds.'

'*Gawd*. Do you do that a lot?'

'Pretty much, yeah. Like, if we carry on at this pace, we'll reach the trees in one minute thirty. If we speed up by half a mile an hour, we should get there some ten seconds sooner.'

'We'll time this pace.'

They were walking across the village green towards a line of beech trees. The grass had been mown and was wet, leaving cuttings stuck to their shoes. Martin had his bag slung crosswise from his shoulder, but CJ was swinging his around on its strap. He was lean, yet to fill out and tall for a fourteen year-old, but he was not as tall and heavy as Castle and not as good-looking either.

'My dad chose my names, Mum says. She tried to stop "Cuthbert", but Dad is unbelievably stubborn. He says it means "famous and bright", and he thinks I'll become famous if I stick with the name. I prefer Jonathan, my middle name, but everyone says it's too long: one too many syllables, so CJ came about.

'I can't stand Castle. He's always looking to throw his weight about and pick on someone, but he'll only do it if those other two creeps are there. He's got his little gang, and he rules the school, or thinks he does.'

'Well if he tries to attack you, like he said, I'll come and help again – I will,' Martin said, and sniffed.

CJ laughed, but it was not a scornful sound. 'I'd avoid him if I were you, he's twice your size.'

'I know. Everyone thinks I'm a weed. I'm skinny, and I can't even do ten press-ups. I can run, though; cross-country's great, but I never have enough puff to finish well.'

'You shouldn't let that phase you, you're much brighter than most of us, Castle especially.'

'Yes, I know, and my dad says everyone's got a strength and it's brains that matter most.'

'Does all the teasing worry you? You know, carrot-top and four-eyes and stuff. They're always having a go at you.'

'It used to, but not any more, not really. Dad said I should ignore them and think how much better I am than those idiots. He says a lot of it is jealousy, because we're quite rich, actually.'

'What's he do, your dad?'

'He's a captain on jumbo jets, and he's teaching me to fly.'

Martin's smile was broad and proud, showing large teeth. 'I'm not old enough now, but when I've got my licence I'll take you up if you like.'

'You're on. That'd be great.' CJ ran his free hand through his hair and gave an enthusiastic grin at the idea.

'He owns a Cessna 172. It's only little, four seats, but it's really cool. I wanted to do the same as Dad, but I don't think my eyes are good enough to be an airline pilot. I can still get a Private Pilot's Licence, though. I love the theory of flight. One day I'll be an aeronautical engineer and design aircraft. That's my dream. What are you going to do?'

'My dad's a chemist and owns his own pharmacy.' The fervour left CJ's voice. 'He has dreams of an empire like Boots and assumes I'll take over the company.'

'Sounds like a good future: your own boss, and rich.'

'Sounds bloody boring. He's always banging on about saving money, investing, starting a pension early and so on. You wouldn't believe what a miser he is. We have no luxuries at home at all.'

'Oh.' There wasn't much else Martin could say.

CJ had not spoken like this to anyone before. This sudden need to voice his private frustrations was surprising. He rambled on, 'You've got to be safe. Health and safety this, health and safety that, hold on to the banister, don't trip on the carpet. I mustn't take any risks, think of the future if I'm injured, on and on, blah, blah, blah. When I took up rugby, we had a hell of a row. He refused to let me play, saying it was too risky, until a teacher stepped in and told him what boys need. He's right in a way, I suppose, you've got to save money at some stage, but it's such a boring idea. Right now I crave adventure. I want to climb mountains, fly fighter jets, base jump off high buildings; anything to give me a kick. I want to find the limit of my courage, the point at which I'm too scared to go on.'

Martin pondered that for a while. 'I never thought of testing myself, but I get your point. I'm lucky, my dad's the adventurous sort, but he always weighs up the situation before doing something risky. He'll do some daft and funny things, but not others. I try to do the same. I meant what I said. I'll help you fight Castle if you need me to. I'll end up with a bloody nose, but I'll be so chuffed from being brave enough to take him on, the feeling will last me forever, a lot longer than the bruise.'

And so a friendship was formed, and a mutual enemy made for life.

3

CJ at 17

SCHOOL – SPRING TERM

The sun was shining for a change. It was warm but the grass and the soil beneath were damp. Brenda Scott was going to fuss about the stains to his trousers. CJ Scott didn't care.

He sat cross-legged on the ground outside the ruins of the thirteenth-century abbey doing two things. The first was a direct result of his father's indoctrination: a budget, which he was scribbling into a new notebook he had bought for the purpose. Would he get the sums right? If he didn't he could run up a huge debt, which was scary. His confidence in his physical abilities and most academic subjects evaporated when it came to money. It made him so nervous, he became ultra-cautious when trying to manage it. He was calculating all the expenses he needed to enable him to begin flying with Martin's dad, Terry.

The Boeing 747 captain had promised to start lessons in the summer. CJ received a measly amount for pocket money, which was never going to cover the cost of learning to fly. His grandfather had left him a substantial legacy, but this was only accessible when he reached twenty-one. Would Terry agree to teach him on credit? Martin said he thought he would, asking only for the cost of the aeroplane. If he did, it would be exceptionally generous of him, but it was still going to be a heavy bill to face when CJ reached maturity.

There was no magic formula; no genie was going to come out of the pot at the end of the rainbow, or whatever. He was going to have to manage it by watching the spend and the pace of his lessons. The idea of buying a car could definitely take second place to flying. Of course, the better he was at flying, the fewer lessons there would be and the less money he would owe. He determined to be good, very good.

He put his cautious, finance-minded bowler hat to one side and donned his adventurous helmet. The second reason for his being at the abbey was the more appealing and immediate need to study the wall in front of him. It was the third time he had done this, and he now knew every detail of the crumbling and broken edge. He noted the grey granite stones that he could not possibly dislodge, and he memorised lesser rocks that looked loose and would not hold any weight, or which were covered in slippery moss and should not be relied on for a good grip.

This is a challenge. It has my adrenalin pumping just thinking about it. It's a risk. I could kill myself, Dad, but what is life without risk? Whatever you say, Dad, I'm going to carry on pushing myself, because it's exciting, it fuels me. In any case, I'm planning this to the nth degree, exactly as you would, should you ever decide to do something wild.

Apart from one long stretch to avoid a fragile segment of the wall, the route up looked safe enough.

He collared his friend after school one day. 'Martin, I'm bored. Let's go and climb the abbey wall.'

'Come on, CJ, you know that's not my scene. I'm a genius at physics and maths not a climber. I heard Mr Butler is giving classes, but it's not for me.'

'You need to get out more, Martin. You're talking about the easy stuff he teaches on the climbing wall at the gym with bloody great handholds. That's a good place to start, but he's been taking a few of us to actual rocks; cliffs, although they're not very high. It's great fun, a bit scary, but it's an amazing feeling when you've done it.'

'No thanks. I'll cheer from below, if it helps. Does your dad know?'

'No way! He'd have a fit if he found out. I'm going to miss out on a weekend's climbing up in North Wales with Butler and the guys, thanks to his stupid attitude.'

'You don't like him, do you?'

'I haven't thought about it, he's just there. Actually, I don't care.'

By 11.30 that night both boys had snuck from their homes and met at the gate to the old abbey. CJ wore a climbing helmet, attached to which was an unlit head torch. He had his *kletterschuhe*, his special climbing shoes, in his hand. Using most of his pocket money, he had bought a pair on Mr Butler's recommendation, because they had a good grip and were therefore safer, but they were too tight for walking in.

A couple of ribbons of cloud drifted past a brilliant gibbous moon. An early January breeze chilled the boys when they stopped moving. The wind brought with it a reminder there was a farm further down the valley.

'Whew! The pigs are strong tonight. I wonder how the monks felt as they sang their hallelujahs, taking deep breaths each time?'

'The hallelujahs would have been expelled with greater force.'

Like CJ, Martin wore dark clothes, although his glasses gave him away when they glinted in the moonlight. He was excited about doing something illegal, even though he was not going to be climbing. He was not nervous at all, glad to be there to support his friend and a little uncertain of what he was expected to do.

The highest part of the ruin was the end wall of the high altar, and it was this which attracted CJ. In its day, the elaborate window, when it was filled with stained glass, must have been magnificent, for it was vast. The basic stone arch which formed the window was still intact, however, and the wall ended a short distance above it. Perhaps forty feet of it remained, which didn't seem much, but it was considered unstable and climbing on any part of the National Trust ruin was forbidden. At the base of the wall CJ changed his shoes.

Martin sniffed and rubbed his eyes. 'It looks very loose. What happens if a stone comes out and you fall?'

'I'll be careful. I've been studying it for a while and I reckon I can get on top without bringing it down.'

'And if you do fall?'

CJ laughed. 'You go running like a greyhound for help. When I get to the top, take a couple of photos to prove it, then we'll go home. Make sure you get the window in the picture, and if you can get the moon through the window with me on top, that'll be great.'

The climb was much easier than anything Mr Butler had had him doing, although his fingers soon lost their sense of touch on the icy stone. The only danger was the loose rocks, but he managed to reach the top of the wall without dislodging any.

'The pigs smell stronger up here,' CJ whispered, rubbing the circulation back into his hands.

After a careful look around and a listen for other people, and when the church clock down in the village struck twelve, Martin took photos of CJ silhouetted in the moonlight on the very top with his arms outstretched.

CJ took the first steps of his descent. He knew it was going to be much harder than going up, and he had to be very careful. While ascending, his head torch had pointed at grips he could use. Going down, he realised the beam was almost useless, as the route was in the shadow of his own body. *I didn't reckon on that. Stupid!*

Tentative probes with each foot blindly sought a firm step, although finding holds with his hands was easy. There was still ten feet to go. A stone moved under his fingers as he gripped it. Quickly, he shifted his weight from his right foot to his left for balance. But the stone kept rolling. It thumped as it hit the grass. His other hand was still secure, but the jolt loosened another rock under his foot. He was going to fall. He twisted round, away from the wall, and dropped to the ground.

'Ow. Shit!'

'Are you okay?'

'Ow, it's my ankle. I think it's sprained or broken. Shit, it hurts!'

With Martin as a support, CJ made it home. They stopped a few times to rest, because Martin was struggling with CJ's weight and the fact that he was a good four inches taller. For CJ, hopping for a long time was hard work and punishment enough. *I must learn a lesson from this bloody one-legged journey home; plan it all the way to the very end, or it'll end in tears next time.*

He laughed. 'That was fun, wasn't it? Thanks, Martin.'

'Phew, it was close though. Suppose you had come off higher up?'

'I know, but I didn't.'

Martin was careless. He let the photo of the lone climber on the abbey wall out into the school community. CJ was forewarned of trouble, because Martin had overheard an exchange between the headmaster and Mr Butler.

'I was passing his office and the door was open. He wasn't amused, CJ, and I'm really sorry. He told Butler to interrogate you climbers.' Martin put on a pompous voice. 'Behaviour like this is contrary to the principles of this school, and I will not have one of my students, a) taking such risks while under my charge, and b) carrying out an illegal act, which would be considered vandalism if the abbey had been damaged in the venture. Think, Butler. Think of the school's reputation if the boy had had an accident.'

CJ laughed at the imitation and waited for Butler's questions. He knew the master would think it was him; the others were good climbers, but too law abiding.

It didn't take long before CJ was looking down on the powerful but shorter man who had always treated him with respect and encouraged individualism.

'CJ, somebody climbed the high wall of the abbey, I hear. Any ideas?'

'Yes, I heard about that.' CJ gave one of his innocent smiles; he found the action made him likeable and relaxed people. It lessened the raptor-like effect of his aquiline nose. 'Probably one of the village lads, they're always up to tricks, sir.'

Butler did not respond in kind. His face was set like the granite he loved so much. 'Climbing an unsound structure without protection is stupid, CJ, stupid, and not what I teach. Whatever his assessment of the risk was, it was well off the mark. The Head has threatened to close our little club down. Whoever did it should use their brains in future, don't you think?'

'Yes, sir. I agree entirely.' Mere words. CJ was at once embarrassed and ashamed of himself. He hadn't followed Butler's careful instruction. He had let the man and his whole climbing community, all five of them, down. *That's the second lesson to be learned from this.*

'Cuthbert!'

'Coming, Dad,' he called from the top landing.

Kevin Scott was standing in the kitchen, tapping his foot on the tiled floor. Brenda was drying a teacup. It rattled as her nervous fingers put it down.

Cuthbert was tall, but he would never reach Kevin's six-foot three-inch raw-boned frame. The older Scott had hollow cheeks and the same angular nose as his son, down which he stared at others through thick, horn-rimmed glasses. This effect was authoritarian, and few challenged it, least of all Brenda.

'Yes, Dad?'

Kevin's fierce glare bored into the boy's charming and innocent green eyes. 'Is this you?' He thrust out a photograph.

The silhouette of the man on the high wall of the abbey could have been anyone, and it would have been quite safe for Cuthbert to deny the connection. But his father would have good grounds for accusing him, which was what, in his way, he was doing. Kevin always had a firm base for his arguments.

'Yes.'

'What the devil do you think you were doing? You might have been killed or injured and brought my company into disrepute as soon as it became known my son was a hooligan. It may still come to that, and I'll have to suffer the embarrassment and loss of customers. You can't go around desecrating National Trust property. And pull your sleeves down, for heaven's sake!'

Cuthbert tugged his cuffs back into position. It was pointless to argue – he would get nowhere. Instead, he stood motionless with his head down in a position of submission and listened to Kevin rant on about safety and taking care and his legacy and the future of his company and a stable life, and God knew what else. All the while his mother did her best to maintain her lowest profile at the stove, stirring a pot which did not need mixing and hoping she would not be dragged into the castigation.

Cuthbert switched off, unfazed by these arguments – they had been made so many times before, and they always amounted to nothing. Mr Butler's words had been far more effective. But with his father, the only way out of this was to grovel and apologise. 'I'm sorry, Dad. It was a moment of bravado. I was only doing something exciting for a change. I won't do it or anything like it again.'

It didn't work, the tirade continued until Kevin ran out of steam and stood panting and glaring at his son. 'Your pocket money will be docked for a month.'

Cuthbert lowered his head again. 'Yes Dad. I'm very sorry. Er … How did you get hold of this photo?'

It was a while before his father stopped glowering. 'It was posted through the letter box with this note.'

It was handwritten and anonymous. The writing was distinctive, untidy and entirely in capitals of varying height and width. "THIS IS YOUR SON DESECRATING THE ABBEY. HE'LL BE PROSECUTED IF THE NATIONAL TRUST FIND OUT." Which implied someone might tell them.

Cuthbert knew only one boy in the school who wrote like that. *Bastard!*

4

CJ at 17

SUMMER HOLIDAYS

'CJ, it'll be a pleasure to teach you to fly, but it can't come free. It costs to run an aeroplane,' Terry said.

'Of course, sir.'

'For heaven's sake, if I'm going to be stuck in a cockpit with you for hour after hour, I'm going to get very tired of being called sir. I get enough "sirs" in the airline to make me feel big and important, I don't need any more when I'm trying to relax. Call me Terry.'

'Thanks.' CJ gave him a sheepish smile. 'Sorry, it's a bit of a cheek to ask, but will it be all right if I do it on credit? I get an inheritance when I turn twenty-one. It's a long way off, I know.'

Thanks to Martin, Terry knew this was coming and had already decided what to say. Honesty was clear in the boy's hopeful face. 'Of course you can.'

It was an easy decision, because Terry enjoyed instructing and would have gone flying anyway, but there was another reason: he had always wanted to provide Martin with a brother. Sadly, one never came, so he was pleased to see the friendship develop between the two boys. It did them both good. Martin had become much more confident and outward-looking since CJ entered his life. And, the more he defended his friend, the more self-assured and assertive CJ became in his relations with others.

As an airline captain, Terry was a good judge of character. He had to be, he had to know how to get the best out of the scores of different first officers he had command over. That meant being on reasonable terms with each one of them, even if he didn't like some, yet also ensuring they knew he was the one who took the final decisions.

He knew that CJ had no one to look up to at home, no one to provide him with any guidance in a world which could overwhelm the innocent. Terry did not know Kevin Scott but, from what CJ let slip, the man was self-centred and focused on his business, and any interest he took in his son's success was governed solely by how it could help him, Kevin.

Terry recognised the adventurous spirit in CJ, and it was not going to be quelled by the boy's father. Somehow, he could not imagine CJ in a business role. The lad was not cut out for it. It was going to be interesting to see what he decided to do with his life: follow his father or go his own way.

That CJ took note of Terry's guidance and inspiration was obvious to the older man, and he was glad to help however he could. He curbed some of CJ's wild ideas and encouraged others through a subtle use of Martin as his mouthpiece much of the time, although he suspected CJ was aware the advice came from him.

Not long after CJ had flown solo for the first time, and Martin was approaching that psychological hurdle at a slower pace, Terry drew the boys together. 'Now listen you two. Exam time approaches. Flying stops until after they're over. Your minds must be focused, your futures depend on it. No wishful thinking, no whining – focus. Right? There's plenty of time to fly afterwards.'

Martin pulled a face, and CJ shrugged.

Terry laughed at their expressions. 'Think about it, CJ, your dad won't spot you being dangerous, and your debt won't increase. A double positive.'

* * *

The chief executive swept into the expansive driveway in his Aston Martin DBS Volante convertible, its V12, 5935cc engine pulsing with latent power. He blipped the throttle to hear the raw sound of the thing. He saw it all – the power, the noise, the house and horses – as symbols of all he, on his own, had achieved with good business sense and careful planning and investment.

It was a warm summer afternoon and the top was down. He had dropped off his handsome young son and beautiful daughter at a sleepover party.

He crossed the hall of his mansion and peered into the gym at the back – she wasn't in there, must be at the pool.

Changed and with towel in hand, he approached the drinks trolley at the poolside. Mixing himself a gin and tonic with a few drops of Angostura bitters, he noticed the half-full jug of Pimm's and the empty glass with a lone slice of cucumber stuck to the side. He watched his beautiful wife gliding through the water with a backstroke, her naked breasts like the conning towers of twin submarines carving their own wakes through the water. He smiled in self-satisfaction and stretched out on the sunbed.

A shadow dimmed the red screen of his eyelids. She was standing there in silhouette and gently wiping herself dry with a towel. She moved to straddle him. The dampness of her pubic hair on his upper lip was cool.

CJ woke suddenly. His crotch was sticky and wet.

'Cuthbert, come into the sitting room, I want to talk to you. Brenda, make us some tea will you, please.' Kevin Scott was sitting in his leather wingback chair, which no one else would dare use, with some papers in his hand. More papers were laid in neat piles on the coffee table in front of him.

It was not always easy to tell whether his father was angry or being his usual humourless self. Cuthbert walked over to the couch and took up his allocated position in the lounge.

'Yes, Dad?' He pulled his sleeves halfway up his forearms and slackened his tie. *What's he want now? There's not more fallout from the climb, surely? Or has Castle found something else to report me for?*

'You shouldn't do that. I've told you numerous times, it stretches your jersey and looks sloppy. And either take your tie off or tighten it properly.' Kevin watched to ensure Cuthbert pulled his cuffs down to his wrists. 'Now listen. We need to submit a university application for you. We won't be able to choose Oxford or Cambridge, overall they're too expensive, but the degree standard is the same at the others. You'll be taking a BSc in business management. It's a three-year course, which will set you up to run Pharma-Scott for a long time to come. I need someone with state-of-the-art skills to expand the business.'

Brenda came in with a tray and put it on the table in the space Kevin had left for it. There were two cups and saucers, a little milk jug and a teapot, all in Chinese willow pattern. The jug had a lace cover held down with a beaded border. To one side was a silver tea strainer in its holder. There were no biscuits; Kevin did not approve of them. As she went out, Brenda straightened an embroidered antimacassar on the back of her allotted chair and left the men to talk.

'Dad, I want to study aviation-related subjects, please. It's my passion, I want to fly.'

'Absolutely not.' The older man glared down his beak, his eyes enlarged by the thick-rimmed glasses. 'Flying is not going to help you run this business. The only degree I will pay for is in business management. Flying is a perilous occupation, and I can't have you at risk. You know I'm going to expand to other branches, maybe take over another small company, and you'll be a key part of that. You'll be well off, settle down and have a family with the confidence there's a solid business behind you and a jolly good income. In order to do that successfully, you'll have to have the right degree.'

Cuthbert listened to the well-worn refrain and, for the umpteenth time, strained to think of a way out of his father's self-centred plans. *I have to hand it to him, though: building up a nest egg, funding a pension for later years and enjoying the comforts of a good woman and maybe some kids is a well-proven path in life.*

But where is the fun and excitement in that? I can dream of being a tycoon all I want, but they're only dreams. Getting to a position where I can sit behind a desk, order my secretary about and wallow in cash will involve following the Gospel According to Kevin, and the journey will be long and hard and joyless. I would have to relish the very act of making money, not only the money itself, and I couldn't care less as long as I have enough.

Aloud, he said, 'Grandad flew, he wasn't in business, and if he did so can I.'

Kevin let out a long exasperated breath. 'Cuthbert, we've been through this before, and it's about time you came to terms with it. My father flew Hurricanes in the war, in the Battle of Britain. That was completely different, it was necessary at the time. He was an ace, they said, but it didn't make him a millionaire – that came later. You're going to help me to run this company and expand it into a pharmaceutical group. That is your calling in life, and I'm not going to listen to any further argument on the subject. One day you'll see sense and agree. Besides which, how are you going to afford the lessons?'

'Grandad left me that inheritance.'

'You know very well that comes in two parts. The first instalment of ten thousand is for you to set yourself up. He meant it to be a start to your future. The second instalment of two hundred and fifty thousand is conditional on you having used the first instalment wisely. It's not something you can fritter away on a frivolous pastime. Anyway, you can't have the first part until you're twenty-one, as you well know.'

'I see using the ten thousand to learn to fly as the beginning of an aviation career, and I'm sure the executors will agree with me. Airline pilots earn good salaries.'

'*No*, Cuthbert. I forbid it. It's irresponsible.'

Seething with frustration at his father's implacable attitude, Cuthbert went to talk to his mother. He yanked his sleeves up over his forearms again as he entered the kitchen.

'Poor boy,' she said. 'I understand how you feel, but your father's right. It's best to prepare for a safe and secure future. Look at Dad and me: we're comfortable and happy in our marriage.'

Cuthbert raised an eyebrow as he gave her a meaningful glance in the full knowledge she was intimidated and submissive to her husband's unyielding will. She either did not notice or simply ignored his look because she had long since buried the truth in an inaccessible part of her mind. She was ironing a floral print blouse, which was almost identical to the one she was wearing and the other three in her cupboard. They only differed in shade. It was the same with her shoes: she only had four pairs and they were similar, as were her skirts and cardigans. Cuthbert knew it was not that they didn't have enough money for her to buy more attractive clothes, it was that his father had deemed it an unnecessary additional expense.

'You'll never see him back down on an argument. Believe you me, I've tried numerous times over the years, and it's no good my trying again over this. Once his mind's made up, that's it – he won't budge. Have another cup of tea, dear, it'll settle you down.'

Later, depressed, CJ was moaning about it to Martin, when his friend surprised him.

'You should do as he says. My dad says the mere act of going through uni shows a future employer you have the ability and drive to do it. Even if the degree is not what you want now, it'll never be wasted. You can still fly while you're there and get a flying job later. It's only three years out of the eighty-five you'll have before you peg out. Let's put our heads together and find the uni that does both our courses. We can get digs together, and that way you can still fly with Dad.'

'I'll think about it, but it seems like giving in to him, and I'm sick of doing everything I'm told.'

'But you won't be, you'll be using the time to further your own ends. Does he know you've been taking lessons with my dad?'

'No, shit no! Don't let that out for heaven's sake.'

5

CJ at 18

SCHOOL – SUMMER TERM FINAL YEAR

CJ sat on the ground a short distance back from the edge of the wood and examined the building in front of him. It was a boring creation, plain like a block of flats with no architectural merit whatsoever. There were three floors, all accessed by a staircase which could be seen through the front door. To the right of the door was a frosted pane window which, on each of the five occasions he had studied it, had been open. The shortest route from where he was hiding to the front door was only about thirty yards, an easy sprint across flat ground. There was going to be a new moon in a few days, which would make it very dark for what he was planning. And this time he had worked out an escape route as well. *Enough! I need to get back to some tedious studying. I've got to spend more time on school work and less on thrills like this. I have an exam to take and a future to decide on.*

The next morning, before they went into class, CJ asked Martin,

'You know that girl in the back row, Jo?'

'Yeah.'

'I think she fancies me.'

Martin tittered. 'But she's always teasing you. She's the one who calls you Cuffy all the time.'

'I know, but she's not nasty about it. I think she's trying to get a reaction, which means she's interested.'

Martin sniffed and rubbed his nose. 'So what are you going to do about it?'

'I told her if she called me Cuffy once more, I'd haunt her in the middle of the night. She laughed at me and said, "You wouldn't dare, Cuffy."'

'Knowing you, that was a mistake.'

'Too right. She's one of the weekly boarders and, as part of the dare, she told me where she sleeps. And to add to the challenge, she told me one of the girls in her room has the hots for Castle.'

'Whoah! She's trying to get you into trouble.'

'No, she's testing me.'

'Are you thinking of sneaking in there? Castle will make sure you're crucified if that other girl sees you.'

Two days later, after a very black midnight and with Martin keeping watch from the wood, CJ removed his shoes and left them with his friend. The front door would be locked, but the toilet window on the ground floor was still open. A flitting shadow, he made the crossing from the wood to the girls' dormitory block.

The window gave easy access, and CJ crept up the stairs in his socks. The staircase and the upper corridor were dimly lit. Jo's room was on the first floor. He turned right at the top and came to the bathroom. Its door was ajar and the light was on. What if a girl was in there? He'd be caught when she came out. He stepped back and pushed the door gently, slipped inside and listened. The cubicle doors were all open except the end one. There was the tinkling of someone having a pee. The only safe place was in another cubicle. He pushed the door to, but didn't latch it. The other toilet flushed. He waited, scared his breathing was too loud, and trying to hear over the resonation of his heart. A sound of running water, a paper towel being pulled. *Come on!* Silence.

He peered out into the corridor again and moved to the second door on the left. Jo had told him she shared the room with three others and her bed was in the far right corner. Her place was marked in the top right position on the name plate. The other names were familiar, but he had no idea which one was stupid enough to admire Castle. Slowly, carefully, he turned the handle. Another glance left and right; the corridor was still clear. If he were caught doing this, there would be hell to pay. A lot was riding on whether the door knob made a noise.

It was silent until the last fraction of the turn, then it squeaked. He stayed rigid, listening, and prepared to run like crazy. Nothing. He pushed the door with his finger tips, but the latch had not disengaged. The knob squeaked again with another twist. Again he froze, ready to bolt. *This is bloody scary, but it turns me on. I'll probably be expelled, Dad will probably have a heart attack, and Mum will probably have a breakdown. But Jo is pretty and enticing, and worth it.*

With another slight squeak, the door opened wide enough to let him through. He left it there. The curtain was open, allowing a smattering of light from the main buildings to provide some visibility. He stood still in the doorway, letting his eyes adjust to the gloom. Clothing was strewn across the floor. A gentle chorus of snores came from two beds. A soft voice was muttering something. It was Jo. He was poised to run. *No, she's talking in her sleep.* He slipped a note out of his pocket and put it on her bedside table so she couldn't miss it when she woke: *I was here!*

He tiptoed towards the door. A sleepy voice to his right said, 'What ...?'

A shiver of discovery ran through him. He stepped away, tripped on the clothes and thumped down onto his forearms. No time to wait for the scream, no time to close the door, no stopping at the stairs. He took them three at a time, almost falling, dived head first out of the window and ran for the wood, laughing with relief and excitement.

Martin met CJ the next morning as classes were assembling. 'You look like the dog that caught the cat at last.'

CJ laughed. 'And got away with it.'

A sudden shove knocked him into Martin. He turned, angry. Castle had a sneer on his face as usual.

'Trying it on with underage chicks, Cuffy? You're gonna be expelled. I'll make sure of it and kill myself laughing, you little turd.'

'What are you on about, Castle? You're full of shit as usual.'

'You won't be talking to me like that much longer, little Cuffy. You're on your way. I reckon they'll tell the cops as well. Sneaking into girls' dorms, trying to get your end away. Little perv.'

'Whatever you're talking about, you'd better have some proof, or you're going to be a laughing stock.' CJ walked away as if he didn't care. But doubt nagged at him. Had he been recognised, or was Castle having a go?

Jo gave him a secretive, admiring and soft smile in class. Her face no longer had its rather teasing, playful, challenging look; now it was warm. At the break, CJ inclined his head at her to meet him outside.

'So you made it.' She reached for his hand and squeezed it. 'I made a private bet with myself that you would.'

CJ wasn't sure how to proceed. This was the first time his emotions had been aroused by a real girl – it was an exciting, rather good feeling, but it scared him. His heart sounded louder than it did last night. What was he supposed to do next?

He took refuge in a practical question. 'What happened after I escaped? Did anyone see me?'

'Oh yes, we all did, but I'm pretty sure no one recognised you. You were out too fast. I didn't know what was going on at first. I woke to the crash, and I saw this bloke get off the floor and vanish. I guessed it was you, but Laura, the gossiping moron that fancies Castle, saw your note. She took it off my table before I got to it. She's bound to think it was you, and she's sure to tell him. She's a cow.'

'She has already, but if they can't prove it, it doesn't matter. You won't tell will you?'

Jo squeezed his hand harder and gave him a wicked grin before she went away. 'That depends.'

CJ watched her go. *Whew!*

During the morning break the next day, CJ was summoned to the headmaster's office. This was it. Castle must have snitched on him – bastard. The boy himself stopped CJ on his way.

'You're for it now, you little perv. We won't be seeing you around here any more, and bloody good riddance.'

'Drop dead, Castle. I can't be expelled for something I didn't do.'

A thin veneer of bravado. Had he gone too far this time? His future lay in the balance. A whole range of repercussions would be in store, including missing out on university. If he told the truth, he'd be expelled. If he lied, he might get away with it. If he was found to be lying, the punishment would be no worse.

'Enter.' The headmaster's harsh voice cut through the door in answer to his knock.

He walked up to the desk. The Head was obese with a florid complexion. When he was angry the redness intensified. And now he was very red indeed. He was wearing his gown, which he only did on formal occasions and when he was going to take disciplinary action.

'You sent for me, sir?'

'Two nights ago, a boy stole into a girls' dormitory and left a note. He was seen, and two pupils have reported that the person was you.'

CJ put shock on his face and opened his mouth to speak.

'Was it you? Did you break into the girls' accommodation block and into the dormitory?'

'No sir, I did not. I'm at home every night, and my father can verify that.'

'You were identified, Scott. You cannot deny it.'

He had to be very careful how he phrased his replies. The wrong word could prove he knew more than he would if he were innocent. To ask which girl had received the note and what she had said, would land him right in it. 'The witnesses must be mistaken, sir. Who are they?'

'I'm not going to divulge that, but one of the girls in the dormitory saw you, and one of the boys saw you out at midnight that night.'

'And what was he doing at that hour, sir? That's not normal, and how do you know it wasn't him? It certainly wasn't me, and I challenge anyone to swear they could positively identify me.'

The Head studied him in silence.

Outrage had to be shown, anything less could be construed as guilt. 'Sir, if you believe it was me, you'll have me expelled, won't you?'

The Head neither changed his expression nor acknowledged the question.

'That's serious, sir, and it will affect my future. You cannot take that action without being one hundred percent certain I was the one. Somebody is mistaken or lying, and I know exactly who the boy is. We have an ongoing feud.'

After another interminable stare, the Head lost some of his colour. 'All right, Scott, you're dismissed. You had better be very careful in your remaining time here, another incident like this and severe action will be taken.'

CJ couldn't resist the last word. 'I don't have to be careful, sir. I have to remain normal.' He left, gently closing the door behind him.

Castle was waiting at the end of the corridor, a smirk on his face. 'Going to clear out your locker, you little shit?'

'Ha, ha.' CJ gave him the finger.

The Hawker 4000, powered by two Pratt & Whitney PW308A turbofan engines which had a combined 13,800 pound-force of thrust, had reached its cruise altitude of forty-two thousand feet on its way to New York. It had left the busy and complicated airspace of Europe behind and was now on a westbound airway at a speed of Mach .82, about four hundred and seventy knots. The pilot workload had reduced. The owner of the Hawker, who was also the captain, gave control to his first officer and left the cockpit to make them coffees. They carried a cabin attendant, but the captain wanted to stretch his legs and think about the upcoming deal he was about to sign that afternoon, a deal which would net him some twenty-four million dollars over the next three years.

He stood at the aircraft-specification coffee machine looking for the Colombian espresso that he liked. The cabin attendant came up behind him, close enough for him to feel her warmth.

He met her eyes, Jo's eyes. Without a word he led her to the rear of the cabin. She fastened her lips on his as he lifted her skirt. She sat back on the pull-out table between the seats and opened her legs.

Damn! CJ had another wet and sticky groin. Hiding the stiff patches on his sheets from his mother was something which had to be dealt with too often these days.

There was a message in these dreams, though, a message of affluence which presented itself as a counter-argument to his adventurous spirit in the ongoing conflict in his mind. But were these aspirations in fact his own, even though he doubted he could face the journey to the top? Or was their origin his father's ambition of a business empire which was continually being hammered into him? In which case they were worthless excursions into sexual fantasy.

The dreams all involved a big shot with a shedload of money, and CJ well knew if he did want to become that tycoon he had better learn to be more cautious and develop a good business sense. He had better follow the Gospel According to Kevin. Or should he?

6

CJ at 19

UNIVERSITY – APRIL

The party was held in a large multi-bedroomed house in a leafy suburb. The place was rented by seven female students who had decided to celebrate the beginning of the last term of the academic year, or for reasons unknown. But who needs a reason to have a party when you're at uni?

There seemed to be an equal number of males and females, although CJ had no partner for the night. He was always on the lookout for someone of substance, as he had not yet found a girlfriend who had similar likes and adventurous tastes to his. Jo had been left behind somewhere when school ended, which was a pity. The one female in the climbing club was a dreadful 'crag hag', intense and with no sense of humour, and there were no girl sailors, sailing being a half-hearted summer pastime he'd taken to.

CJ, always a listener and an observer rather than a social animal, spotted Martin in a corner chatting to Ginny, a pleasant-looking girl in rather plain clothes; friends he could chat to instead of forcing useless small talk with others.

As he picked his way through the milling crowd to join them, he had a brief view of a familiar outline helping a student up the stairs. She was holding on to the banister, her foot wavering and prodding at the next tread as she tried to get a purchase. The burly figure put an arm around her waist, stopped her falling and lifted her from step to step. *What the hell was he doing here? He didn't even qualify for university.*

The music drifting from another room where the main body of dancers were was so loud the conversation elsewhere struggled to overcome it. It didn't matter as most of the students were so well oiled they either didn't hear or couldn't care. A faint whiff of marijuana emanated from one corner, accompanied by peals of hysterical laughter. Men pressed themselves on girls, and girls draped themselves over their partners. A lone couple made tiny movements in time with the music. She had both arms round his neck, while his hands on her buttocks pulled her softly gyrating hips into his. It was so sensuous CJ would not have been surprised if they had sex right there amongst the raucous crowd.

He made some more progress through the throng, then changed his mind. With more than a few beers under his belt, he decided the bathroom took priority over a lengthy conversation. He searched the ground floor without success, the pressure mounting. Upstairs, all the doors were closed, the landing was dimly lit and there was no way to tell which was a bathroom. The place was enormous, at least six bedrooms. Sounds of activity came from one of the rooms, so it wasn't that one. He took a guess and tried the door at the end of the passage.

His pain eased at last! He left the bathroom door open to help any other desperate souls searching for relief; there were likely to be many more as time went on.

A muffled scream stopped him: a cry of protest, of terror, from behind the door to his left. Frowning, he strained to hear. There was movement, but not calm movement: more urgent, even violent. A thump on the floor, followed by another. A scream, immediately stifled, chilled him.

Something was very wrong. CJ turned the handle.

His first glance took in the discarded pale blue jeans on a white rug. A pair of red knickers was still inside them, as if one urgent tug had ripped them off as a single item. Sounds of grunting and whimpering and a bed creaking came from his left. He peered round the door.

A woman was on her back on the edge of the bed. Her top had been yanked up, and her heavy right breast swayed back and forth with the movement. A large forearm pinned her knees up high. A rough hand was clamped over her mouth. She was trying to shake her head from side to side and struggling with the pathetic weakness of the truly drunk: uncoordinated and floppy. Her eyes were squeezed tight as if to shut out the image, even the act itself. Barry Castle, his trousers round his ankles, was thrusting into her, his teeth bared, his jaw clenched.

CJ was stunned. *Is this what it looks like?* He hesitated for too long before the reality dawned on him.

Her eyes opened; widened in terror as she saw him. Panicking, she scratched at the face above her. Castle swayed back and slapped her hard. She tried to kick, but he was too heavy. Crying and pleading again, her words were garbled through distorted lips.

Castle's flat hand resounded against her ear. 'Shut up, you bloody bitch, you've been begging for this.'

Vivid images flashed through CJ's mind: Castle's sneering face above him, his fist raised for another blow, Martin being thrown aside like a doll as he tried to protest, some junior boy shoved out of the lunch queue, another's phone ripped from his hand.

CJ lost it. A red film of rage swamped him. His body took actions; his mind followed.

Two strides across the room. He yanked Castle back by his collar, slammed him to the floor. The bully was shocked, not hurt. His surprise at seeing CJ switched to a sneer. 'Cuffy! You want some too, do you? Help yourself, this bitch is crying for it.'

Castle was hobbled by his trousers. CJ loomed above him. Castle, loaded with hatred, tried to wriggle into his jeans.

'Where'd you find the balls to go for me? You don't do that, Cuffy, nobody does. And that's the last time.'

CJ said nothing. He glared down at the bigger man with no fear. Why not? Castle was so easy with his fists, but CJ's confidence was boosted by his anger.

The woman was sobbing and had fallen off the bed. She crawled towards her pants. CJ kicked them over to her with one eye on Castle, who was struggling to stand with his trousers in one hand. He was almost upright, his intent venomous. CJ had seen that look before and knew what was coming. He had to strike first. The man thumped back to the floor. Using both hands, he clambered urgently to his feet before he was hit again. Blood trickled from his nose, down his chin and onto his shirt.

'Fucking bastard! I'll get you for that,' Castle muttered through his hand as he tried to stem the flow. A crimson spray spattered the white rug.

'Get out, Castle. Rape means prison.'

Another woman appeared in the doorway, her hand covering her open mouth. Castle gave her a brutal shove and barged past holding his nose, blood seeping through his fingers. In his anger, CJ snapped at the woman, 'That sod's just raped her. She needs help.'

'Oh my God!'

'He's not going to get away with this.' He rubbed his hand: the punch had hurt.

7

CJ at 19

UNIVERSITY – OCTOBER

CJ had not seen Castle since the party and the rape, which was a relief. He did not relish meeting the bully on the man's own terms.

The day after that traumatic night in April, CJ had eventually found the victim. At first, no one at the house was aware of her name, or where she was or where she had come from. The girl he was talking to in the doorway gave way to the one who had been first on the scene. She was older than her housemates and seemed to be their leader. Suspicion gripped her face when she saw who it was.

'Hello. My name's CJ, from last night, remember? I'm trying to find the girl who was raped. I want to see that man charged, but I'll need her help.'

Her mouth set into a thin line, the woman said nothing.

'Please. She needs to tell the police what happened. I know she won't want to, but he's been a bully all his life, and it's time he was dealt with.'

'Is that really what you want? You were in the room with him last night. Were you going to join in? Is that what you want to do now, get into her pants with some lame excuse?'

The last thing CJ expected was hostility. 'No, God no! I'm trying to do the right thing. Castle must be arrested. He'll only rape again if he gets away with this. Please try to persuade her. She'll feel better for it in the end, I'm sure.'

The woman continued to glare while she considered his words. Then her shoulders dropped, and her face softened. She took a deep breath. 'You look harmless enough, I suppose. But if you try to take advantage ...'

'No way! I only want to see that bastard punished.'

She stepped back to let CJ up the steps. As he reached her, she held out her hand. 'My name's Libby. I invited Michaela, so I feel responsible for her, and that was my room. I'll ask her if she'll speak to you, but she didn't want to talk to the police.'

'Thank you. If we, you and I, can get her to talk to them it'll be fantastic.'

'Go now. I'll try my best to persuade her, but she's very upset, and I don't know what success I'll have. What's your number?'

Libby called him in the afternoon. 'CJ, she'll talk to you, but only if I'm there.'

When he was shown into the lounge, Michaela and Libby were sitting close together on a couch. There was a comfortable chair next to them, but CJ chose another on the far side of the room with a coffee table separating him from the women. Libby kept her arm round the girl's shoulder and held her hand.

'Michaela, do you remember me? My name's CJ.'

Michaela's cheeks were flushed, and she kept dabbing at her puffy eyes with a tissue. She glanced at him, unable to look for long, shame dragging at her. She dropped her head to fixate on her hand entwined with Libby's. She gave a single slow nod.

'Do you remember I came into the room and fought that man?'

Her head was still down. No reaction.

'I want to see him punished for doing that to you. He has bullied and assaulted lots of people, men and women. It's his nature to carry on like that, and he has to be stopped. To stop him would save a lot of people from hurt and harm. Do you agree that would be a good thing to do?'

No reaction.

'Michaela, I helped you last night. Do you think you can trust me to help you again? Libby will always be there to protect you.'

Libby patted the girl's shoulder. 'Michaela, CJ is your friend. He wants to help, and I think you should trust him, but you will need to tell the police everything. I'll be with you all the time you talk to them, and if you don't want CJ to be there, he'll wait outside.'

It took an hour, but the combined persuasion of CJ and Libby eventually convinced Michaela to bring a charge against Barry Castle.

CJ's disgust at the previous night's experience still lingered; anything to do with Castle always left him with a bitter taste. Needing a complete change of scene, he drove with deliberate calm to the airfield, switching his focus to his next flying lesson with Terry.

Castle had been arrested the day after they talked to the police and had attended a hearing at the magistrates' court, where he was told he would be bailed and put on trial at the Crown Court at a date to be determined.

It took six months.

CJ waited outside the Crown Prosecutor's office for the man himself to turn up. It was hard to believe it took so much time before a case could get to court. In that interval, Castle could have committed multiple assaults if he felt like it – and maybe he had. It would be in his character to relieve his anxiety over his dismal future by giving some innocent person a hard time.

The rapid clacking of hard-heeled shoes echoed along the corridor. The prosecutor rushed up, breathing heavily. He pushed open his door, beckoning CJ to follow him in. The man plonked a heap of files onto his desk and collapsed in his chair with obvious relief. 'I'm sorry to keep you waiting. It's been a hectic morning.'

'No problem.'

'How are you feeling?'

'Nervous, to be honest. Appearing in court is scary enough, but the prospect of being pulled apart by the defence in front of everyone is even worse. I mean, I don't know whether Michaela consented or not and, as you said last time, the defence is going to press that point.'

The prosecutor raised a finger at him. 'Whoa! That's not your concern. You stick to telling the court what you saw and did, as we discussed. Nothing else, no speculation. There's enough medical evidence to show the act was forced. No need for you to worry about it. Having said that, your statement is critical. Without it, the case remains a matter of his word against hers.'

'I know, but still …'

'I'm sorry to rush you, but I have to be back in court in a few minutes. Next Wednesday. Please be there in good time, and we'll have a last word before it kicks off.'

CJ left the building no more confident than when he went in. It was all very well being calculating and sure of yourself when physical action was required, but the potential embarrassment and shame of failing in front of a full court and the national press was truly frightening. If only the self-assurance he felt with physical challenges could be employed to conquer his fear of ridicule – if only.

Was this a pointer to help him decide his future? Should he follow his strengths and lead a physical life? The trouble was he was most unlikely to make any money taking that route, and if he were injured there would be no future. He had better man up to the challenge facing him on Wednesday and stop being a wimp with, as he imagined it, the world watching.

It was Friday. There was time enough to psych himself up to the task. If he overcame this irrational fear, he'd be the stronger for it. And, he reminded himself, Michaela was going to be even more nervous; he was getting off lightly.

Meanwhile, he had an essential flying exercise to complete: a milestone in his training curriculum.

Terry was waiting for him at the flying club when CJ arrived that afternoon. He assured the lad he could have the aircraft on Saturday at two. They would go up in a short while to practise emergencies again, in spite of the odd rain shower which had been forecast. CJ could then focus on the task of planning for his exciting and all-important first solo navigation exercise. He confirmed his booking for Saturday with the secretary and watched as she wrote it into the programme. Collecting his kit, he happily walked out to the Cessna with Terry.

Neither of them noticed the large man sitting in a scruffy armchair, his face hidden behind an amateur flying magazine.

Barry Castle stood and watched instructor and student until they vanished down the row of little aeroplanes. The secretary was on the phone and taking some details down on a scrap of paper. She smiled a question at him as she hung up.

'I was hoping to hire a Cessna 172 tomorrow morning.'

'Oh. We only have two, I'm afraid. One is booked and the other is private. The owner doesn't hire it out. Sorry.'

Castle put on his most charming face and said, 'No worries. Thanks.'

The situation couldn't be better. No mistaking the aeroplane. He had less than twenty-four hours.

On Saturday afternoon, CJ cycled out to the airfield, glad for the chance to get his blood moving and hoping the exercise would help him overcome a strange and unusual bout of nerves. These weren't the nerves he'd had before he embarked on his first solo flight. Every aspiring pilot suffers from those: the first time alone in an unnatural environment, no instructor to rescue the situation before he makes a fatal mistake, and being in control of a machine he was still getting to grips with. No, this was a trepidation CJ could not explain. After all, he had been flying solo for some time, he was used to it, the fear no longer had a hold over him. In fact he relished the prospect of being alone and in control, a master of his own ability, even if it was only for an hour at a time.

The flying school was a hive of activity, it being the weekend. An atmosphere of unbridled enthusiasm filled the room as students of both sexes milled around, teased each other, or boasted without foundation. There was laughing and joking amongst some, although one quiet lad, who was due for his first solo flight, was looking distinctly anxious. Empty coffee mugs and magazines about flying littered the table. The notice boards had safety and technical and general news items pinned to them. The hard-pressed secretary was trying to juggle bookings to accommodate a difficult situation.

CJ had begun preparations for his flight on Friday afternoon, when he checked the weather and planned the route Terry had given him. He worked out the times he should be at the turning points and the headings he should keep to between the points, taking into account the forecast wind. He identified any diversion airfields he could go to in case he had an emergency, and calculated the fuel he would use and added a reserve.

On Saturday morning he went over the whole plan again, especially the weather, and confirmed in the little Cessna's logbook that the plane was serviceable and not carrying any defects. Confident he had been thorough with his flight planning, he did not understand why he was still apprehensive. He acknowledged part of the reason could be because this was the first time he had been let loose outside the training area on his own, and the possibility of getting lost was always there, not to mention the likelihood of straying into a controlled or restricted area and being told in no uncertain terms to bugger off – although not quite in those words. But, prideful, he was more worried Terry would find a fault with his planning.

His instructor led CJ away from the hubbub and into a briefing room. Examining the lad's preparation, he at last said, 'Hmmm.' CJ waited anxiously for criticism, but Terry gave him a pat on the shoulder. 'Looks good to me, good work. Now, go and check my aeroplane and get out of here. Oh, and don't bend it, please!'

CJ grinned at him, more confident now. But something still niggled. What could go wrong? His fear of getting lost was actually one of failure – after all he could always resort to the GPS to find where he was. But Terry had insisted he navigated by reading the map and confirming his position from the ground. 'A GPS can fail,' he had preached. 'You must learn the basics first.'

CJ confirmed the high layer of cloud which was forecast. He subdued his nerves as he walked out to the aircraft, weaving his way through the ranks of other little aeroplanes waiting for the abuse which students might inflict on them. There was a collective creaking from this fleet as they rocked gently in the light breeze. Another student was standing on the wing of his Piper, about to climb into the cockpit. He waved at CJ, who raised his headset in his left hand as his other was laden with the flight bag.

He focused on his preflight inspection of the aeroplane. Terry had taught him well, giving him a good knowledge of the Cessna for someone so young and inexperienced. He knew all sorts of technicalities of which other students in the club, with less experienced instructors, were ignorant.

He opened the engine cowling and appreciated the mechanical smell of the thing. He checked the oil level, had a general look around, could find no fault and closed the cowling again. He checked the fuel for the presence of water, which would cause engine problems. He examined the tyres, inspected the control surfaces and tested them for free play. All good, he said to himself, now eager to have this preparation out of the way and get going.

There was no question CJ was as diligent as he knew how to be, but he was still inexperienced.

He climbed into the cockpit and secured his kit so it would not move around during the flight. The pre-start checks done using the check list, he confirmed all was clear around the aircraft and turned the key. The engine fired after two turns, settling into its familiar noisy rumble. The noise excited him, and he was keen to be off.

He taxied out to the runway, stopped short of it and carried out his run-up check at full power. All was good, so he throttled back and asked permission for take-off.

Fred, in the control tower, told him he was clear to go and added, 'Don't get lost, CJ!'

The lad gave an automatic and brief smile, but this was serious stuff, and his attention had to focus on the task at hand. He lined the little aeroplane up on the long runway centreline – his route to happiness. He opened the throttle slowly at first; oil pressure and temperature were in their green arcs, so he applied full power. The Cessna charged down the runway. His eye was on the airspeed indicator. Fifty-five knots; he gently pulled back on the yoke. Sixty knots; he pulled back a little more. He was airborne.

CJ and his Cessna, his team, passed through six hundred feet above the ground. The runway was well behind him. He set the climb speed and was ready to turn onto the heading for his first leg once he reached a thousand feet. The engine was belting out its comfortable roar. Another check of the instruments and his confidence increased. With the good start to this exercise, his nerves were well behind him, forgotten with his attention to the flight.

His focus switched to navigation. He noted the time and set his heading – he was on his way! He kept monitoring his instruments to ensure all was well, and kept scanning the sky, looking out for other aircraft.

The first turning point was not far; he saw the monument on the hilltop about three miles ahead. He folded his map to display the next leg and twisted round to see out to the right, under the wing, ready for his turn.

Flash! Bang! An impossibly loud explosion from the engine.

He gasped and whipped his head back to the front. Thin white smoke was billowing out from the cowling, curving around the windshield. The engine sputtered. The oil pressure zero. A sudden silence.

CJ reacted by rote, talking himself through the actions Terry had put him through so many times. *Lower the nose, keep the speed, maintain control and go through the checks for engine failure. But why the smoke? Engine fire! A pilot's worst fear. Must get on the ground now! Set a hundred knots, it might blow the fire out, shut off the fuel.*

His mind raced as he searched for a flat area to land, but the surface was hilly. *Aim for the valley, that way I can't roll down a slope on landing. But the only valley within reach is filled with trees. Trees or hillside? Trees, I think – at least I'll stop.*

A popping noise in front distracted him. More smoke. *Where the hell did that come from? It's inside! Shit, I've got a serious problem.* He coughed over and over as the stuff clawed at his throat. *What's the bloody speed, I can't even see the instrument, an arm's length away. What the hell is going on? This is not how it's supposed to be – fires don't produce this much smoke. Never mind the bloody cause, you idiot, focus on landing! But I can't see to land!*

Cough, cough, inhale more smoke, cough. Eyes streaming, he opened a fresh-air vent – it made little difference.

'Mayday, Mayday, Mayday.' CJ coughed out the aircraft registration on the radio. 'Engine and cockpit fire. Going into trees.' In his desperation he forgot to give a position. He didn't call again, he had to concentrate on trying to see, trying to make the best of the imminent crash.

Only trees and low hills were visible through the side window. The Cessna was below the top of the hill to his left with a wood somewhere below him. He was getting lower, the surface getting nearer, the crash getting closer. A brief glimpse ahead, only trees were in the valley bottom. The view was obscured again. Bizarrely, he noticed fine detail in the branches almost level with the left wing. He fought himself, trying to keep his head. *Stop panicking. How high am I? Reduce the speed. I can't see. I can only fly by my memory of what lies ahead. But that doesn't tell me where I am now. Any moment, surely.*

A clatter, almost a rattle, was accompanied by a hesitation in the aeroplane. The first strike of the tree tops. Green fingers reaching up to claw him out of the air. He flared for landing. *Is it too late? Is it too soon? Oh shit!*

8

CJ at 19

OCTOBER

Mild concussion and a broken arm was what the doctor said. He could have added a face which looked as if it had been hit with a brick, bruised ribs and a deep cut on the right leg – plus a persistent headache and a desire to sleep.

It was Sunday morning, and CJ was gradually coming to terms with his unfamiliar surroundings. He had never been in hospital before and was sufficiently alert to be curious. He scanned the ward and absorbed the atmosphere of scrubbed cleanliness. It was more cheerful than he expected, with a pale blue floor, off-white grey walls and brightly patterned light blue curtains. There were five other beds in the room, all occupied by older men. One was watching TV, but the others were asleep or unconscious, or possibly dead.

A cheerful nurse, efficient and in her fifties, came in to make sure he was in the land of the living. He tried a weak joke on her. 'Do I get a bed bath?'

She wasn't having any cheeky student nonsense. 'We've a lovely big male nurse for that.'

'Oh! Actually, I'm not that dirty.'

'Not in body, maybe.' She laughed and rushed off to the next patient.

He lay back and dozed. Semi-conscious, he tried to shut out vivid images of smoke-obscured instruments as he struggled to see where he was going. That glimpse of trees flashing by on the hillside above him had been frightening, as was the first snapping noise of twigs on aluminium – a sharp rattle at first, then harsh bangs as they dragged him down. It was over in seconds, but the visions would stay in his mind forever.

As the afternoon visiting time was reached, Terry, with Martin and Ginny, now firm partners, came through the ward door. They scanned each bed in turn, but it was Ginny who spotted him. 'There he is.'

CJ beamed at them as they approached and gave a weak wave. Ginny could be Martin's sister; they both had thick-rimmed glasses and ginger hair, although Ginny's was drawn back in a long neat ponytail, while Martin's was scraggy. He had been trying to grow a beard since they'd been at university, but it was red and scruffy and feeble and did nothing for him. He had developed a habit of running his finger and thumb across his top lip outwards from his nose to the corners of his mouth, in an apparent effort to train his measly moustache. What were their kids going to look like with all that ginger in their genes?

'How's the victim? You're a very lucky chap,' said Terry.

Martin was holding a plastic bag. He stroked his moustache and glanced around. Within the bag so it was out of sight, he opened four bottles and handed them out. 'Cheers,' he said. 'Your health depends on this.'

'My health won't be so good if they catch me drinking. Thanks though, I need it. Terry, I'm so sorry, I don't know what happened, there was so much smoke. I couldn't see, and now I've stuffed your aeroplane.'

'Nonsense. It was fully insured, so don't worry. It was definitely not your fault. The accident investigation will carry on for a while yet, but they've confirmed there was a smoke bomb planted behind the instrument panel. The aircraft was sabotaged – someone tried to kill you, or us.'

A short, thoughtful silence followed.

'It was quite cunning, actually,' Terry continued. 'The smoke grenade was put into a tube with the safety pin removed. Somehow, they don't know exactly how yet, the grenade fell from the tube and triggered. They think a similar arrangement was done in the engine compartment, but that had a flash grenade which must have made a loud bang. There must have been timers involved somehow, but they're still searching the wreck.'

'There was a tremendous bang from the engine, and white smoke. That was before the smoke in the cabin. I could see nothing outside except through the side window. I should have yawed it, I suppose, but I didn't think of that – sorry.'

'Good job you didn't, you might have stalled it. And don't apologise – I certainly don't blame you, I'm just thankful you're alive. It could well have been otherwise, but you kept your head and did a good job.'

'Huh.' CJ protested for a short while, before changing the subject. 'How did I get here? I don't remember anything.'

'Your Mayday call was picked up and relayed to Fred, who got everything going. I worked out where you should be and Gerry Simpson – you know, the chap with the little helicopter? – he took me there and we gave the exact location to the rescue services. You were very lucky there was no real fire. If you hadn't switched the fuel off, you'd be toast now.'

CJ attempted a weak grin. 'Actually, in a way I feel rather good and excited about it. I experienced a crash and got away with it. It's almost something to be proud of.'

Martin rolled his eyes. 'Here we go again, bloody adrenalin junkie.' He gave CJ a meaningful look. 'Don't forget you have to give evidence against Castle on Wednesday.'

The empty bottles clinked in Martin's bag as they left the ward.

CJ watched his visitors to the door. It was obvious that Ginny and Martin adored each other. What a pair! He was glad for them, but envious too.

It wasn't that he was lonely, it was more a matter of not having a well rounded life, and Ginny and Martin's happiness often caused these reflections. He was glad when his mother interrupted.

Brenda Scott appeared at the door. She hesitated as she looked around, as if she didn't want to intrude in a men's ward, before tiptoeing over to his bed. CJ hid his amusement in his sheet.

Brenda pulled the chair closer to the bed. She was petrified of disturbing the other patients and kept her voice at a whisper. 'Your father's absolutely livid, dear.' She patted at her hairdo. Not that it needed it, it wasn't going to go out of shape except in a hurricane. 'He refuses to visit you. He said if you were not dying there was no need for him to come. He did ask if you were all right, though.'

Cuthbert shrugged out of habit – it hurt.

Brenda leaned over to mop up a water drop on the side table. 'We had no idea you were taking flying lessons. You know he thinks it's not safe, and he needs you to be healthy to succeed him.'

'You mean he's determined to leave a legacy in which his name is prominent. Tell him not to worry – I'll erect a statue to the founder of the empire of Pharma-Scott!'

Brenda ignored that. 'You'll have to give it up dear – life will be impossible at home if you continue. You're ruining his vision of the future. How are you paying for it? Isn't it terribly expensive?'

Having ensured there would be no after-effects from his concussion, CJ was released from hospital on the Tuesday. Wednesday, the day of the trial, came all too quickly.

He sat in the witness's waiting room in a kind of mental agony. In spite of his breakfast, an ache of hunger tore at his stomach. The sling held his arm in a position that sent stabs of pain through his ribs, the puncture in his leg kept reminding him to take it easy, the ugly bruises on his face were sore, and a headache came and went.

Maybe Michaela's testimony would be so powerful they wouldn't need his, and he would be able to go home. Fat chance. Waiting for him was a torture chamber of a court with wigged and gowned aggressive people who were going to rip his evidence to shreds, make him look a complete idiot and leave him so embarrassed he would not be able to appear in public for months. His face would be plastered all over the national newspapers. He would be a laughing stock – the pathetic witness who broke down as his lies were exposed. Only they weren't lies. He had to remember that.

Michaela was in there telling her story. He knew it must be agony for her to relive it and be ripped apart by the hostile cross-examination. Her shame was being made public. *Why do women feel shame after rape? It isn't their fault, they are victims. It's the rapist who should be ashamed. If Michaela has the courage to testify, then so should I. Get a grip!*

His name was called. He stood and limped through the door into the court. He was shown to the witness box and asked to swear to tell the truth. He ignored the Bible and affirmed he would.

The judge was a heavily jowled man with thick glasses, who dominated the room from his prominent central position. A jury of ordinary folk faced the witness stand, men and women. *They may look normal, but they are the ones who are staring at me, trying to determine if I'm going to tell the truth. It's them I have to convince.*

Other eyes bored into him; Barry Castle's hostility radiated from the dock. Castle, CJ could deal with. His confidence returned as he gave a contemptuous glare at the rapist. *I'm here because of you, and I'm going to do my best to see you put away.*

The judge peered at him over the top of his spectacles. His voice was deep, loud and authoritative. 'I understand, Mr Scott, that you were in an aeroplane crash a few days ago.'

'Yes – er, Your Honour.'

'Thank you for appearing in spite of your injuries, which look to be painful. Are you sure you're fit enough to testify? Would you prefer to sit?'

'I'm fit, Your Honour. I can stand, thank you.' The brief exchange settled him. The judge wasn't as imperious as he looked, up there on his throne.

Even so, the formality and ceremony of the court, the wigs, the gowns and the absolute power of the judge forced respect for the proceedings and lent court officials the authority to take other participants out of their environment and subjugate them.

His attention was taken by the prosecutor who calmed him and put him more at ease. He gave his testimony as he remembered it, without embellishment. As the words came out, he gradually became more confident and relaxed. This was not as bad as he'd imagined – so far. He spoke to the jury, but was acutely aware of Castle's unwavering scowl.

The defence barrister stood and, for effect, took a few paces out and back from his position as if in fierce consideration of his words. He had a grim expression and was forbidding in his wig. He asked a few mundane questions as he warmed up and tried to fool CJ into relaxing. Then:

'Mr Scott, you have been Mr Castle's enemy since you were at school together. My client has made several attempts to reconcile with you, but you turned your back on him. He does not understand why. I think you are vindictive, Mr Scott. You are willing to put an innocent man in jail purely to satisfy your hatred, aren't you?'

What the hell is this? What rubbish!

Castle looked down from the dock with a smug expression at CJ's discomfort. The barrister glared at him as he waited for a reply.

'Answer the question, Mr Scott,' a deep voice said.

Hate? At what stage does dislike become hate? 'No, I don't hate him, I merely think he's despicable. And he hasn't—'

'You have physically attacked my client on at least two occasions, have you not?'

'Yes. One was—'

'Why would you punch someone if you didn't hate them? I think you're lying, Mr Scott. You have seized this opportunity to take your hatred out on Mr Castle, using a flimsy story about rape as the vehicle.'

'No! I witnessed—'

'What you saw was consensual sex. You saw a young woman screaming in the throes of passion, and because you wish to see evil in everything my client does, you have taken this opportunity to have him convicted of a very serious crime.'

'No! That's rubbish.'

Castle was on his feet in the dock, the officer behind rising to restrain him.

'Liar!' Castle yelled before he was forced down.

The barrister continued as if nothing had happened. 'Note that my client has declined the opportunity to lay a charge of assault on you for hitting him on that occasion. This goes to show his good nature in the face of extreme provocation.'

This was bullshit. This man was fabricating a situation, and to make it worse, Castle was openly grinning at him.

'You are lying, Mr Scott. Perjury is a very serious offence.'

This had gone far enough – to hell with courtroom etiquette. One way or another he had fought the bully through school and was having to do it again. But this defence lawyer was now bullying him. That made it a fight. All fear of embarrassment, of making a fool of himself in public, evaporated. He raised his eyes to the jury and spoke over the head of the barrister.

His voice was loud. 'I. Am. Not. Lying.' He pointed across the court. 'That man was a bully at school, and I could produce scores of pupils to verify that. He raped Michaela in a further act of violence against an individual weaker than himself. That is the absolute truth.'

'It seems to me that Mr Scott's obviously uncontrollable anger is a reaction to being exposed for the liar he is. No more questions, Your Honour.'

The smugness had been wiped from Barry Castle's face. The man's hatred followed him as he limped to a seat to observe the end of the trial. He turned to the dock to challenge the animosity. Castle's natural good looks had been transformed into something a lot less pleasant.

CJ took a seat next to Libby. She clasped his hand for a few seconds. 'Well done. I know that was difficult for you, but you came across well.'

They only had to wait an hour before the jury returned. Guilty. Castle was led away. As he reached the door he turned to give CJ a final look which plainly said the war was not over.

At his sentencing three weeks later, Castle was given six years. He was told he would be able to apply for release on licence after half his time, but he would be on the sex offenders' register for at least fifteen years. It was no wonder he entered prison a bitter and vengeful man.

9

BARRY CASTLE

PRISON – OCTOBER

Castle seethed with anger, day after day. His hatred of CJ Fucking Scott, abbreviated in his mind to CFS, was the flame under a pressure cooker, and if he saw the man it would be as if the lid were lifted suddenly, the contents boiling over. His mind raced in so many directions at once, he confused himself as he hunted for ways to take revenge.

The glossy cream walls of his cell were devoid of decoration except for a notice board for pinning pictures of wives, family members and girl friends – true, or exotic and imaginary. Each inmate had a small set of drawers, and there was a desk and two hard chairs. Next to the door were a basin and a stainless-steel lavatory. On top of one of the cupboards a small TV sat on a kind of bridge under which was a row of toiletries. The furniture was flat-pack and the bunks steel-framed. The room had the stale odour of continuous human occupation.

The focus for Castle, though, was the window with its thick steel bars and a flimsy blue curtain which was gathered in the middle and tied with a piece of string. It represented the outside, freedom, and the place where he would be in three years, where he would be able to get his own back on CFS.

The cell was already occupied by a scrawny young man with a protuberant Adam's apple, a wiry nerd of an individual who was the epitome of the type he had picked on in school. Castle was twenty-one, Eddie a bit older. Eddie introduced himself when they first met, but Castle ignored him, and he continued to ignore the little man for almost two weeks while he cooled down.

Castle's initial dislike of Eddie was not unusual; it was a reaction he applied to most other humans, anyway. There were several reasons for this in Eddie's case, though: he already occupied the top bunk, so Castle had to accept the lower one which he found annoying, because he felt it every time Eddie climbed up or down; his visits to the toilet were revolting (what breed of microbes did he harbour in his gut?), and he always chose breakfast time to do it; his need for continual chatter; and the fact that he was always in the way when Castle wanted to move around the narrow cell.

'Look, mate,' said Eddie. 'I dunno what your beef is, but it ain't my fault. You're hostile, and it's making me nervous. We gotta live like this for years. You might think of talking, you know, so we can get along a bit? I mean, I don't even know your first name.'

Castle gave him a withering look, but did not reply. Instead he scratched a nervous itch in his crotch, a habit which stayed with him for life, along with that of taking extreme steps to ensure his nose was clean.

One night, Castle came to terms with his outlook for the next few years and opened the conversation for the first time. It was late and the light was out. Moonlight from the narrow window reflecting off the glossy paint of the cell wall was the only illumination. In the dark, Castle said, 'What are you in for then?'

'Bloody hell, it speaks! Identity fraud.'

'Huh.' Castle fell silent. Eddie's breathing settled into a quiet rhythm.

'So how do you steal someone's ID then? What do you need?'

'Aagh! I was just asleep. Well, obviously you need their name, when they were born – the place even – address and email addresses, previous addresses, bank account details, PIN numbers, National Insurance number, any passwords you can get. Basically anything you can get your hands on. The more info you have, the easier it is.'

'Hmm.' Castle lay awake for a long time. He had two years, eleven months and thirteen days to put a plan together.

His mother came to see him regularly. Eva found the prison visits daunting, which made Castle concerned. Before he was born, one wet night his father had skidded his motorbike into a oak tree. His mother had found it hard to cope with a job and look after her son on her own. Particularly so because, without his dad's supervision, Barry was a rebellious child and an even more difficult teenager.

Belatedly, he now realised how much she had sacrificed for him when he was young. She was the only person he cared about and, to make up for his earlier difficult period, he always made an extra effort to help and care for her.

'How are you, Mum? Are you coping?'

'Oh, I'm okay. A bit lonely without you around, but that's how it is.'

'And the neighbours, how are they treating you with me in here for rape?

She shrugged her shoulders. 'Actually, everyone is sympathetic. They don't treat me any differently than before.'

Castle knew she was lying about people's attitude, but there was nothing he could do about it except brood. *Thank you, Cuffy Fucking Scott – there will be a reckoning!*

In the thousand long nights he spent in his prison bunk, Castle's thoughts often strayed to his past. His dad had been doing his national service in the BAOR, the British Army on the Rhine, during the Cold War, when he met the pretty German girl. They married and, when his old man was discharged, they returned to live in England. Eva's English was halting at first, but she soon came to speak it with only a trace of German remaining in her accent. It took a few years for attitudes to soften, but in due course the neighbours accepted her for what she was and not a mere daughter of the enemy.

Whenever she could afford it, Eva took Barry over to Bielefeld to stay with her brother's family. He liked them. He liked his aunt, and he even liked his strong and forbidding uncle, who was a sharp contrast to Eric, his mother's ex-boyfriend. He was much calmer under his influence. And he came to adore his cousins. They spoke reasonable English, but were unsuccessful in teaching him German.

'You like beer, Rolf?' They liked to use his German middle name, which his mother had wanted to be added to his English identity.

'I dunno, never had it.'

'Come, we go to the park and we buy some beers and have a good time. Yes?'

'But, can you get beer – you two?'

'*Ja,* we are sixteen. Is legal for us. You, we hide!' Giggles.

They became close, even though they were almost two years older than him.

One afternoon, their bedroom door being ajar, Barry caught a glimpse of one in her bra and panties. He watched her for a few moments, fascinated and aroused. A shove from behind, and he stumbled into the room. The other one closed the door behind them and grinned at her sister.

'What are you doing?'

They didn't answer. They only spoke to each other, and in German.

They pushed him onto a bed and calmed him with smiles and soft words he couldn't understand.

'Hey, you two, what are you up to?'

They tittered as they brushed their hands across his skin, feeling his ribs, stroking his throat, tickling his ears and smoothing his hair. He tensed at first, but his friends were so kind to him he soon relaxed. The whole experience was quite pleasant.

'Give me your hands, cousin Rolf. Don't worry, we will not hurt you.'

One of them tied his wrists to the bedhead with the cord from her gown. When he was secured, they both caressed his forehead and cheeks. They were his best mates, and their playfulness was not threatening.

'Sweet young Rolf. He is pretty boy, no?'

'*Ja.* I could eat him with *strudel* and cream.'

With a wicked little look, the one who had shoved him locked her eyes on his and with slow, enticing movements shed her dress. Her figure was identical to the other's, slim with small breasts and a tiny waist. Their bras were the same, black and lacy, their panties the same. What were they going to do? He was almost fifteen, he was excited and nervous, but he trusted his cousins.

His belt was undone. His fly unzipped. His heart was pounding. Four hands pulled his trousers down.

'Hey, what …?' His words were silenced with a kiss.

His underpants were next. He was exposed and trapped with sixteen year-old girls sitting one on each of his legs. They played and massaged him to heaven and laughed in delight at their success.

From there on, their relationship became much deeper. They let him fondle their breasts, nothing more than that – they were cousins, after all. They quizzed him on his secrets, and because he was in love with them he was honest and told them how he bossed and bullied others to get his way and dominate the school.

'Why you bully little boys, Rolfy? What makes you do that?'

'It's natural isn't it? Me mum's boyfriend use to bully me. He said it would toughen me up. He said it was the natural way of things, for the strong to make the weak work for them.'

'He hit you?'

'He hit me, swore at me, told me I was stupid, made me spend most of the time in my room.'

'That's terrible. And Auntie Eva? What did she do?'

'She never knew. Then one day she saw my bruises, and she cried, and she told Eric he was a bastard, and he had to get out of the house. He hit her too, then.'

'Oh, poor Auntie Eva. That's terrible, Rolf. What happened after?'

'I'll never forget it. She was lying in the corner of the kitchen all crumpled up. There was blood coming from her mouth. I called the ambulance. Eric gave her a black eye and a broken jaw. The cops took him away. I never saw him again.'

They were all quiet after that.

Barry asked, 'And you? You could rule the school, 'cause there's two of you.'

'Oh naturally, Rolf, we do. We rule only because we are strong, and we can. We are the queens, all the girls respect us. So, Rolf, will you keep a secret? You'll never tell anyone what we tell you now, will you?'

'No, we're best mates. I'll never tell on you.'

So they confided what they dreamed of doing.

'What? You're joking, right?'

'Oh no, we're deadly serious, cousin Rolf.' They both giggled. 'You want to join us?'

'No, I couldn't do that, but will you tell me how it goes?'

10

CJ at 21

TWO YEARS LATER

'Cuthbert, come into the sitting room. I have some exciting news you need to know about. Brenda, may we have some tea, please.'

To combat the miserable January weather outside, his mother liked to maintain a high temperature in the house. Cuthbert shook his head at the "exciting" news to come and pulled his sleeves up to his forearms. *It's late for tea; I'd much rather have a beer to cool off.* What was exciting to his father was utterly boring and of little interest to him. Kevin Scott had never mentioned the crash in the twenty-seven months since it happened, nor asked how his son was. He had gone into a state of denial over it. His focus was fixed on his grand plan for Pharma-Scott, with Cuthbert there to back him up, educated and primed to take over when Kevin retired in the glory of his name and on his carefully selected investments. Cuthbert was well aware his father would still keep a watchful eye on him, though. There was no possibility of him losing either interest or control. He threaded his way through the furniture to reach his own chair.

Instead of sitting in his normal position, Kevin paced the room in an unusual state of excitement. But discipline came first. 'Pull your sleeves down to their proper position, for heaven's sake. This is brilliant, Cuthbert! The expansion of Pharma-Scott has begun. I've agreed a merger with Quercus Pharmacy wherein I will have a sixty-five percent shareholding.' He gave a rare, self-satisfied contortion of his face, his best attempt at a smile. 'I am going to appoint you as an executive director. Michael Hines of Quercus will be the financial director, but with your business management qualification coming up, you can keep watch on him. Not that I don't trust him, but better to have one of our own camp with a keen interest, since he's got some old-fashioned views. The Hineses have a daughter, Lisa, nice girl, pretty. She's graduate with a Master of Pharmacy, MPharm, so she can manage the technical side in the future.'

'That's good for you, Dad, well done.' Cuthbert was caught off guard by this announcement. Things were moving in a direction he was very reluctant to take, and at an alarming pace. It would be best to keep quiet until he understood what the future held.

'I think it's fitting we can celebrate this merger in the same month you turn twenty-one. What a birthday present, eh?'

Cuthbert stifled a reply. *Some birthday present! The best present is Grandad's money, because I can now repay Terry and fund my flying.*

'Anyway, to celebrate, I've invited the Hineses around here for dinner on Saturday. Better for everyone to get to know each other during a social occasion, rather than across a boardroom table, don't you think?'

The dreaded night.

Usually, it would be Cuthbert's task to respond to a knock on the door, but he was reluctant and slow. His father leapt out of his chair and beat him to it. Kevin showed the Hineses into the living room and made the introductions. They formed a line abreast after they passed through the door, as if for a family photograph, the parents on either side of their daughter.

Cuthbert discerned an innate sensuality in her. Or was it only her tight-fitting dress, amplifying a good and full figure, which gave that impression, because she was otherwise quite demure? He could not distinguish her pupils, her eyes were so dark. She wore thick-rimmed glasses, the frames of which swept upwards to a point at the hinges. The style did not suit her. Her hair, almost black, was straight and long and fell to her waist. Her skin was pale, and her lipstick dark. *Give her a nose ring and a few piercings and she could pass as a goth. The glasses aside, though, she's actually quite attractive. She's certainly worth a go – maybe there's a positive side to this after all.*

He watched his father's performance during the evening. The man had never been so cheerful. He was grandstanding, playing the corporate boss indulging his minions with his wisdom. It was pathetic. He was also not-so-surreptitiously keeping an eye on him and Lisa, who had been seated next to each other at dinner. But while Kevin tried to keep his glances casual, his mother spent most of the meal with an expression of maternal sweetness at a potential romance, even though they had barely spoken to each other.

The next morning, swallowing a spoonful of cornflakes, Kevin said, 'Well, what did you think of Lisa, then?'

Brenda issued another sugary smile before Cuthbert shrugged his shoulders. 'She seems nice enough.'

'Are you going to ask her out?'

'I hadn't thought about it. Maybe,' he lied. *No maybes about it. Yes. If I'm not mistaken, her sideways glances at the dinner table and the occasional touch of her thigh on mine, not withdrawn immediately, means she's open to an invitation.*

Brenda did her bit to encourage him. 'You don't have a girlfriend at the moment, Cuthbert, and she seems very nice.'

Cuthbert refused to give his father the satisfaction of seeing the success of his very obvious plan on the horizon so early in the game. 'She's okay. I wouldn't say she appeals to me enough to consider a relationship. I'll think about it.'

His father grunted his annoyance with Cuthbert failing to fall in with his plans yet again, but he passed no comment.

Later, when Kevin had gone out to get the newspaper, Brenda put a tentative hand on Cuthbert's shoulder. 'Dear, your father thinks a good relationship between you and Lisa is important to the joint company.'

'He's made that very obvious, Mum. If he thinks he can get me to marry her in order to cement the merger, he's got another think coming. Times have changed, our society no longer arranges marriages for non-romantic reasons. I don't know what Lisa thinks, but I find it insulting.'

'Oh dear. It's not as bad as all that. You must make up your own mind, of course. But will you please try to form a friendship with her, if only to keep the peace? It would be nice if you did get along well, though.'

'Two things,' CJ said as he and Lisa strolled through the park on the way to the pub on their second date.

'Mm?'

'Please stop calling me Cuthbert and use CJ or Cuff like all my friends do, and, if we go out often, please can we keep it low-key – as far as my parents are concerned, at least. The thing is, my dad is becoming thoroughly irritating over this merger, and he seldom stops asking me how we are getting along. He wants to be sure we're friends to ensure the future is rosy. My mother spends her time nervously padding around hoping everything is going to be all right, and trying to placate Dad when he thinks we don't like each other. It's a nightmare.'

'Okay, no problem.' Lisa groped for his hand. 'But I want to call you Cuthbert when in front of your dad. It'll keep him happy.'

When he thought about it much later, CJ was proud of the very short time it took for him to bed Lisa – or had she had the same designs on him? Young and inexperienced they might have been on the first occasion, that did not last long, for they were not shy to experiment, each meeting the other's expectations and taking things another step further, causing Lisa to quote the cliché that they had exhausted all the ideas in the *Kama Sutra*.

CJ was enjoying himself. He was having plenty of adventurous sex with no strings mentioned. They got on well together, he and Lisa, as their enjoyment of each other was not confined to sex.

They had similar tastes and listened to the same contemporary music, although Lisa was not as keen on some genres which CJ liked, such as folk, as she let him believe. They went to movies they both enjoyed, and to parties with each other's friends and made new acquaintances. They went on a couple of picnics in the country, although Lisa was not happy when CJ almost collapsed laughing at her reaction to a walker's dog stealing her sausage, and again when she squealed in horror at the ants invading the spread. She pretended to laugh about it, so CJ failed to notice how the events exposed fundamental differences between them.

His father hated shopping, he considered it a woman's job and never helped. When he accompanied Brenda on such a trip one Saturday afternoon, it was obvious he was making himself scarce and leaving the house to CJ and Lisa.

CJ was lying back on the pillows, content after a lengthy bout of gymnastic intercourse. Nestling in his shoulder, Lisa voiced her dream. 'I want a big family one day, I think four kids are not too many and should be lots of fun. Two boys and two girls to balance them out.'

CJ shot out of his drowsiness. *What was this?*

'CJ, will you do something for me?'

Alert for trouble, he was cautious. 'Depends.'

'Will you give up flying? It's so risky and you've already had one accident. Next time you may not be so lucky.'

'You should stop worrying about things which either don't exist or carry no risk. What are the chances of my having another accident when most pilots go through life without ever experiencing a major emergency?' He wormed out from under her head and went to the bathroom.

When he came out, he stood stark naked in front of the window with the shock realisation she thought they were deeply involved and was now hinting at marriage. This was far from his idea of a future – he was not ready for that.

'CJ, come away from the window, people can see you.'

He put his hand flat and horizontal on a level with his pubic hair, and registered the height of his organ against the window frame.

'Come here,' he said.

Lisa crawled over to him on all fours. He turned so his penis was at her face, and she grabbed it.

'Look out of the window.' He pointed. 'What can you see?'

'The sky.'

'That's why there's no risk of anyone seeing you giving me a blow job.'

She giggled. 'I see your point.'

* * *

CJ's overview of the situation was simple and cynical. Pharma-Scott officially swallowed Quercus Pharmacy on the 26th of May. With Quercus no longer in existence, its staff became employees of the Pharma-Scott group, or, to put it less delicately, of Kevin and Cuthbert Scott. Michael and Lisa Hines were directors, of course, but with their minority stake they had less influence.

Three years out of CJ's life had been wasted earning a business management degree to support this potential conglomerate. To make it worse, his father had hauled him into the firm as soon as he'd graduated. 'What do you want to take a holiday for? The company needs your expertise right now.'

His father was as easy to read as a children's book in overlarge lettering. He imagined his Cuthbert was looking forward to taking up his position in the new company. The man was confident his 'famous and bright' heir would have Lisa crawling around in her adoration of him to such an extent Cuthbert would have no difficulty in getting her to vote down her father with his conservative views.

But CJ was also certain Michael was banking on his daughter being able to influence him when necessary, such as when the insufferable older Scott tried to force through a board decision which was, in Michael's view, unwise.

With Kevin's odd subtle hint about keeping the Hineses firmly in their minority role on one side, and Lisa hinting at how they could sway board decisions in the direction they (she and her father) wanted, Cuthbert was the rope in a tug of war. It was annoying, not least because he would give anything not to give a damn.

11

CJ at 22

JUNE – A YEAR LATER

A little over a year after the merger, Kevin had booked his son onto a week's course in Oxford on some management thing. CJ was unsure what it was or what he was supposed to bring back to benefit the empire. It would fall into place at some stage; there was no need to sweat over it. As he stepped up into the train, he looked forward to five days away from home and away from Lisa. *My life can't carry on like this forever. I feel a change is coming. I don't know what, but I need space to think.*

His relationship with Lisa had taken a turn. They had been uncommitted in their affair for about eighteen months. They were both in it for the fun and the sex, weren't they? They were getting on pretty well, but as for the rest of their lives, that was stretching things a bit. She was very likeable, but the overwhelming desire for her which Jo at school had aroused in him was missing. Of course, that had been puppy love, and now, as a young dog with more experience, it was different. Lisa, on the other hand, kept dropping hints about marriage with increasing frequency and seemed to assume the union would occur at some stage. She kept trying to discuss her plans for a family with him, but he had so far managed to avoid these conversations with not-so-subtle changes of topic.

The marriage might be okay if the sex was anything to go by, but of course that was a feeble argument. A worry was that she liked his father, she liked his stability and his desire for money and a comfortable life in his old age. She admired Kevin's drive to build a pharmaceutical empire, and that he wanted it to stay in the family, and CJ was going to inherit it all. She had told him this, clinging to his arm as they strolled through the park one rainy day.

A serious discussion with Lisa about what she felt and what she expected of him was going to have to take place.

CJ was one of the first in the carriage, so he grabbed an aisle seat at the end with the doors immediately behind him. Other passengers were boarding, halting his maze of thoughts about relationships. A few grappled with shopping bags, bumping him as they passed, before waiting impatiently while some in front faffed around, struggling to lift their stuff up onto the racks and get seated and out of the way.

A commotion began between the doors behind him. Twisting round in his seat, CJ saw a tall man with both hands up in front of his chest in a placating gesture. Another advanced on him, shouting, 'Get away from me, get away.'

The tall man pleaded, 'Please. Calm down, I'm sorry. I didn't mean to push you. I didn't mean to get in your way. There are lots of people here, there's going to be pushing.'

'Mark, please, leave it.' A middle-aged woman called out as she fought her way past CJ. Untidy hair, drooping bloodshot eyes and a miserable expression could not disguise that she was Mark's mother. She tugged at her son's arm. He shook her away, still staring at the tall man. 'You want to fight? I'll headbutt you. You want me to headbutt you? I'll give you a headbutt!'

'Mark, please love.'

Mark was mentally disturbed in some way. *What the hell had the tall man done?* He stood with his open hands still up there, palms outwards, wondering how to deal with this. *How do you deal with the irrational?*

Mark carried on shouting, and those passengers who were trying to board retreated and went further down the train. The tall man tried to get off as well, out of the way, but Mark wasn't going to let him. He moved to block him, shouting again, the words accompanied by a spray of spittle. 'Why are you stopping the train leaving? I'm going to headbutt you. You want a headbutt from me? The train's gotta leave.'

'Mark, darling, please.' The poor mother was distraught. It was plain her strength had been sapped by too many years of caring and trying to win an unwinnable battle to calm her son when he drifted into his own chaotic world.

The entrance to the carriage had emptied but for the two men. On the platform, people had massed around the door and were staring in at the confrontation. CJ's pulse raced, his mouth went dry. Intervention was inevitable. He shifted his position, ready to get up.

'Fuck it,' yelled Mark. Illogically, he yanked on the red emergency stop handle above his head. 'Why isn't the train going? The train's gotta leave. We're going to miss our bus.' He jumped across the carriage and pulled the opposite red handle as well. The tall man saw his chance and leapt out onto the platform.

'Why aren't we leaving? We're going to be late, we'll never catch the bus now.' He was standing next to CJ, shifting from one foot to the other and shaking the seat with his hand.

Still crouched as he rose, CJ tried to promote as calm a front as he could. 'We can't go now because you pulled the red handle. We'll have to wait.'

'Who the fuck asked you?' screamed Mark, noticing CJ for the first time and glaring down at him.

'Mark, darling! Please!'

CJ was distinctly vulnerable below this troubled person. He was almost upright when Mark punched him, a downward blow which thrust him back into his seat. It hurt. Angry now, CJ pushed himself up again and got the same treatment. Mark was over him, a threatening fist pulled back in case he tried again. CJ put a defensive hand out at Mark and thrust upwards with his other from the arm rest. Mark was quicker and landed another punch on CJ's face. Blood trickled over his upper lip as he struggled to find a way out of the situation.

From ahead, a hand shot between Mark's legs and grabbed his

balls, hard. He screamed and whipped round, lashing out at the unseen attacker. A head of short fair hair caught a clip of his fist, but the hand clung on tight to its prize. CJ seized his chance, leapt upright and pinned Mark's arms to his side. The man fought. He was strong and threw CJ about as he struggled to hold on. A Transport Policeman appeared beside him. Another came down the carriage from ahead.

'All right sir, we've got him now.'

Mark's mother burst into tears as she followed her captive son onto the platform. Panting, CJ watched her leave. *How incredibly sad. Poor woman, how does she handle that on a daily basis? How many years has she been trying to control Mark?*

A nurse in the row ahead grinned at him. 'Works every time!'

'Thank you, I couldn't see how to get out of that.'

She delved in her bag and produced some tissues. 'Here, let me mop you up. You're a bit of a mess. Where are you going?'

'Oxford, some hotel, I don't remember which.'

'Me too. I've a flat not far from the station. Come back with me and I'll clean you up. You can't walk into a hotel looking like that.'

CJ studied his reflection in her bathroom mirror. *She's right, I'm a mess. People will think I've been in a pub brawl.* He gave a short humorous snort. There wasn't much difference between his face now and Barry Castle's after he'd punched it. Castle; the man will only have about four months to go if he's behaved himself.

With tender strokes, the nurse cleaned the blood off his face and stuck surgical tape on a cut over his left eye. As she patted the plaster flat, she laughed. 'And I thought my shift was over.'

They sat on opposing chairs beside her kitchen table. Her face was close to his, her breath sweet, her eyes focused on what she was doing, not on him. They were grey, and her hair was a genuine blonde. She was short and solid – not fat, but big boned with broad shoulders. Everything was proportioned and in the right place – nice, cuddly and strong.

'There you are, good enough to go home, not good enough to avoid questions, though. You want a glass of wine? I haven't got anything else.'

'I'd love one, thanks.' CJ got up and went into the tiny living room. She followed with two glasses and a bottle of plonk and sat on the arm of his chair.

'Cheers.' CJ raised his glass to her. 'Thanks again, for an unorthodox rescue and for repairing me afterwards. Oh, and for this too.'

'Are you feeling all right?' She leaned towards him, putting a hand on his arm. 'Do you want to stay here tonight, rather than your hotel?' Her expression contained no hint of her preferred answer. Perhaps she didn't have one, and it was nothing more than an honest and open question. Doubtful.

'Yes please, are you sure?'

She leant down and kissed his bruised lips, 'I'm sure.'

The bottle dead and an hour and a bit later, CJ rolled back onto the pillow.

'What's your name?'

'What's it matter? There's you and there's me, no one else here, so why do we need names?'

'True.' He paused. 'So you'll be You and I'll be Me.'

'Yes,' she giggled, 'I'll be Me and you'll be You.'

'Okay You, would you like Me to give You another dose of the same?'

'You can dose Me all night – if he can!'

12

CUTHBERT and JONATHAN at 22

JUNE

CJ lay awake in the early hours. Tenderly, he felt his bruises. What the hell was he doing here? He had stepped out of the rut of his life, naked and exposed somehow, into another world. What was to be made of this? Did it change anything?

Terry and Martin had visited when he was in hospital after the crash.

'You kept your head and did a good job.' Terry had said.

'That's not true,' CJ replied. 'I didn't keep my head. I was scared stupid – I suppose I panicked. The feeling of losing control, of not being able to do anything to rescue the situation, it's bugging me. I feel ashamed of myself. I should be better than that. I didn't think clearly.'

Terry's answer had been firm. 'You didn't panic, CJ. Anyone would have been scared, that's nothing to be ashamed of. Do you think the young pilots, your age, your grandfather in fact in the

Battle of Britain, weren't scared? The expert defusing a terrorist bomb? Of course they were. The point is, they overcame their fear and kept their heads. You overcame yours. You kept control of the aeroplane until it hit the trees. You didn't stall it, or dive it into the ground. You kept it level. There was nothing else you could have done. No one could have done better: I could not have done better. I mean that.'

'Maybe, but I've got to come to terms with how useless I felt at the time, how out of control I was.'

Almost three years had passed since that conversation. At some point, CJ had put his imagined failings behind him. Apart from being incredibly lucky to survive the crash, he had been exhilarated by it. *I have a need to repeat that feeling. I want to confront my fears and experience the thrill which comes with facing them. I want to feel the pride which follows again and again.*

But what brought these thoughts to his mind now? *It's because nothing much has happened since the accident to provide any stimulation.* He was bored with his existence – extremely bored. Yes, his relationship with Lisa was great, it was warm, but it trundled on through time without intensity. It couldn't be called a fire; the flames held little heat.

But today? Being thumped was hardly exhilarating to most people, but his injuries were insignificant, and the excitement it brought, followed by this casual, light-hearted fuck, brought CJ alive again.

He sat up, ignoring the sleeping body beside him. He had a choice, and he was poised to make a momentous, life-altering decision.

He had dared to take a brief deviation from his father's straight and narrow path and had been rewarded. His memory of the crash had been revived, invigorating him. *I was free at that time, free! Whatever the outcome might have been, disastrous or not, I had been in control of my own destiny. And I'm free now, unrestrained by the shackles at home. You, whoever you are, sleeping happily, have opened my mind: there's more to life than Dad's Gospel. You don't know it, but you've shown me a gateway to freedom, you've opened a door to a myriad of opportunities for something different. I don't have to go back to the confines of Lisa and Pharma-Scott. No, I don't. The question is, should I?*

His mind switched from one choice to another and back again. Jonathan, the natural adventuresome part of him, wanted to go one way, far away, and Cuthbert, his brainwashed cautious side, felt he should take the stable path, the prosperous path.

What about those enticing teenage dreams, the wet ones, and the fantasies which caused the result. Cuthbert, the chief executive with all his money and his yacht and his jet, and what he did with the beauties who hung onto his every word (and penny). For those fantasies to be realised, first the money had to come, and the money wasn't going to come unless he knuckled down to some hard and unpleasant work.

When Jonathan had climbed the abbey wall, he had stood on top of the crumbling stonework, more than forty feet from the ground in the middle of the night. He had taken deep breaths in the cool breeze – and coughed at the smell of pigs. He had balanced there in the moonlight, the king of the castle looking out and down upon his world. Martin's face was a pale tennis ball far below. He'd spread his arms in freedom and embraced the darkness and the thrill of having conquered something in himself, knowing death was certain if he succumbed to vertigo. That too had been invigorating.

When Cuthbert had climbed the abbey wall, he'd been incredibly lucky. To stand there swaying on the apex of an eight-hundred-year-old wall of loose stonework had been brilliant and thrilling, but what would have happened if he'd been discovered? If he'd slipped, he might have died or been severely injured. Either way, his career would have been ruined. To threaten the future with risky adventures was silly.

Jonathan recognised this night's escapade was insubstantial, but it was a welcome relief from being confined in the dungeon which Lisa was creating. Marry, four kids in the first four years. She wanted him to devote his life to following the Gospel According to Kevin. In contrast was his puppy love, Jo. He had won her schoolgirl heart through a daring raid which threatened the consequence of expulsion and a ruin of his future. He had lied about it – but what the hell? It was only a prank with no criminal intent. And it too had been exhilarating.

Cuthbert could get used to Lisa in the long-term. She was pretty, and they had good sex; not quite on the scale of this one-night episode, but damn good all the same. He should be able to temper her demands to have children too soon, and make her see that if they were going to enjoy life while they were young, then kids would have to wait. He would have to persuade Lisa that, as the director of pharmaceuticals or whatever title she wanted, the way to the top was for her to work with him and, when necessary, decorate his arm and impress their investors into signing whatever it was they had to sign.

The only other girlfriend he'd had was Jo at school. His breaking into her dormitory had been another adrenalin-pumping adventure, and he admitted it gave him an enormous sense of achievement. But he had almost ruined his future with that one too. Thrills were all very well, but there was a time to grow up and put a career first.

Jonathan had a powerful need for adventure and excitement. How was he going to satisfy that in the mundane life they wanted for him? Without the odd physical threat to spur him on, the shot of adrenalin which kept him alive, he would stagnate and become a miserable, bad-tempered husband and father.

Cuthbert the Cautious: If he rejected the Gospel, what would he do for money? How would he ever become rich? There was Grandad's inheritance, but that would not last forever, and he needed it for the flying which would give him his one escape from a humdrum existence. But if he put his reservations behind him and followed the Gospel to the letter, he would be on the path to prosperity.

He had been very, very lucky to survive that crash, and such luck was unlikely to recur every time he risked his neck. So would it be fair to his family, and would he ever become the high-flying executive if he chose not to be as cautious as his father?

Once he had made his money, he could be as adventurous as he liked. He could have his yacht and his jet – who was going to stop him? The good life lay in the long term. His father would be happy, and his mother would be happy his father had stopped fretting about his legacy. Lisa would be ecstatic, and would at once set about feathering her nest for a rush of children. To follow Kevin's Gospel would keep everyone happy. Except himself, maybe.

Jonathan the Brave: Was Lisa the right person anyway? There was purpose in her actions; she was prostituting herself to drive their thus-far uncommitted relationship in a direction of her choice. This nurse, You, was so different from Lisa. She was only out for fun, and she wanted nothing other than for him to have fun with her. No complications, no agenda, not even a name. She had not only shown him sex was available, it was out there, ready to be had, but that there was far greater depth to life than he had experienced. As promiscuous as their behaviour was, it had opened his naive eyes to a wider world of relationships, and he saw that they did not have to be confining.

I shall be treated as a pariah; but better that than chains.

13

JONATHAN'S WORLD

JUNE

On that Oxford night, their first urgent session lasted as long as it took for the wine to warm. They then set about exploring each other with a sense of fun Jonathan had never before experienced. They laughed and romped and You giggled and uttered happy, indescribable sounds.

Later, her gentle snoring was the only indication she was lying there. It wasn't loud enough to disturb the vital thoughts rebounding through his head and barring sleep.

After tossing the options around, he relaxed, comfortable with his decision. His choice was made. He was not going to settle down until he found the right person, and that person would be one who wanted to live the same life he did. In spite of the good time they were having, Lisa was not for him. *Give me ten years, and I'll consider whatever similar options are on the table, but not yet.*

The problem is how to explain this to Lisa and Mum and Dad.

Dad is going to go ballistic, Mum will collapse in tears, and Lisa might get vicious.

Whatever, I cannot do something which doesn't suit me – it'll have dreadful consequences later on, particularly if there are children involved. It's a far worse route to take. Better to be bold now than commit to a relationship that's destined to be unhappy.

So Me rolled over and prodded You into life.

'Can I stay the week?'

'You bet!'

'You mean, Me bet, don't you?'

You laughed and stood on tiptoe to kiss him before she left for work.

The course his father had booked was boring and irrelevant to his new future. What he was going to do next in life took precedence over the course material – that and what Me and You were going to get up to that night.

You was great, she treated sex as a jolly adventure, bouncing around on top of him with gay abandon and wriggling about, all the while laughing and making pleasurable noises. Sex for her was huge fun, and she gave as freely as she took. He knew this was only a happy interlude, it was never going to last, but neither of them were going to have any regrets. If they met in forty years, spouses in tow, there would be no embarrassment, only laughter.

On Friday morning they sat eating toast and drinking coffee before she left for the hospital and he, later, for his course.

She pushed the butter over to him. 'Just the right amount of time, don't you think?'

'Yes, you're right. Much longer and we would find something to argue about. We can go our different ways and remember there were only good times. How many other people can do that?'

She reached out and touched his cheek. 'You'll make someone a great husband one day, you're a good man.'

They kissed for a moment and hugged for longer. She picked up her bag and went out of her front door, leaving him to lock up and post the key back through the letter-box. He watched her walking down the street until she reached the corner. She looked back and waved. He smiled with satisfaction at the pleasure and lack of complication of it all.

* * *

Jonathan arrived home after his parents had finished their supper. He declined his mother's offer of food, having already eaten a sandwich.

'How was the course, Cuthbert?' Kevin Scott was nursing a cup of tea at the kitchen table, his eyes wide and expectant.

Jonathan regarded him without feeling. His father's bubble of enthusiasm was going to burst, but there was no point in even a white lie. 'About as boring and unimaginative as it could be,' he said with some savagery.

His father slammed his cup onto the table. 'What? I paid a fortune for that course. I'll demand my money back.'

'Oh dear!' Brenda offered.

'There was nothing wrong with the course, I suppose. But to get any value from it you have to be interested in the subject and, as I've tried to explain over and over again, I'm. Not. Interested.'

'Now look here, Cuthbert …'

'No, Dad, *you* look here. I'm tired of repeating myself to you, I don't want to follow in your footsteps – the whole concept bores me to death. It's not for me.'

Kevin had slumped onto the table with his head in his hands, shaking it slowly. Brenda tugged a little lace handkerchief from her cuff and held it to her eye.

'*Get out.*' It was said quietly from between Kevin's fingers. He jumped up, knocking his chair back. A vein in his forehead was pulsing. He stabbed his finger at the door, shouting this time. '*Get out.* Where are your family values? After all I've done for you, after the future I've laid out for you, you throw it back in my face. If you can't recognise what I've given you as my son, then there's no place for you in this house. You're no longer a member of this family. *Get. Out.*'

Brenda's hand was up to her mouth. She was trembling and had dropped her handkerchief. She reached out a tentative hand to touch Kevin's shoulder. He shook her off.

Jonathan glared back. 'I'm going. Freedom is in sight at last. And from now on, I will not answer to Cuthbert – my name is Jonathan.'

In his room, he fumbled under the bed, found his secret bottle of whisky, took a long swig and coughed. The bottle dangling from his hand, he stared around the room from the doorway, looking at the place where he had spent almost every night of his life, seeing it from a new perspective. This was the last time he would be in there. He would no longer come up here to go to bed or to listen to music or read in private. The room had to be cleared of the essentials he would need; the rest could be left.

He phoned Martin. 'Can I come and stay with you, please?'

Pulling his rucksack down from the top cupboard, he tossed it onto the bed. Things he had collected – mementos, odd hats, the books he wanted to keep, his camera, his pilot's log book, photos of his friends, even the pictures on the walls – they all reached out to him, begging to be taken along, but he had to be selective. He stuffed as much as he could into the pack and a holdall. He could come back later when his father was out to get anything more he needed.

It would not be right to leave Lisa hanging in limbo. He would have to tell her to her face they did not have a future together. There were going to be tears and angry words, but that could not be helped. Once he knew what he was doing, he would write individual letters to them all.

He closed the front door quietly and walked out into the night.

14

CUFF'S LIFE

JUNE–SEPTEMBER

On that Oxford night, their first urgent session lasted as long as it took for the wine to warm. They then set about exploring each other with a sense of fun Cuff had never before experienced. They laughed and romped and You giggled and uttered happy, indescribable sounds.

Later, her gentle snoring was the only indication she was lying there. It wasn't loud enough to disturb the vital thoughts rebounding through his head and barring sleep.

After tossing the options around for ages, he was still uncomfortable. His self-imposed pressure weighed on him.

If he rejected his dad's idea of happiness, everyone else would suffer. His father would go bananas, and his mother would worry herself sick. And Lisa? She would be devastated. For her, it would be a personal rejection, even though they had made no commitment.

There was something at the heart of the Gospel which was

unsound: it went against every fibre in his make-up. But if he changed his outlook, he should be able to come to terms with the life. A serious effort would have to be made with Lisa, for example – a commitment. He would try. Of course, to maintain sanity he would still fly and let off steam occasionally with aerobatics, which he had every intention of learning.

But first, Me needed to leave You and check into the hotel his father had booked for him. He had to get out of this flat right now, at two in the morning, if he was going to commit himself to the cause, because if he delayed he might stay.

So he eased himself out of bed, gathered his clothes and went to the bathroom to wash.

'Are you leaving already?' You's murmur was muffled by her pillow.

'Yes, I have to. It was great, truly great, but I have to go.' He leaned down and kissed her one last time. She looked good and inviting, tousled and sexy. He forced himself to stand upright.

'Aw, too soon. Thanks anyway. Look after yourself.'

'Dad, can we talk, please?' Cuthbert was standing at the kitchen door. Brenda was at the sink washing the breakfast things, and his father was drying them and putting them away. Relieved at the opportunity to stop, he sat at the kitchen table and looked up.

'Dad, I've come to terms with what you want. I'm going to accept the directorship you offered me, and I'll do the best I can to make a success of the joint company.'

A rare but brief smile flickered across Kevin's face. 'Good man, Cuthbert. I knew you would see sense in the end. There's a bright future ahead, and you'll be the boss one day. A pharmaceutical empire is your future.'

'There are two conditions, though.' The determination in Cuthbert's face said there was no bargaining to be done.

Kevin Scott was not accustomed to making concessions. His face reverted to its usual authoritarian expression. 'Conditions?'

'If you intentionally call me Cuthbert once more, I will leave. You can call me CJ or Cuff like everyone else, but never Cuffy, because that's diminutive, and never, ever Cuthbert.'

'But your name is Cuthbert. It means—'

'Famous and bright, I know. You've told us a thousand times.'

'Huh! What else, what's your other condition?' Kevin's pale face was flushed and getting darker. A vein at his temple pulsed.

'You will never again try to stop me flying.'

'But … but it's so dangerous. I need you safe.'

'The only reason you need me safe is because you want the legacy of your name on the company after you retire. I'm more likely to be killed going to work than in the air. The choice is yours – you either accept my terms or I'll leave today.'

With no intention of provocation, purely habit, Cuff turned his shirt sleeves up one fold as he watched his father's reaction. The man's face went puce, his fists clenched, and his mouth opened and shut a few times as if he had difficulty in finding the words he wanted. No one had ever managed to better him in an argument. No one had issued a take-it-or-leave-it demand to him before, and now it was his very own son who stood there challenging him – Cuthbert had always done as he was told. It was hard for Kevin, with his own argument being untenable, and the situation therefore unacceptable.

Wincing, Kevin clutched his left arm. 'I'm going to lie down. I … I feel dizzy.'

Brenda's eyes were wide. 'Cuthbert, what have you done?'

She rushed out after her husband and turned the corner to the stairs. Cuff followed with a sense of foreboding. Brenda's foot was on the bottom step. Kevin had almost reached the top. He had paused his struggle to climb and was clutching the banister, panting with exertion.

It happened so slowly. First he cried out in pain and let go of the rail, pressing his hand to his chest. He doubled over and staggered, turning enough for them to see the agony on his face. His foot slipped, and he pitched headlong down the stairs to land at Brenda's feet, his head lying against her leg at an impossible angle.

A week after the funeral, Cuff and Martin were sitting at an outside table at The Gargoyle getting drunk. The sun was warm and the Thames flowed by slowly, allowing hopeful swans to keep station without effort. Cuff threw a piece of crust into the water.

'You shouldn't do that, bread is bad for them,' said Martin.

'I blame myself,' Cuff said. 'I should not have been so confrontational. He couldn't handle people disagreeing with him, particularly when it came to his dream.'

'You had to say what you had to say. You can't take blame for asserting yourself. I'm sorry to say this, but he never allowed you any of the freedom of choice others of us have. He dictated your future, and I think you were very loyal to follow in his footsteps, on a path that's contrary to your nature. Do you miss him?'

Cuff paused before answering. 'No.'

'How's your mum coping?'

'Not very well. She's confused and doesn't know what to do. She wants to sell everything to raise money she thinks we don't have. I don't think she loved him, he was not a lovable person, but he was her rock, and now she's alone. It doesn't help she blames me for causing his heart attack.'

Cuff paused and drained his glass.

'This entrenches me more deeply in the bloody business. I'd love to pack it in and bugger off somewhere, but I can't leave it now. I'll have to look after Mum, and there are employees with jobs.'

'And Lisa.'

'Yes. She's being very supportive, I must say. She's been great helping with Mum.'

They fell silent and watched the swans for a while. Martin asked, 'Another beer? It's my turn.' He threaded his way through the tables to the bar, already a little unsteady on his feet.

Martin returned and put the beers down on the table. 'I was thinking, isn't Castle due out soon?'

'Don't remind me.'

It was a tearful Lisa who told him. She had been there. 'She was very confused. I could hardly make sense of what she was saying. She seemed to be in some sort of trance almost, vague, out of it. We were talking as we walked along the pavement towards the zebra crossing. Then she saw her bus on the other side and stepped into the road. I tried to grab her, but missed. It was horrible, Cuff. The driver had no time to react. It was awful to see. I don't want to think about it. I'm so sorry.'

Cuff was stunned. At first he didn't believe it. *Mum, gone so soon after Dad!*

As he told Martin, 'Mum's death overshadows Dad's. He was such a dominant person, but so emotionally remote, he's hard to miss. Mum was a good, harmless soul. She's always been there for me, not very effectively, but she tried, and I've never given her credit for that.

'I suppose it was my fault Dad died, so it's also my fault she followed. She was so shocked at the loss of her support. She didn't understand. She didn't know what she was doing. She was living in a trance, fumbling along until she strayed blindly to her fate. Dad had never let the poor woman have a full and happy life: so sad when I think about it. I tell you what, though, it's going to be a problem running the business without him. I've never paid any attention to how it's done.'

People commiserated with him, and one even expressed sympathy for his complete lack of family. Cuff was puzzled at first; he had always been alone in a familial sense, so it never occurred to him to think of the loss in those terms.

Lisa was a rock; she gave Cuff an extraordinary amount of support in comfort, organisation of the funeral, disposal of assets and dealing with solicitors and insurance companies. He was grateful for the help, and the more she did the more he came to rely on her to the extent that they became a team – like man and wife.

Later, when he was in a bitter mood, he asked himself if her actions had been calculated, if she had been laying down the bed for her marriage, her family, and her future.

It was easy to slip from that weak and reliant state to agreeing to marry. In spite of some lurking reservations, though, Cuff did just that, but only after he insisted on a serious conversation on the way it was going to work.

'Lisa, we get along well, we love each other. There's no reason we can't have a successful life together provided we recognise there are some no-go areas for each of us: serious stuff. If we breach these boundaries, there's going to be disagreement, and we could fall apart.'

She hesitated, looking worried. 'Okay. That's sensible, I suppose. It'll give us some ground rules. What were you thinking of?'

'I want kids,' Cuff said, and her expression switched to delight. 'But not for three years.'

Lisa jerked back as if he'd hit her. Her face fell. 'Why? Why wait so long? Oh Cuff!'

'Lisa, don't cry, for heaven's sake. I'm only twenty-two. You're a year older. Our whole lives are still ahead of us. We have plenty of time before it's too late for you to have children. There is so much of the world to see, so much to do together, so many adventures to excite us, all of which would be hindered by the presence of a child. My basic nature is to live on the edge. If you don't allow that, I'll be very difficult to live with, I'll likely rebel against the marriage, and I'll come to hate myself.'

'I see.' She paused, thinking, while Cuff waited. 'What other demands do you have?' she ventured.

'I must continue flying. It's an absolute passion. You'll have to let me indulge in it, same reasons as before. That's all. What do *you* want?'

Lisa sniffed and dabbed at her eyes. 'Nothing. I think I'm going to lie down for while, I've a headache.'

Lisa was easy to damage but quick to repair. Cuff, however, was not certain whether she did consign any differences between them to the dustbin, or whether her overriding desire to have a husband smothered them under a temporary cloak which would be withdrawn when strategically necessary. So, despite conditions and tears, the union was agreed and arrangements were made for a ceremony as soon as it could be held.

Their marriage began well. With the death of his parents sufficiently far in the past, they had a quiet ceremony and reception on a beautiful Saturday in September. Martin, of course, was best man, and Lisa's firm friend Sheila was bridesmaid. Michael Hines adored his darling daughter and told the couple he had every intention of hiring an eighteenth-century mansion-turned-hotel for the reception. Onc glance at the estimate put paid to that idea, so he was forced to settle for a marquee on the edge of a village cricket field. It made no difference. Martin's speech was brilliant and contained the joke that, as their nemesis was about to be released from jail, so Cuff was going into chains. Most people laughed, but Lisa gave only a token tight-lipped smile.

They went to a Greek island for their week's honeymoon and came back tanned and invigorated for the future. All was well while sex was prominent in their lives; any little problems could be worked out or forgotten or forgiven in bed. They had fun too: parties and movies and the theatre occasionally, plus weekends away and country events.

It was all fun for the first two months, and Cuff relaxed into his new way of life, comfortable with the decision he had made.

82

15

JONATHAN'S WORLD

SEPTEMBER

In early September, Castle was told his cousins were in the country. He signed the Visiting Order and waited impatiently for them to arrange a date.

One afternoon, his cell door opened with the familiar metallic clacks.

'Your visitors are here,' the prison officer said and smirked. 'Better smarten up, and you can give me their numbers.'

Castle hated all the guards. 'I might do that,' he said, knowing what would result and looking pleased for once.

In the Visits Room, he was told to sit at a table as usual. Wives and children and brothers and friends entered and rushed to meet their loved ones.

Hannah and Anna stilled much of the conversation as they came in. Frustrated males showed lascivious interest as the twins crossed the floor. Castle hugged them both together in a little huddle, under the watchful eye of an officer and some hard stares from jealous prisoners.

In Germany all those years ago, he had given up trying to identify each one, and took to addressing them as a unit – *Zwillingsmädchen*, twin sisters. The way he bowed to their nationality but shortened it to *Zwillings* made them laugh. Now, they looked as happy and confident as usual.

'How's things? How're your plans shaping up?'

'We have had success, Barry. Only one, but it was fun, and we feel good. It was in Prague and was very easy. Poor man, we have a big advantage as we are identical and beautiful and charming. It conquers the most suspicious people, actually.'

Castle shook his head in wonder at them. Clever girls, weird tastes, but fascinating. 'I want to hear all about it, one day. But you must be careful. In English we say pride comes before a fall.'

'*Ja*, we know this, actually. We are very careful. Don't worry.'

'Will you do something for me, *Zwillings*? It should fit your plans, and I think you'll enjoy it.'

At The Gargoyle once again, Jonathan took a table outside on the deck above the river. He ordered beers and waited for Ginny and Martin to join him. He was still staying with them and kept himself occupied with a job as a barman most evenings. By day, he flew to keep his hand in and planned his travels, which were due to start in a couple of weeks.

A family of six occupied the adjacent table. Loud voices, a booming male and a squeaky mother with giggling kids. He watched them idly, thanking heaven he was not going to be in that situation for many years yet.

'Cheers,' Jonathan said as his friends arrived. 'It's a fantastic day for drinking.'

'Skol,' said Martin, who liked to be different.

Ginny raised her glass.

Two young people in red jackets came out onto the deck and scanned the area. Jonathan glanced up at them before they took the table behind him. Why did they have their hoods up on this brilliant afternoon?

'Here, I've drawn up a programme. Whether I'll stick to it depends on events, but at least I've listed the sights I want to see, starting in Bolivia. All I've booked are the flights, everything else is suck it and see.'

Ginny said, 'This looks wonderful, Jonathan. I haven't even heard of some of these places.'

'We should come with you, but we can't.' Martin took a large gulp of beer. 'You'll keep us up to date, won't you?'

'Of course I will.'

Ginny folded the paper and handed it back to him.

'No, you keep that programme, so you know roughly where I am. I'll print another copy.'

Martin bought another round. When that was half downed, Ginny said, 'Jonathan, sorry, we need to go I'm afraid. Martin, we're going to be late.'

Martin sniffed as he always did and blew his nose. 'Do we have to? I'd much rather get drunk with my friend.'

'We said we would. Come on.'

As they reached the car park, Martin was searching his pockets. 'I think I've dropped your programme. I wonder of that couple have it.' He pointed over the cars to the deck where the two red-hooded people were studying a sheet of paper.

'Don't worry about it, I'll print you another,' said Jonathan.

16

BARRY CASTLE

SEPTEMBER–OCTOBER

In the last few days before Eddie was released, five months ago, Castle had been stewing over what he was going to do when it was his turn, and abruptly realised time was running short to get more information out of the little weed. He was lying in his bunk while Eddie was sitting in a chair.

'Look Barry,' said Eddie after a series of repeated questions, 'I've told you all I know about nicking someone's ID, but if you want to commit fraud, you're going to have to use your nous, 'cause I don't know what you have in mind, and I don't wanna know. I've learned my lesson, and I'll not be doing it again. I'll tell you what I'll do. I'm going to introduce you to the guy who helped me. He'll charge a bit, but he'll do all the donkey work, hack computers, give you hands-on advice. He's bloody good. I only ended up here 'cause I fucked up, not him. I'll tell him about you and tell you how to get hold of him. All right?'

'Okay. How will I know what's happening, when you'll give me the information? I'll be out in October.'

Eddie laughed. 'Trust me, I'll do it. I might even come and visit you for old times' sake.'

Barry Castle was released from prison in October, three years after he entered it. He walked away from the vast, dark, threatening door with his confident, swaggering and odd gait of short strides. He stopped after a few paces, looked up at the grey overcast sky and breathed freedom, appreciating the cleaner air outside the walls. A tall chestnut tree stood at the edge of the parking area. Already a few leaves were turning bronze, but Castle passed under it without an upward glance. Trees were for country yokels, whereas he was city bred; somehow that made him a more advanced human being. He was carrying his minimal possessions in a holdall and heading in the wrong direction.

His mother had been waiting in her car, the wipers flicking the Scotch mist away. She got out and waved. She hugged and kissed him, and he threw his bag onto the back seat. On the way home she asked, 'What would you like to do now? Have you given more thought to what you're going to do for the future?'

'Right now, I just want to go home and get drunk. I've got options, and I'll think about them over the next few days.'

Although her English was almost indistinguishable from a native, Eva would sometimes use the odd German word as if she could not release her past. The disappointment in her voice was clear. 'You've had three years to do that, *Schatz*. Never mind, it'll take a little while to get used to life.'

Castle did not respond. He could not explain to his mother, because she would be horrified, but he was excited that at last he could put his plans into action. He knew very well what he was going to do.

She interrupted his thoughts. 'You know Bert, who runs the car dealership?'

'Yeah.'

'Well, I was telling him you'd be looking for a job and he said you should go and see him, have an interview.'

'Does he know I've been inside?'

'*Ja*, but he said we all make mistakes and anyway, from what he heard, you weren't totally responsible. The girl had asked for it, he said, and he couldn't see how it would affect you selling cars.'

'Second-hand car salesman. That's not really a good job is it?'

'You can't afford to be picky. You're charming, you're a handsome boy and on top of the salary there's commission. We'll get you some smart clothes, create a good impression. You should talk to him at least.'

'All right, Mum. Thanks.' To change the subject he said, 'How are my cousins?'

'Oh, they're well, I think. You can't speak to them, because they're backpacking in South America. I don't know where. I'm so glad you all like each other, they're such sweet things and good fun.'

Castle looked away from her to hide his smirk. She didn't know how right she was.

17

CUFF'S LIFE

BARRY CASTLE – OCTOBER

Castle picked up the phone and took a deep breath. 'Right, Cuffy Fucking Cuthbert Scott, it begins: your enemy is moving in. I'm going to take you apart pound by pound and juicy bit by juicy bit.'

The phone was answered on the third ring. 'Yup?'

'Eddie told me to call you,' Castle said, his voice hoarse and nervous.

'I don't know any Eddie. You've got the wrong number.' *Click.*

Castle knew he had to ring again in an hour's time, so wasn't concerned.

On his second call, the receiver was picked up, but nothing was said. He heard breathing on the other end and what sounded like a keyboard being tapped.

'I'm calling about Eddie, Eddie from Winchester.'

'Ah. And you are?' The voice sounded young, high pitched, almost female. It conjured an imagine of a youth with a sparse immature beard, acne and skin which never saw the sun.

'Basil Rampart.'

'Sandford Lock. There's a bench near the notice board on the island. Nine tomorrow.'

'Okay.'

Click.

The seat was on the opposite side of the Thames. There was no one there the following morning. He crossed over the bridge and hurried to the bench, pulling up his hood both to ward off the drizzle and to hide. He was wearing grey tracksuit bottoms, and they were getting very damp and cold. There was still no one there. Uncomfortable outside his home environment, he scratched at his crotch and sat down to wait. It was certain he was being watched, but he wasn't concerned. The hacker could not afford to take chances, and neither would he under the circumstances.

'Don't turn around.' The same voice as on the telephone came from behind him. 'How's Eddie?'

'He recommends you highly. I'd like your help too, please.' Castle rarely used the word 'please', it was foreign to his lips and sounded strange.

'What do you want from me?'

Castle explained. If only he could see what weed he was talking to.

'What information have you got?'

'It's all on this paper.' He held a folded sheet up above his shoulder.

'Stay there. Keep looking at the river.'

The paper was taken out of his hand and he heard the figure retreat back into the trees.

'Cuthbert Scott, known as Cuffy and an address. There's not much here, not even an accurate date of birth. January has thirty-one days in it, you know.'

'It's all I can get. Eddie said you work with almost nothing.'

'The less info you have, the more it costs. Call me tomorrow, I'll let you know if I can use this.'

'Okay, what time?' He was talking to the trees.

The next day at around lunchtime Castle phoned the number again.

'Yup?'

'It's Rampart. You told me to call.'

'Oh, right. Yeah. I think I can work with this, but it's going to take a while. Plus there are two jobs ahead of you. I can maybe make a start next week.'

Castle could not keep the disappointment out of his voice. 'Oh. I thought it was a quick thing.'

'No it isn't. And I'm not going to start until you cough up a deposit. Five hundred, and I'll tell you what the final figure will be when I've got more into it.'

'Shit!'

'No shit. It's your choice, I've got plenty of work. Cash. You can leave it in the rubbish bin next to that bench. Tell me when it'll be there.' *Click.*

18

JONATHAN'S WORLD

OCTOBER

The journey time from London Heathrow to Santa Cruz de la Sierra in Bolivia via Madrid is about sixteen and a half hours. It is a long trip in an economy seat by any standards. Jonathan slept little, so took full advantage of the free alcohol. He was tired and restless by the time he arrived in the early morning.

His efforts to sleep had been disrupted by the physical needs of his neighbours and recurring recollections of his struggle with Lisa. With her at the kitchen table, he had paced the room. To soften the blow, he first explained why before revealing he was going away.

Lisa's face had been getting more and more drawn as she listened to the reasons. With his words of departure, she burst into tears.

'You bastard, you fucking bastard! You used me, and now you've dumped me like a piece of rubbish. You selfish bloody, bloody ...' She leapt to her feet and thumped his chest with her fists. Whirling around, she grabbed a knife from the rack.

Jonathan backed away, glimpsed the breadboard, seized it. Lisa lunged. The knife rammed into the wood. He slapped her across the cheek. Her eyes widened and went blank, and she slumped to the floor on her backside. She curled into the corner where she landed, sobbing. Jonathan put the board back on the counter, the knife still lodged in it. He tried to help her up, to be kind to her, but she shoved him away.

'Lisa, try to understand what I'm say—'

'You've ripped my dreams of a family to shreds. You've robbed me of the future. You led me on; we were going to be married.'

'I, *we*, never made any commitments. You know that. You deluded yourself, Lisa. I never promised you anything. I thought we were merely having fun together.'

'You selfish, selfish bastard. I hope you rot in hell!'

That knife was embedded in the breadboard by half an inch, at least. The image was still vivid, and it had been too close for comfort.

The distasteful subject of money had been something else he could not avoid. He still had plenty left from the first instalment of his grandfather's legacy, even after paying Terry for his flying lessons. He withdrew the lot, bought a money card to use in South America and closed his account. There was still the second instalment of the inheritance, which would be available when he was twenty-three. The executors of the will had been told he would apply for it at some time in the future, when he had made a decision on what course his life was going to take. Grandad had been clever in insisting on a solid plan for a business before the full legacy was made available.

South America magnetised him. He was attracted by the Altiplano, the great plateau upwards of twelve thousand feet of altitude which stretches along the Andes from southern Peru through Bolivia and touching into Argentina and Chile. Bolivia was cheap, which was important, and cheerful and a great start to his life of adventure. School geography had tempted him with images of Lake Titicaca and the Salar de Uyuni, both on the Altiplano, and he made it a goal to explore them.

It pained him, but his flying had to take a back seat for a while. He needed his money to travel, and to carry on flying in foreign countries would incur all sorts of bureaucratic hurdles over licences and medical examinations and language issues. Maybe he could find a hang-gliding club or try kitesurfing later when he reached Peru.

That evening, struggling to stay awake with the jet lag weighing on him, he wrote. To his father he sent a strong letter emphasising the finality of his decision. There was no hint of affection in it. To his mother he was softer and apologetic, and ended it with *'Love'*. To Lisa he was more regretful and tender, but firm, preventing any thought on her part that there was a possibility of him changing his mind. She should forget about him and move on, the letter implied, ending with *'Yours'*. It took him a long time to write much the same thing in three different tones, because he took great care to be as kind as possible.

The ageing Boeing 727 adopted a steep approach to the Juana Azurduy de Padilla International Airport at Sucre. With a short runway and an altitude over nine and a half thousand feet, it needed to be steep. High ground passed by the cabin window as they neared the surface. The view reminded him of the last glimpses of the hillside he'd had before his crash and made him nervous, but the pilot put the big aircraft down right on the threshold, hard. The immediate roar of the reverse thrust and the maximum braking had the passengers hanging forward in their seats and the overhead baggage bins rattling and squeaking under the strain. The brakes were only released as they turned to backtrack to the terminal, the wing swinging out over the grass at the end of the runway. *Whew! There's no room for error here, it must be like landing on an aircraft carrier. And these pilots do it every day.*

The lengthy aristocratic-sounding names the Spanish gave themselves fascinated Jonathan, and he wrote the airport name in his notebook as he rode the bus into the town. It dropped him and several other passengers in a square which was part car park and part bus and taxi station.

Always on the lookout, Jonathan noticed a couple of fair-haired girls dwarfed by huge backpacks hovering near the ticket booth. As he joined the queue, they slipped in behind him. He grinned at them, and got sweet smiles in return. He asked for Potosí, took his ticket and walked away to find a toilet before identifying his bus amongst all the other colourful ones.

Helpful people pointed him to a bright blue vehicle with golden artwork on its side. Wary of thieves, he carried his pack to the rear and stowed it on the rack. The back row of seats beckoned because the centre one would allow him to stretch his legs into the aisle. The two girls from the queue were on one side and a Quechua couple on the other. A local man was about to take the seat, but one of the women must have said something, because he moved and allowed the foreigners to sit together. Jonathan thanked him. He nodded in return.

'Hello,' the two girls said in unison. They were in their twenties and quite pretty.

'Hello.' Jonathan pulled his sleeves up and settled in. 'You're sisters, twins.'

'Yes,' they answered in unison, 'we know that, actually.' German accents. They were dressed in identical jeans with the fashionable tears at the knees, and black T-shirts, which undoubtedly had the same logos or quotes, but these were covered in red down jackets. Four red canvas shoes covered four small feet set in a neat row on the floor.

'I'm Jonathan.'

'Hello Jonathan, I'm Anna.'

'Hello Jonathan, I'm Hannah.'

'There must have been confusion in your family when your mother called, if you misheard, that is.'

'No, because we would both answer together, actually.'

'Something tells me you like to play games with people and confuse them.'

They laughed. '*Ja*, that's true. It's good fun.'

More passengers were boarding. Quechua women in their colourful dresses and bowler-style hats; children, rosy-cheeked and tanned from the high altitude and clear air; and an elderly couple with leathery, sun-wrinkled skin and who might have been much younger than they appeared, seated themselves for the long drive.

There was a stop at a roadside tea shop. The old couple got off first, followed by everyone else. Some piled into the shop for refreshments, while others took long grateful drags on their cigarettes and kicked at the dust. Hannah and Anna disappeared in search of a toilet, and Jonathan followed a few equally desperate men.

Afterwards, he bought some tea and a packet of huge maize kernels each for the girls. They were nice and very friendly, and they livened up the bus ride. Like him, they were going to Potosí and Uyuni before visiting the Salar, and were excited at the unique prospect of spending the night at the salt hotel in the middle of the flat.

By the time they reached Potosí, Jonathan and the twins were getting along famously. He had pinned them down to their names by virtue of their seat positions at first, but after the stop he could not be sure if they had changed places, and they were having a lot of fun over his confusion.

'There must be a way to tell you two apart?'

'Oh yes,' said Anna, or was that Hannah?

The other one was teasing. 'But it's in a private place.'

'There's too much opposition in you two – I give up and apologise for any mistaken identity.'

'We call ourselves Black Widows.'

'Widows so soon, both of you – or do you kill after mating?'

They laughed in unison. 'Not one or the other, we just like to put fear into the hearts of men. You have a place to stay in Potosí?'

'No, I was going to ask a taxi driver.'

'We have a place booked, but it is a little expensive, actually. If you want, we could share, and also the cost.'

Jonathan's heart changed gear. He agreed, with a weak attempt to keep his enthusiasm hidden. *Wow! Where's this heading? Don't be presumptuous, they'll have you for toast if you put a foot wrong.*

His feet remained firmly in the right place and they didn't toast him, but later they made him the meat in their sandwich.

'This is the stuff dreams are made of,' he told them, but admitted he was knackered. They did not understand the word, so he had to explain how it could refer both to testicles and exhaustion. They thought that was very funny and teased him and kept him close: their toy.

Or was he? During the next leg of their bus journey, they had him sit between them. They were all laughing and telling silly stories, but occasionally the girls spoke across him to each other in German. It made him feel disadvantaged. It was understandable that the twins considered themselves a unit, but as they were travelling and sharing their bed with him, they should not make him feel so excluded. He caught them exchanging glances now and again, but could not see a relevance to the discussion when they did … *Maybe that's what twins do?*

From the 1890s to the 1940s there was a British-built railway which was used by the mines to carry minerals to the port of Antofagasta for export. When the mining industry collapsed in the forties, the railway fell into disuse and the engines and rolling stock were left abandoned on several parallel lines in what is now the well-known Cementerio de Trenes. This train cemetery is walking distance from Uyuni, but it was getting late so Jonathan and the twins took a taxi.

Under the deep blue cloudless sky, steam engine after engine lined one particular track, the rails themselves part buried in sand and stones. In the dry air this ancient machinery had hardly rusted in over sixty years, but it had been robbed of whatever steel was easy to remove. Huge driving wheels were aligned in perfect rows, but without their coupling rods. The ends and tubes of most boilers had been taken, leaving the supporting frames like giant cutting plates from a mincing machine. On other tracks were engines listing to one side where the rails had sunk into the surface; box cars, now skeletons stripped of their side panels; dismantled carriages; wheel bogies on their own, some off the tracks in the dirt or piled on top of each other; and enough scrap metal to make a man in the right place a millionaire – but not here.

It was the engines which most fascinated Jonathan, and he explored them for photographic opportunities, of which he saw many. Rising from a crouch beside a set of driving wheels, he looked around for the twins. He hadn't seen them for a few minutes. It was of no concern, it was easy to be out of sight behind some steel hulk. He smiled to himself. *I'll surprise them. I'll creep up on them and give them a fright.* He looked under the trains for their legs. He walked along the line of engines, squeezing between them to look down the aisle separating the tracks. Nothing. He crossed to the next line towards a set of useless rolling stock and again checked under the cars. Nothing. They must be waiting for him at the taxi. He went back to his queue of engines. Another photo presented itself to him, and he crouched to take his picture from a low angle.

'Hello.' The voice was from the cab above him.

'Hello Jonathan,' came from the engine cab on the adjacent line.

He started, and his shot was ruined. 'Oh hello, you two. I was wondering where you were. I want to take this photo before we go, if you're ready.'

There was no reply, and he knelt again, his attention occupied by the symmetry of the line of wheels and the orange evening light which amplified what small areas of rust there were. A shutter-click later, he stood and was checking the picture on his camera monitor.

'That's good.' The voices murmured in both his ears. They were on either side of him, their arms linked together behind his back as they studied his work. It was uncanny how these two would each say the same thing unrehearsed. It was unnerving how they could move together so silently. He hadn't heard them come down from their cabs, nor heard the one cross to him from the other track.

That night in Uyuni after a few beers and a good meal at over twelve thousand feet, Jonathan was lying weak and defenceless on the bed. Anna, naked, was astride his chest, the hot dampness of her crotch on his skin. Hannah was riding him, gasping with deep rhythmic moans as she clung on to her sister from behind. He was trapped, unable to move with his approaching orgasm and was struggling for oxygen in the thin air with Anna's weight constricting his chest. Above her small, firm breasts, the nipples erect, her face was framed by her hair, which fell on either side, casting a deep shadow. From that oval of darkness, her eyes glinted as they focused intently on his.

She had him pinned to the bed by his shoulders. Her fingers brushed over his skin as they crept inwards to his neck with a gentle, almost loving, touch.

The pressure of her thumbs was light at first. So light, he ignored it. Until it increased. More and more. He panicked. Hands together, elbows apart, he formed a wedge that he drove up between her forearms breaking her grip. With a violent thrust, he bucked his hips. Anna was thrown forward, her breasts smothering his face. Hannah landed on the floor.

'Don't do that!' Panting, he shoved Anna off.

Hannah was angry. 'What's wrong with you? That was the worst moment to do something.'

'Don't ever put your hands round my neck again.'

'I'm sorry, Jonathan. Some men like that, they say it increases their pleasure.'

'Well I bloody well don't. It's hard enough to get air up here as it is.'

Anna gave her sister a brief hug. 'Sorry, Hannah, I spoilt your fun. Jonathan, sorry. Let's make up, please. It's my turn.'

He calmed himself and allowed them to restore his confidence and start again. He lay awake for a long time afterwards, though, deflated. Even so, his sleep was postponed as he recalled how Anna's eyes were empty and devoid of expression when her fingers had tightened around his throat.

The largest salt flats in the world, the Salar de Uyuni is a unique visual experience with 'flat' being the operative word and the colour white being a glaring, dominant, inescapable fact. A thin layer of water from recent rain created a perfect mirror that blended sky and distant clouds into their reflections and made it impossible to discern the horizon.

Other tourists were playing around, taking funny photos and getting in a silly mood, their reflections so perfect that people appeared to be floating somewhere above an indeterminate surface.

Anna stepped out of the vehicle first, followed by Jonathan. It was hard to tell up from down at first, disorienting. He almost fell and clutched the car door for support. Anna giggled and hung on to him until Hannah reached them, dragging her hand on the vehicle for reference as she came around from the other side and joined their hug. Last night's upset was behind them, but Jonathan caught another brief, conspiratorial smile between the girls as they broke up.

Back in the car, the twins placed Jonathan in the middle between them. Anna's (or Hannah's) hand rested on his inner thigh. Hannah's (or Anna's) hand rested on the other thigh. As the driver continued across the flats through the film of water along a route only he knew, the hands gradually crept up to Jonathan's crotch. He laughed at them and settled back to enjoy whatever they were planning. Nothing. The hands stayed there, each with a light pressure on his erection, but did not move.

'Wait for your salt bed, Jonathan,' said the twin on his right.

'*Ja*, be patient. Put this thing down, you're wasting it, actually,' teased the other.

The salt hotel was a let-down. The fascinating, but unattractive, place was located in the middle of the flats. A low building, its walls, floor and furniture were constructed from salt blocks, most of which, like liquorice sweets, showed separate layers of brown sediment laid down through tens of thousands of years. The shallow-pitched roof was covered in a sparse layer of thatch. Set against the incredible brightness of the Salar, it was an ugly example of how man could ruin nature.

'I'm not feeling so good.' One of them was rubbing her stomach after dinner. Her mouth was twisted at her discomfort.

'Oh Anna, so sorry. Is it the food?'

'*Ja*, it must be.'

Jonathan grunted. 'My gut is also churning around. Let's hope it doesn't get worse.'

'*Ja*, that will be terrible.'

'I'm going to bed, girls.'

'Me also.'

'So, you can take a break tonight, Jonathan. Build your strength up again.' Hannah laughed at him as she put her arm round her sister and led her off to bed.

Although uncomfortable and tossing and turning most of the night with a gurgling stomach, the blessing was that Hannah was right: he was getting a rest from these two for a while. They were super friendly and intimate most of the time but, now and again, there were those looks between them and hard expressions on those pretty young faces.

Or is that my imagination?

They caught the tourist bus to La Paz. It was a night ride over mostly gravel roads, but the vehicle was large and comfortable with a toilet, and hot drinks were available. The twins sat in the row in front of Jonathan, while he was next to a small Korean man who did not speak English but smiled and nodded a lot when he was awake and snored when asleep.

It was the second night in a row that circumstances had liberated him from physical contact with the twins. Their intimacy was something he could not help enjoying at the time, but once released he felt free. Although, was he? In the middle of the night he woke to see the glint of an eye regarding him from the row ahead. He winked at it, whomever it belonged to, and it retreated into the dark.

This episode in his life would soon end. They would go their way, and he his. Should he part company with them in La Paz? It would stop his inexplicable feelings of unease. On the other hand, he was indulging in amazing sex with two women at once, twins at that. His youthful testosterone levels were to blame, of course, telling him that if he gave up now, he would rue the decision for the rest of his life. After all, how many other young men can boast of such exploits? *Although much more of it at this altitude, and I could have a heart attack.*

When they reached La Paz the twins did something odd, putting another question mark on their behaviour. In the tourist office, they pored over brochures of likely accommodation.

'What about this one? It's a low cost, actually,' said Hannah.

Anna peered at her sister's pamphlet. 'It's not so bad in the photos.'

'It's probably dreadful and run-down at that price, but any of these will be the same. Let's try it,' Jonathan said.

After the short taxi ride, they pulled him away from the hotel entrance. 'Jonathan, you book in, please. We want to see something.'

'Okay, but why don't we all check in, you leave your packs and go off and I'll see you later.'

'No, we don't want to do it that way, actually. We need our packs for the moment.'

'Please get the room number and meet us round the corner in a few minutes, Jonathan.'

He gave them a puzzled look. Previously, in Potosí, Uyuni, the salt hotel, in the cars and everywhere they had been, the girls had made no effort to conceal the fact they were a threesome, but here at this nondescript establishment in a back street in one of the highest cities in the world, they chose to keep out of the way. Why be worried about girls in a man's room in a seedy dump like this?

He shrugged his shoulders and put on a matching expression. 'Whatever.'

The answer was sweet smiles.

After checking in, he found them. 'Room twenty-one. You go off and have fun. I didn't sleep on the bus, so I'm going to have a nap.

I'll see you later.'

Jonathan slept until lunchtime. He was uneasy and unable to trace the cause. There was nothing wrong in what they had done, perhaps they wanted some time to themselves, but why the nonsense over the check-in? If they were trying to hide, why? This unease was identical to that he had had before his aircraft crash.

He counted out some notes, stuffed his share of the room cost in between the sheets, picked up his pack and left down the fire escape.

19

JONATHAN'S WORLD

OCTOBER

Jonathan gazed out of the window of the bus, trying to get a clear view between the smears of hair oil on the glass. The vehicle ground its way uphill, its gear train issuing disturbing noises, as it headed out of La Paz for Lake Titicaca.

In this suburb on the outskirts of the city, soulless flat-roofed houses and blocks of flats followed the contours of the steep mountainside in a shambolic pattern of ugliness. With no attempt made to hide them, rickety sewage pipes dropped several storeys down the side of buildings or short cliff faces. *Some of these buildings are not even upright. The architects of this lot should be put up against the walls of their dreadful creations and shot.*

The sky was overcast that day, one of the few he had experienced, but it was high stuff and did not threaten rain. The grey was relieved by the decorated buses and trucks which, honking at pedestrians and each other, moved past roadside stalls displaying all manner of goods in a kaleidoscope of reds and yellows, greens and whites and blues. The bus stopped a couple of times before it left the city to offload or take on more passengers. *What people are they – Aymara? They're supposed to be the most prevalent in this area.*

Jonathan was heading for Copacabana, a tourist Mecca, an ancient lakeside town which manages to cater for both a steady stream of backpackers and locals with hotels, hostels and bars, as well as the traditional attributes of a country settlement. To get there from within Bolivia, the bus had to stop in Tiquina to let its passengers cross a narrow strait in little boats while the bus itself travelled on its own barge.

A middle-aged American lady was puzzled. 'Why don't we stay on the bus? This little boat don't look safe to me. I mean, look at that engine, it doesn't even have a cover.'

No one else replied so Jonathan did. 'A few years ago, many people lost their lives when a barge capsized, and they were trapped inside their bus. You should watch it and hope for the best.' He laughed. 'Your bags are on it.'

There was no wind, and the water was calm all the way to the far shore. As their little ferry moved out of the dock, another two buses from La Paz arrived to wait their turn for the crossing. Their passengers disembarked, and Jonathan searched amongst them for the twins.

They had given him an experience which was never likely to be repeated in a lifetime, but it had drained him. Since that night in Uyuni, without realising it, he had been on his guard. But now, the ride from La Paz, the absence of a language he could understand and therefore listen in to, the green of the countryside, the peace of the lake – all contributed to his tension oozing away. He was comfortable in a closeted world of his own for a while. With the little ferryboat, some laughter from its passengers and the excitement of arriving in a new place, he recovered his sense of freedom, not quite believing the twins had had such an effect on him. *It was fantastic, but I'm not sorry to have left them behind. I'm now on my own and out of danger. Danger? Why on earth did that word spring to mind?*

In Copacabana, Jonathan searched for somewhere to stay, and found a decent bed in a clean room with its own shower and toilet. Watching his budget, he was concerned that this was going to cost a few bolivianos more than he wished to pay, but was too tired to search for another place. It was set a little higher up the hill than most of the town and had a magnificent view out over the bay and jetties below.

He set off to find somewhere to get a drink and eat.

The bar looked out over the beach onto Lake Titicaca. It was late afternoon and a faint orange glow was building in the crystal sky. Scores of small pleasure boats and canoes were drawn up on the sand, faced by a row of tiny narrow restaurants which served the world's most delicious trout with chips at plastic tables. A lot of laughing and screaming and splashing came from a struggle to push a trio of girls into the water.

The lighting in the bar was dim, but enough to see there were very few locals amongst the tourists. Spilt beer pooled on the counter, the barmen too busy to wipe it up, and the cigar and cigarette smoke from a group further along assailed his nostrils. Apart from that it was a comfortable atmosphere, if noisy, and he was content to sit and listen and watch, but he was going to need a pee soon and did not want to lose his seat. Draining his beer, he signalled the barman for another.

A group of American men were making quite a noise, with one particular individual standing out by virtue of his sharp voice. They were already drunk, which it's easy to become at the high altitude of the Altiplano.

Jonathan stroked the moisture off the Paceña bottle and read the label yet again. It was time to think of what he was going to do with his immediate future. He needed an income while he continued to travel. At the moment he was in holiday mode – what if he switched to exploration mode? Exploration with a view to turning an income.

I can write pretty well. I should make some money selling my travel stories. It sounded like a good plan to start with, and he could see how things developed. *From now on, I'm going to record every day's activities to give myself material. I can be paid through my money card which will simplify my finances. And, if it's not too naive a thought, I might be able to save a little.*

'Hi,' said a quiet female voice behind him. The 'hi' was clipped, the accent indeterminate. 'Is this chair free? I can't see another.'

She was leaning down towards him, putting their heads on the same level. Her eyes were ice blue, pale – the kind of eyes which appear as empty as the Arctic, leaving the observer to read into them whatever he or she determines.

Absorbed in his thoughts, Jonathan had not even noticed his previous neighbour had left. 'It's free on one condition,' he said.

The girl raised a full untrimmed eyebrow in a question. She had a slight seen-it-all-before expression on her face as if to say, *Here we go again – another smart-arse going to try it on.*

'I need to go to the bathroom. Please keep my seat for me.'

'Oh, sure.' She flashed a row of bright teeth at him and turned to the barman.

As he made his way back to his seat, Jonathan observed his new barstool neighbour. Her long pale hair lay in two braids taken from the sides of her head to join together at the back, allowing the rest to fall free. She had a strange accent; not German, certainly not Dutch; Nordic possibly, or maybe Russian? Her light tan reminded him of the twins who, they had told him, spent a lot of time naked as they sunned themselves on the East Frisian Islands.

The American table was becoming louder, and the worst individual was mouthing off about other nationalities. Some Europeans nearby were visibly annoyed. The relaxed mood in the bar was deteriorating.

'Thanks. Are you travelling alone?' Jonathan sat down while watching the looming hostile situation.

'Yes.' The word was sharp and backed up by a brief nod.

'Me too, I want to go to Cusco next. They say it's beautiful and interesting. That's only to start the trek to Machu Picchu, I'll spend some time and look around the city afterwards.'

'Yes.'

'Would you like another beer?'

'Yes.' There was a long pause before she added, 'Thank you.'

The nationalist rhetoric was becoming louder and more insulting. Jonathan stood. 'Excuse me, I'm going to ask them to tone it down. Someone's going to start a fight if this carries on.'

'Please don't.' Her grip on his wrist felt like a handcuff. 'I will go. You will be the first one hit, because men are stupid!'

'I ...'

Her face said arguing was out of the question. She was right, anyway.

'Hi there.' The noisy American was addressing the girl. 'I'm Carl. You wanna drink? Join us over there?' He positioned himself almost between them with his back to Jonathan, effectively excluding him.

'I'm talking to my friend here,' she said, 'and I have a drink.'

'Aw, c'mon, we're having a great time over there. You look pretty bored with him.' He tossed his head in Jonathan's direction.

That tightening of the gut, the speeding pulse which comes before a confrontation. Jonathan got to his feet, half a head taller than the stocky intruder. The girl stood too. Up until then he had not seen her fully upright. She was a giant, much taller than him, a good six foot two. She reached over Carl's head and pressured Jonathan onto his stool. Then she stepped between the two men, put her fingers on Carl's chest and gave him a slight shove, a flick of her wrist. He stumbled back a few steps, surprised. He sniggered. 'Oh, you like it rough, huh? We can do rough all right.'

Jonathan got off his stool again. 'Go back and sit down, you're intruding.'

'Aw, get fucked, pretty boy. You don't wanna mess wi' me, I was a Marine.'

Jonathan knew what he meant, but could not resist. 'What's that?'

The headbutt was easy to see coming, because Carl was drunk and slow. Given their relative heights the blow wasn't going to be very effective anyway, but he had time to sway back and Carl's forehead hit his chest. Jonathan did nothing, he was going to be heavily outnumbered if this man's friends got involved.

The girl shoved Carl away and stepped between them again. 'Stop!' she shouted. 'Stop now!'

The bar went quiet. People were watching, and a few couples moved towards the door. Two other Americans left their table and approached. Jonathan's mouth went dry, this was going to get bloody. But they gripped Carl by his arms and pulled him away. One grinned at the pair and said, 'Sorry 'bout that. He gets outta control sometimes.'

The girl followed them to the table, towering over Carl. 'You are very rude. I don't like rude people.'

Jonathan was both relieved the situation had fizzled out and very impressed by her. 'That was well handled. You've had practice, I think.'

'If you interfere there will be a fight, and I can look after myself.'

'I can see that all right. I'm Jonathan Scott.'

'My name is Gudrun Einarsdóttir.' Jonathan's expression must have told her an explanation was necessary. 'I am the daughter of Einar. And for your next question, Iceland.'

Fresh off the bus, the self-named Black Widow twins had found their room and went off to search for the nearest bar. Now, sitting unnoticed at a corner table in the shadows and ignoring the hubbub of noise and the milling crowd, they were watching events with considerable interest. Anna looked at Hannah, and Hannah looked at Anna, and they reached an unspoken agreement.

Gudrun and Jonathan had another Paceña each, but he was struggling to keep his eyes open. He admitted it to himself, but did not want to leave this intriguing woman. He had to secure a future arrangement.

'I'm so tired, I'm going to have to go to bed. Will I see you again?'

'Yes. If you like.'

'I was thinking of going to the Isla del Sol tomorrow, would you like to come with me? We could meet at the ferry at eight?'

'Yes, but let's eat first at the café across the road after seven.'

'Great. Are you going to stay here now?'

'No, I'm tired also.'

Their guest houses were close to one another, and Jonathan left Gudrun at the steps to her room. A strange mixture of contentment and anticipation settled on him as he carried on towards his own. He was on the brink of something good.

Jonathan walked down the hill to the café the next morning, curious as to how the day would turn out. Meeting someone in a bar after a couple of beers have loosened the tongue and softened the perceptions was all very well, but being cold sober in the broad light of day could result in a different impression altogether.

He was not disappointed, though. Gudrun was even more appealing than he recalled. She was wearing hiking boots, jeans and a loose denim shirt under her jacket. Not only was she tall, she was proud of her height which she accentuated with a knitted black-and-red beanie with ear flaps and a huge bobble on the top. She was magnificent.

Neither said much as they ate breakfast, but there was no uncomfortable feeling attached to that. It was later, on the little ferry, when their conversation picked up.

Embarrassment at what he was going to say was certain, but curiosity reigned. 'Excuse me, er … but you remind me of someone, someone well known, but I can't place who.'

'Maria Sharapova? I am asked that a lot. Too many times, it becomes boring.' An almost imperceptible, wicked little smile flittered on her lips for a moment. 'So I tell them it is the other way around, Maria looks like me, because I'm a centimetre taller than she is. But I know it's meant to be a compliment, don't worry.'

In spite of her comment, Jonathan had been put in his place. *What a stupid thing to say. I want to be different for this woman, and I go and repeat what has to be a cliché to her.* He fell silent for a while, and she switched the subject to the dubious state of their ferry.

The boat dropped them at Challapampa on the north end of the Isla del Sol, their plan being to walk to the south end to pick it up for the return trip in the afternoon.

Neither of them took notice of the passengers disembarking from the larger ferry which docked at the same time, and they took no notice of the score of walkers who followed them up to the Inca ruins above the village.

The trail runs south along the spine of the island. There is little vegetation, only the odd clump of short trees and some bushes. The hillsides are, for the most part, terraced and have been for centuries as the Inca, and all those who followed them, grew crops on every slope.

They chatted along the hike, walked side by side where possible and shared their single sandwich, all the while absorbing information about each other. Above Yumani, as the path descended to the southern dock, Gudrun stopped and faced him. Because she was a little lower down the slope, their faces were level.

Her pale eyes fascinated him. *Eyeballs themselves have no expression. It's the way the tiny muscles control the lids and cheeks and skin around the eyes that provides clues to a person's emotions – her emotions. Eye colour itself has nothing to do with expression, yet some people are put off by pale eyes, thinking there is something empty or evil in them.* With Gudrun's ice-blue irises, it was like staring into a bottomless crevasse, but only if he ignored the gentle rise of her cheeks and the slight deepening of tiny crow's feet when she was amused – and how could they be ignored?

'I like you, Jonathan.' She gave him a brief kiss on the lips and turned back down the slope.

'Wait,' he called. 'You can't do that and walk away. Wait there a moment.'

She faced him again, and he grasped her chin and kissed her softly. It lasted forever. Breathless, they broke apart. Eyes were locked on eyes, reading, probing. Her arm went round his neck and pulled him close again.

'You want sex?'

'What? Er … Bloody hell. You mean here?' *Jesus!*

'Not exactly. On the terrace below, over there behind the trees.'

'Well, yes. Of course.' What else should he say?

She took his hand and led him off the path and down the hillside. Behind the terrace wall she said, 'Why are you shocked? I like you, and you like me. You turn me on, so I want sex with you – is okay?'

'God yes! We can't lie down here, though, there are too many rocks.'

'So we do it another way.' She laughed, and unclipped her belt.

'Am I like other Icelandic girls?'

'I don't know any others.'

'We are supposed to have a reputation of being very easy with sex, sleeping with men after a few hours and a few beers. "First you must sleep with a person then you can date them," is what they say. Those may be the girls in Reykjavik who are part of the bar scene. You know, drunk on the weekend nights, sleep with people, they don't know who. I don't know if it's true, probably not so bad, but it's not who I am. My father owns a horse farm, I am a country person. I don't like Reykjavik that much. If you had wanted sex last night, I would have said no. I need to know I can trust you, I need to like you before we have sex.'

'But after one day you can't say know me, I might be lying about everything to you.'

'No, you are not lying. I trust you – you are a good person. I can feel it. And why waste your life when you know about a person?' She raised her eyebrows with her question, challenging him to disagree with her.

'I'm leaving you in Cusco.' She laughed in delight at his change of expression. 'I agreed to meet some friends in the city. They sent a message saying they will be there earlier than they planned. So I will not hike to Machu Picchu with you. When will your trek be over, when will you be back in Cusco?'

He counted on his fingers. His mouth had gone dry with disappointment, and he swallowed before speaking. 'Should be a week from today if I leave tomorrow. But I can skip it and stay with you.'

'No. Do the hike – you will regret it if you don't. Don't be so sad, Jonathan, I will see you after your trek. I will wait for you in Cusco. I'll send a text to tell you which bar it will be.'

Jonathan led the way back to the path. Before they reached it, he stopped below a terrace wall and listened. Chattering voices were coming down the trail towards them. To emerge from the bushes off the path together would invite the obvious conclusions and knowing looks, so they stayed out of sight until the women had passed.

It did not take long to descend the path to Yumani as it zigzagged down the steep slope. Before they boarded, Gudrun needed the toilet, and she disappeared inside a small building. After a short while waiting for her, Jonathan decided to go too.

Gudrun came out. A blonde woman was standing outside the men's entrance and trying to entice a tethered llama to take an interest.

'Waiting for your man?' the woman said.

'Yes. We have walked from the north, what about you?'

'Also. It was very good. This is a nice place, actually.' The woman looked along the beach to the waiting boats. 'That is our boat, I think, the third one.'

Gudrun joined her, putting her back to the toilet building. 'I think ours is the first one. It's only small and I worry that the outboard engine will fail. There is a spare one, but it looks broken to me.'

The woman laughed. 'I hope you make it back this week. Well,

I'm not going to wait here, I'll go to the boat and he can find me there. Have a good trip.' She skirted round the llama and strode down to the jetty.

Gudrun watched her go, then turned back to see where Jonathan was. *He's is taking a long time. I hope he hasn't got a tummy problem.* Time was passing and the boat would be leaving soon. The blonde woman's boat moved away from the jetty, increasing her sense of urgency. At the toilet door she called, 'Jonathan, Jonathan. We must go, are you all right?'

There was no answer. There were no other men about, everyone was down near the boats. Peering round the toilet entrance, she wrinkled her nose at the smell of urine and went inside. He lay dead still on the floor by the basin, a brick beside him.

'My God!' She saw the blood on the back of his head and held it off the floor as she gently turned him over. He groaned and tried to get up.

'Jonathan, can you hear me? Have you broken bones?'

'Mmm, no. I'm okay.' He was dazed, though, and struggling to focus. Blood trickled down the back of his neck.

'Can you stand? There's no hospital here. Can you make it to the boat?'

'Yes.' But he didn't sound sure.

'Come, put your arm round my shoulder. We must go outside to stop the ferry before it leaves. We must get you to hospital in Copacabana.'

'Ah!'

'What is it?'

'My wrist. It's painful.'

Gudrun lifted him off the floor, and they staggered out of the toilet. She yelled down to the water, '*Socorro!* Help!'

Some men looked up, dropped their tools and came running. They took Jonathan off Gudrun and half-carried him down to the ferry.

'*Gracias, mucho gracias.*' She thanked them as they lifted him into the boat and carefully sat him down. Passengers made space and he lay on a bench.

A man came back from the bow. 'I am a doctor,' he said. 'Let me see your friend.'

Gudrun watched anxiously as the doctor probed and asked

questions. Before he finished, he said, 'He has had a heavy blow to his head and will certainly have a mild concussion, but I don't think there is anything more serious than that. He must go to the hospital for a better examination as soon as possible. I have some supplies in my bag. I will dress that wound to keep it clean.'

'Thank you so much.'

'No need. I am a doctor, it's what I do.' He went back to his seat, adding, 'He also has a sprained wrist, I'm sure it's not broken.'

20

CUFF'S LIFE

OCTOBER–NOVEMBER

The opportunity for Cuff to take up aerobatics arose after he and Lisa had been married for about two months. Terry had said he would instruct him in the art, but they would have to use a special type of aircraft, and he would search for the best option. Knowing Lisa's opposition to flying in general, let alone aerobatics, Cuff avoided telling her.

The thrill of this new flying discipline flowed through his veins long after each session was over, stretching well into the next day, by which time he was longing to be airborne again. The thrill aside, perfecting his spin recoveries, hammerhead stalls, barrel rolls, inverted flight and loops was the initial aim, with the goal of precision aerobatics on the horizon. Aerobatics would make him a better pilot, one more in tune with his machine and therefore more capable and the safer for it. It was not enough, though; he wanted to be the best. After these sessions, which Lisa must have thought were tedious circuits of the airfield, he was always fired up and buoyant. This mood probably gave her a false sense of security, imagining he was happy in their life.

Lisa had changed since they'd been married, and that was after only some six weeks. Before the wedding she'd been devoted to pleasing him and doing whatever he wanted. Now, increasingly, she was becoming a real nag, demanding the same things of him over and over again – like his father. It was as if, having snared her man, she could bend him to her will and achieve what she wanted. The fact that he resisted these demands made her less amenable.

Have I changed as well? Is some of this my fault? Not much, not enough to account for her attitude, anyway.

What might be his part in the deteriorating relationship, was that he was becoming fed up with the routine of his life which, without doubt, was affecting his attitude at home. Not only was there no change in the pattern of their working days, there was no possibility of any variety in their lives at all. From Monday to Friday and sometimes Saturday, the same things happened: breakfast, office, snack lunch, office, home for dinner, have a drink or two, watch a snatch of TV maybe and collapse into bed exhausted from the lack of stimulation.

This life is what I had foreseen in following Dad's Gospel, it's just what I was scared of. So why on earth have I chosen this path?

Lisa only worked mornings. Sometimes she was in the pharmacy and sometimes she was out talking to drug companies and other suppliers, so there were times he did not see her at all during the day. In the afternoons she occupied herself with a weekly tea with her friend, Sheila, and in other unknown ways, but she always had dinner prepared by seven o'clock. Why always at seven? There was nothing unreasonable about the time itself; it was more that he was subject to its control. The predictability of it and the bland food, which was its substance, made life comparable to that of a family dog.

However, everything was calm until Lisa became broody in early November.

Terry had introduced him to the flick roll for the first time one afternoon. It was a difficult aerobatic manoeuvre to do with precision, and it was going to take some time before he was adept at it. In spite of the challenge, Cuff was fired up with the new movement and was running through the aerodynamics of it in his mind while driving home.

'Hello.' Lisa's voice was tense as he entered the room. Cuff took a deep breath; a difficult discussion loomed.

'Did you have a nice flight?' She didn't wait for an answer. 'I can't see what's attractive in going round and round the circuit practising take-offs and landings. Surely you're good enough at it by now?'

'Yes, I think I am.'

'Well since you are, you can give up flying, you've nothing else to achieve.'

'You're never good enough until it's perfect. In any case I enjoy the whole feeling of being airborne, acting like a bird, slipping the surly bonds of earth and all that, seeing the world from above.'

'Cuff, it's dangerous.' Her voice cracked. She was going to cry again – it was becoming more common. 'You could be killed in your next accident, and I don't want to bring up my child alone. It's not fair.'

'What child?' His anger flared. 'We've been through this over and over again. I'm not prepared to be a father so early in our marriage. We have years yet.' He thrust his head forward at her. 'Are you still taking the pill?'

Lisa nodded, sniffed and dabbed her eyes with a tissue. 'When do you think you'll be ready to have a baby? It's a feeling that's gnawing away at me. My biological clock is ticking. I can't help it. It's a female thing. I want a child.'

Cuff pursed his lips. Was she ever going to let this go? His impatience rising, he took a beer from the fridge and opened it under her watchful eye as she waited for his answer.

'That's nonsense, you've at least ten years before you need to worry about your age. We agreed before we married we weren't going to have children handcuffing our lives until we've had time to explore the world, have some fun, do some exciting things together.'

He yanked his sleeves up, picked his jacket off the chair, took the beer in his other hand and strode to the door. He stopped and grumbled spitefully, knowing it was going to upset her, yet unable to stop himself. 'At the way this is going, that'll be never.'

Lisa howled and let her tears flow.

21

JONATHAN'S WORLD

OCTOBER

Jonathan regained full consciousness after the hour and a half's trip. But he had some difficulty concentrating, was a bit groggy and had a splitting headache. Concussion was a strong possibility, and he knew he should take it easy for a few days, which might mean missing the five-day hike to Machu Picchu which included the Dead Woman's Pass at almost fourteen thousand feet – not good for concussion.

The little launch glided up to the wooden jetty at Copacabana. Gudrun let the other few passengers disembark before taking Jonathan's hand and helping him ashore.

Two policemen and two female officers were standing on the beach, smart in their dark green uniforms. They approached.

'You come,' said one.

'Why? What's the matter? This man needs a hospital.'

The doctor noticed and walked over to speak to the police in

Spanish, showing them Jonathan's head wound. All Gudrun could understand was *'el hospital'*.

A high-volume conversation in rapid Spanish ensued. The most senior policeman ordered one car to take Jonathan to hospital and the other to take Gudrun.

'Vamos!' A female officer tugged at Gudrun's sleeve. There was no arguing to be done.

The crowd on the beach realised something interesting was going on and gathered round. Gudrun looked at Jonathan, her eyes riddled with questions.

'I've no idea,' he said, 'we'd better do as we're told.'

'Will you be all right?'

'I'll be fine. I'll find you later.'

Jonathan watched the two females take Gudrun by the arms, but she shook them off and got into the waiting car. He allowed his escort to guide him to a different vehicle. The man was quite considerate of the tourist's condition.

When they arrived at the hospital, the policeman ushered him into a waiting room. Every seat was taken and some patients were even sitting on the floor. Jonathan resigned himself to hours of waiting while he nursed his head. But the policeman used his authority and pushed him through to the front of the line. In five minutes he was in a curtained-off cubicle on his side, facing the wall while his scalp was examined.

The doctor spoke in the typical, almost whining accent of Latin American English. 'Ya don't have no serious damage to ya skull. I cain't get ya X-rayed tonight, and even if I did there ain't nothing to be done. Ya gonna have concussion, no doubt about that. Only cure – rest for at least forty-eight hours. When ya gonna be home?'

'No time soon, I'm … drifting along.'

The doctor grinned his approval. 'Best way, relax. Ya have repeated headaches, ya go get a better check-up than we can give ya here, okay? Sorry I cain't do more.'

'Okay, thanks.'

'The nurse will clean and dress that wound and strap yo wrist. Then you can go with these gentlemen. What's goin' on anyway?'

'I don't know, I haven't got a clue.'

The doctor shrugged and left him alone. Jonathan's main concern was Gudrun and what she might be going through.

Half an hour later, Jonathan was led into the police station, which was clean and organised except for some individual desks. Gudrun was seated at one end of the room with an officer diminutive beside her and half a mug of tea on the desk. She had waited, and waited, not knowing what was happening. Jonathan gave her a thumbs up as he was shown to the far end of the room. He was going to ask if she was all right, but was hurried along to where an officer with more insignia of rank waited for him. Gudrun appeared nothing worse than bored.

'Good evening.' The high ranker spoke careful English. 'You are Señor Jonathan Scott?' Like many Bolivians, he appeared to have part Spanish and part indigenous ancestry.

'Yes, what's this about?'

'What happened to your head?'

'I have no idea. I was in the toilet and someone hit me from behind, I suppose. I don't know why.'

'Please, I would like to know your movements last night.'

Jonathan told him about the bar, and that he'd gone back to his room at about nine o'clock, adding, 'Your English is excellent, by the way. I'm sorry, I don't know the police ranks – are you a captain?'

The officer was a straight-face man; he inclined his head at the comment. 'Thank you. At the bar, who did you meet?'

And so the questions went. Jonathan told him the truth, including the near fight with Carl.

'So no real fight? If not, how did you injure your hand?'

'No, there was no fight. He tried to butt me with his head, but I moved and his friends came and took him away.' Jonathan shrugged. 'He was drunk, it was nothing.' He pulled his sleeves up and waved his bandaged wrist. 'This happened today – I think I fell on it when I was hit on the head. Please tell me what the problem is, why you are questioning us.'

'Señor Carl Schwitter was murdered last night in his room. You had a fight with him. You may have killed him.'

It took a moment for that to sink into Jonathan's slow-functioning brain. *Carl, dead, murdered! Bloody hell!* He stared at the captain, wordless for a moment. 'That's ridiculous. I went back to my room at nine as I told you. Miss Einarsdóttir will confirm that, because we walked back together from the bar. How was he killed?'

'Wait there. Would you like some maté?' The captain did not wait for his answer, but gave the tea order to an underling anyway, crossed the room and took a seat opposite Gudrun.

It was Jonathan's turn to be bored. The paracetamol the doctor had prescribed, he had paid for and the police had collected for him at the pharmacy, did not do much to alleviate his headache. His eyes kept closing.

The captain came back to his desk. 'How are you feeling?'

'I have a headache, and I want to sleep.'

'Señorita Einar's daughter – I can't say that word – is suspected of the murder of Señor Carl Schwitter.'

'What? That's ridiculous.'

'He was murdered a little after midnight, you both agree that you left each other at nine, so she has no alibi. In addition, a witness saw her going to the man's room twice last night.'

'No. The witness must be mistaken, she would never do something like that.'

'How well do you know the lady?'

'Umm … We only met last night, but that's irrelevant. I trust her. She's not a killer.'

'Also, who hit you on the head? Are you sure it was not her? You never saw who it was.'

'But why should she do that? We were establishing a good relationship. I'm sorry, Captain, but you're wrong about this.'

'The Señorita will stay here under arrest. You may go, but I will hold your passport. You will return tomorrow before nine to report. If you do not come, I will think you have run away and will have you arrested.'

Jonathan was staggered. What was there to say, except, 'Who was the witness who says he saw her? May I speak to her?'

The captain was unsympathetic at first, then relented. 'Only one minute. I will be present.' He did not answer the first question.

With the captain leading the way, Jonathan walked to Gudrun, put his hand on her shoulder and squeezed. 'I'll get you out of this, don't worry. Is there an Icelandic embassy in Bolivia?'

'The Danish Embassy in La Paz represents us. They will let me contact them. I'll be all right, don't worry. You must rest, it's important to save trouble later – with your head.'

* * *

Out on the street, the cold air hit Jonathan and banished his lethargy for a while. What witness had seen Gudrun going to see Carl? It had to be one of the other Americans, because they knew which room he slept in.

They would be drinking. He was silhouetted in the doorway of the first bar he went into, with the street lights at his back. Glancing round the room, he saw no sign of the three Americans, but his eye was caught by the pair of blonde girls at a table in the corner. *So they did make it here.* Jonathan ducked back out of the door, hoping they hadn't seen him. He found the Americans in the bar where he had met Gudrun.

'Hello, I'm sorry to hear about your friend.'

All three faces turned up to him, and all expressions turned from morose to angry as they saw who it was.

One of them got up and confronted him, his face inches from Jonathan's. 'You've got a fucking cheek, man. Your goddam woman murders Carl, and you come in here and apologise like all she did was kick over the garbage.'

'Please.' Jonathan held out his hands in a sign of peace. 'I came here to tell you there is no way Gudrun would have killed Carl. There is something else going on. Look at my head – I was attacked on the island this afternoon, and it wasn't by her.'

'Look, buddy, I don't give a shit what happened to you. What's a bump on the head when a guy's dead?'

One of the others put out a restraining hand. 'Brad, let him talk, he's got something to tell us.'

Brad needed to take out his grief and frustration, and who better than the murderess's accomplice. His chin was thrust out, his breathing noisy, but only his beer fumes assaulted Jonathan's nostrils.

'Thank you. Please hear me out.' He pulled up a chair from the next table and sat, leaning forward to get their attention. 'Is it true one of you saw a fair-haired woman going to Carl's room last night?'

'Yeah, me.' Brad was shoving his beer back and forth across the table, slopping it over the lip of the glass. He didn't seem to notice. 'She went there twice.'

'Twice? Are you sure?'

'Yeah. I saw her go in and I thought, Wow. Like Carl's got some go in him, since he was so drunk. Then I went back inside to get another cigarette and have a piss. When I came out again, maybe ten minutes later, there she was again, knocking on his door.'

'Are you sure it was the woman I was with last night? If I showed you some other blondes, could you tell them apart?'

'Well …'

'Brad, please. You've given a statement that may wrongly convict an innocent person. If you're not one hundred percent certain, you could be responsible for ruining the life of a young woman. She would rot away in a Bolivian jail for years. Do you want that on your conscience?'

'He's right Brad, are you sure it was the tall chick? There's plenty of other blonde tourists here,' said his friend. To Jonathan, 'You have someone in mind?'

'Yes, but we must hurry before she goes for the night.'

They went into the other bar, Jonathan in the lead, the others in a tight group behind him. Only one of the twins was at the table in the corner, but there were two beer glasses and two plates of food. Jonathan said, 'There, Brad, in the corner – could she be the one?'

'Well … jeez, I dunno, maybe.'

'Wait please – something else is going to happen in a moment.'

They waited. Brad became impatient. 'What's the hold up? I told you that could also be her, I'm not sure.'

'Please. Remember, a young woman's future is at the mercy of a few minutes patience. Something will happen very soon.'

From the toilets, came Anna or Hannah to join her sister.

'There was no second visit by the same woman, was there? What you saw was identical twins arriving ten minutes apart.' He resisted the temptation to tell them he may have ended up like Carl if he had not been alert to her hands tightening around his throat.

'Jeez! Hey, I'm sorry, man, I'm sorry. Carl was my best buddy and I'm upset. Your girl was so impressive, she was stuck in my mind, she was the only one I thought of last night.'

'Brad, will you please tell the police captain as soon as possible? If those two are guilty they'll try to leave on the first bus in the morning. They must have missed the last one today. It must be done tonight.'

Brad's friend said, 'Consider it done, buddy. C'mon Brad, we gotta duty to perform.'

The night had settled in. The police captain had gone home but, after a lot of persuasion, the sergeant got him on the phone and he promised to intercept the twins before they left town. He would not release Gudrun until the situation was resolved the next day … maybe.

Jonathan set out to find his bed. His head was pounding; God knows what it would be like without the paracetamol. Every step a thump, he plodded along the street in the general direction of the guest house. His mind numbed from the misery of his condition, he took a while to register the light footsteps tapping on the pavement behind him. They were neither gaining nor falling back. At a corner he stopped, and, head in hands, leant wearily on the building. He glanced back. Two figures turned left into an alleyway. It was impossible to see who or even what they were. He walked on. The footsteps resumed, a little quicker in pace, or was he being paranoid?

Damn! He had missed the side road that led to the guest house. The only way was back towards his pursuers or to try to go round the block, if there was one. He turned right and found himself on a street that looked familiar, but could not place it. Trying to get his bearings, he walked on, conscious of the steps behind him that were sometimes inaudible, sometimes definite enough to give a faint echo from the houses.

He knew where he was at last, because he had already explored this famous feature: on the path to the Cerro Calvario. To most tourists, this was the only route up and down the hill, but there are two less distinct paths, one to the north and one to the south. It being well after dark, if the steps followed him, he was a prey and, unless they were muggers, the only predators were the twins. His headache was still there, but it receded as he raced through the implications. That piercing stare of Anna's when she straddled him in her nakedness – was that the look of a killer? Had these two done the same to poor Carl? Was the Black Widow joke not a joke at all? And why were they after him now?

The route to the Cerro Calvario starts under an arch above a set of elongated steps from the end of the street. It reaches a saddle then zigzags as a rocky path up the slope past fourteen crosses, each where pilgrims stop to offer a prayer. At the summit is a line of seven shrines set on plinths which are about the shoulder height of a man. They represent the seven *dolors*, or sorrows, of Mary and sit well to the left of the walkway. On that side, little stone caves have been built where the devout can leave a burning candle shielded from the wind. The *dolors* lead to a larger shrine higher up a short set of steps. When the large shrine is reached, there is no reasonable way down the hill in the dark.

Jonathan had spent well over a week at this altitude. He should have been acclimatised, but his rapid climb up the rocky path and his pounding head lent a lie to that belief. He stopped by one of the little crosses to catch his breath and listen. Nothing was visible in the dark, but a faint rattle of stone on stone told him they were still there.

The reflection of the enormous moon on the lake was stunning, a highway of silvery light stretching from the far shore directly to the Cerro Calvario. He appreciated it, but did not stop to admire it, he ran on up and to the seven shrines. At the third he glanced back – the two dark figures were still advancing, and had reached the first *dolor*. They would be confident they had him trapped, because one was likely to advance along the wide walkway, while the other kept pace with her, but go along the narrower cliff side of the shrines. That way they could see him leave whichever way he went and block his exit should he hide behind one.

At the sixth *dolor*, he ducked behind it and waited. The lesser-known path down to the lake on the north side of the hill ran from opposite the seventh shrine. The southerly path was out of the question for a quick escape in the dark.

He crouched behind the plinth. They would be timing their advance to reach each *dolor* at the same moment. Had they seen which gap he had chosen?

A car horn beeped a few times in the town below, Latin music and the odd shout and laughter in the streets carried up on the breeze, but his breathing was louder than any other sound nearby.

As the Black Widows pass each shrine, they'll know they are getting closer, and when they reach the fifth one, the one before mine, they'll know there are only two left where I'll be hiding. They'll be ever more cautious.

A pebble fell on the cliff side. *They're almost here.* His mouth was dry, his breathing rapid, his aching head forgotten. He kept low, his knees bent ready to spring, his right side against the plinth. The only escape route was across the walkway. He wanted the twins in full view before he moved. They would not creep into position, giving him time – they would pounce like cats and together, one on either side to block his escape.

One was there. He charged at her before her sister could catch him from behind. He ran her over, knocked her flat and sprinted. Across the walkway, over a low wall and onto the northerly path. He bolted, scree running down the slope. How he never broke an ankle was a miracle. He fell once, and an agonising pain shot through his injured wrist, but his head stayed safe.

He skidded sideways to a stop. There was no sign the twins were following him, he heard nothing. He sat down to collect himself for a moment, picked a pebble out of his shoe and quivered; the stress and shock were setting in.

A few deep breaths and he was thinking again. The narrow path he was on met a broader one that contoured the hillside above the shoreline and found its way back into the town. Provided they were not waiting for him there, he should reach his room safe and sound. *Just as Dad would have wished.* That was almost funny.

22

JONATHAN'S WORLD

OCTOBER

Barry Castle's interview with Bert, the car dealer, had gone well. He had dressed smartly, and his mother said he was ever so handsome in his navy blazer with his pale hair. His tie, the first since he had left school, was red, which signified power.

Bert had taken exception to his behaviour, though. 'Barry, no bloke that's looking at a Bentley or an Aston with a good-looking bird in a fur coat 'anging on his arm is going to buy from you if you scratch your bollocks like you've been doing. It's offensive, and my girls aren't going to like it either. Do it again, and you'll be on the first bus home – right?'

For once in his life he blushed. 'Sorry, I didn't realise.'

'All right. Now, the job's yours, if you want it. Sell some of these beauties, which you will if you switch on the charm, and there'll be a fat commission in each deal. You'll have to kick your heels for a few weeks, though, it don't start till the end of next month.'

That was a disappointment. Castle needed to find some temporary employment, preferably part-time so he could continue with his plans for the destruction of Scott.

He walked to the corner store to buy some milk, eggs and the day's papers. The local one would show what jobs were available in the area, and a copy of the gutter press would give its juicy reflection of the news.

He stopped outside the shop, absent-mindedly scratching himself as he looked through the situations vacant column, but found nothing without having to stoop to menial tasks he considered to be beneath him. The community notice board usually had several new offers, but that bore no fruit for him either, except for someone looking for a gardener. That was too much like hard work, so he wandered back home hoping his mother had left for her office by the time he reached there.

Once in the kitchen, he made himself a bacon sandwich, poured on some brown sauce and guzzled it in five mouthfuls. Belching, he sat down with a mug of coffee and reached for the national paper.

The headline screamed at him: *"BRIT HELD FOR BOLIVIA MURDER"*. And there was a picture of Scott with a bandage on his head. Interesting, very interesting. It looks like the cops got him first. Pity, the girls would have had fun. He read the article again.

Our correspondent understands that a British man, Jonathan Scott, who is on holiday in Bolivia, has been arrested in the town of Copacabana on the shore of Lake Titicaca. Scott is alleged to have got into a fight with an American tourist and subsequently killed him.

The paper presumed that Scott's head injury was gained in the fight and someone from the British Embassy in La Paz was on their way to offer consular support. The paper presumed too much, but Castle did not know that. If it was in the paper, it must be true. They wouldn't dare to print a lie, would they?

So Cuffy is calling himself Jonathan is he? Well he can now be Johnny Fucking Jonathan, JFJ.

He sent a text to the twins to Skype. They appeared as pretty as ever, although they had both dyed their hair a dark brown. He said they were better as blondes.

'Rolfy, *Liebling,* right now it is necessary, but we agree with you. A shame – we cannot get to your friend, because he has been taken by the police. Now we need to leave Copacabana very quickly – tonight, actually.'

To Lisa Hines, the tabloids were a national scandal. They made up stories and embellished facts to sell more copies rather than tell the truth. On the other hand Stacy, the fifty-something cashier on duty, lapped up the daily fiction, especially the misbehaviour of celebrities.

'Stuffin' 'ell! 'Ere, Lisa, you seen this?'

'No,' Lisa had no idea what the woman was talking about. She was still bitter over Jonathan's rejection, and was often in a foul mood. Today she had a lot to do and could not be bothered with Stacy's daily reportage.

'Well, I think you'll be very interested in this, dear.'

Lisa tutted and walked over to the till.

'Good grief!' Her hand went to her mouth. 'It's CJ, calling himself Jonathan. He's killed someone, and he's in jail. Good grief!' she repeated, as she stared at the paper for a full minute. 'Bastard! He can rot there for the rest of his life as far as I'm concerned.' She cast the paper back at the cashier. 'Sorry.'

Stacy laughed. 'You can keep the paper as a memento, if you want.'

'Thanks, Stace. I will when you've finished.'

She walked back to her office humming to herself. *This is news to be shared with Sheila this afternoon.*

Martin Beale also thought the paper was appalling. The fact that someone could make money out of selling such trash was one of the few things that annoyed him, and the fact that there were people out there, millions of them, who bought the rag was truly upsetting. There was another tabloid that produced equal rubbish, but the only thing that made it better than its Marxist cousin was it was more right-wing. The level of truth between the two could not easily be determined, however. He could not escape the headline, though, as he glanced across the news stand. He studied the article, before putting the paper back and picking up his usual read.

'Bloody hell, Jonathan! What have you done?'

The tea shop tried, in a half-hearted manner, to be Victorian, but could not make the final effort with every detail. Lace-fringed table cloths were laid on unsteady tables from the fifties. Fine china cups and saucers were accompanied by cheap stainless-steel spoons and cake forks, and embroidered napkins were being replaced by paper ones when they wore too thin. Victorian-era photos, prints on the walls and ornaments on the shelves were the most authentic witnesses to the age.

Lisa and her friend Sheila faced each other over a pot of what the menu described as, *delicate first-flush Darjeeling leaves, dried and steeped in water at 95 degrees Celsius for 3 minutes.* To accompany the tea was a plate of four huge scones and individual dishes of thick strawberry jam and clotted cream. This regular afternoon event was their weekly sin, but it was absolutely delicious and not to be missed. It also gave her an opportunity to profit from sharing her woes with her old friend and long-time confidante, who had a propensity to dispense ill-considered advice at the worst possible moment.

Sheila was somewhere on the wrong side of forty, although she pretended to be ten years younger. She could not hide the sun damage to her fair skin, though, which was brought about by hours on expensive beaches paid for by her first two husbands. With attractive features, she had an hour-glass figure.

'Lise, darling,' she had once advised, 'you need to lower your neck line and lift and squeeze your boobs together. Works wonders. I love to flaunt my cleavage in front of men. I lap up their frustration when they can't burrow their heads down there. Power, Lise, it's all about power.'

On another occasion Sheila had said, 'After three marriages, I'm well qualified to help you through your emotional and relationship problems.'

Sheila was shameless but fun, and Lisa relied heavily on her experience, even if it was the result of numerous mistakes.

'Jonathan's been arrested for murder!'

'No! Good heavens.' Sheila leaned forward. 'Tell! I need to know all about it.'

Lisa handed her a copy of the paper. Sheila snatched it from her, put her cup down and scrabbled in her bag for her reading glasses. 'I hate wearing these in public, they make me look old, but this news is not something that can wait. It has to be devoured now.'

Lisa sipped her tea as she watched for her friend's reaction.

The readers came off and disappeared into the bag. Sheila picked up her cup again. 'Huh. What do you think, Lise darling?'

'I'm glad, I hope he rots to death in jail. My only regret is I did not have anything to do with it.'

'*Hell hath no fury* ... I think that serves as closure for you, darling. Now what you need is a young, muscular lover with six-pack abs to carry you off for a while. I shall search around. You don't mind previously owned, second hand, used do you?'

'You mean your cast-offs?'

'Mmm.' Sheila grinned wickedly. 'He'll come with a personal guarantee of satisfaction!'

'You lack any semblance of morals Sheila. No thanks, I'm after a husband not a playboy.'

'Only until Mr Right pops up, darling – temporary relief to keep your hormones active.'

23

JONATHAN'S WORLD

NOVEMBER

The alarm beeped him into wakefulness – almost. Jonathan lay still for a while. Was the pounding in his head any less than it had been when he had at last collapsed under the blankets at around eleven? His escape from the twins had stimulated him so much, it had been a long time before sleep overcame him. He struggled out of bed, wanting to stay there, knowing he should. As he stood, his head spun and a wave of nausea swept over him. He barely made it to the toilet. Food was out of the question, but a cup of strong coffee later, he wandered down to the police station.

The captain was already at his desk. '*Buenos dias*, señor. I said nine, you are early.'

'*Buenos dias*, Captain. I wanted to know if you had found the German twins the Americans told you about, and to tell you what happened to me with them.'

'We have not found them yet. They checked out of their hostel late last night. I have men watching the bus station, but they have not been seen there.' The officer gave him a sharp glance. 'What information do you have?'

Jonathan told him of the lack of expression in Anna's face when her hands increased their pressure on his throat, and how they avoided being identified with him at the hotel in La Paz, while the captain scratched notes into a little book. When he stopped and looked up, Jonathan asked, 'When will you release Miss Einarsdóttir?'

'Now, she is our only possible suspect. I have asked for detective assistance from La Paz, and some forensic officers will be here soon. If they do not find a link to Señorita Einar's-Daughter, she can be released without her passport, but you must both stay in Copacabana until we have more evidence for the investigation.'

'May I see her, please?'

'No, is not possible now. Maybe is possible this afternoon when the team from La Paz have been.'

The telephone rang, a hideous jangle which reverberated through Jonathan's head. He sat back and listened to the rapid exchange, after which the captain thumped his desk and scowled.

'A boat was stolen this side of the water at Tiquina sometime early this morning. It was found on the other side.'

'You think it might be the twins?'

'Is possible. Officers are trying to find a man who gave them a ride from here. Is too far for walking – more than forty kilometres, so they take a car. Then they steal a boat. Is possible.' He swept his hand over the desk in a sarcastic gesture. 'Now they are somewhere in Bolivia.'

Jonathan regarded the other man across the desk. Was this situation going to drag on and it be forever before Gudrun was released?

The captain appeared to be lost in thought, but he soon returned to the present. 'Señor Scott, I think you should go back to bed. I don't wish to insult you, but you look very bad. It will be some hours before we can make a decision. Come back this afternoon. Have a long siesta. The señorita is well and comfortable, do not worry.'

A constable came up to the desk and handed the captain a note. The officer read a little, glanced up at Jonathan, and carried on reading to the foot of the page.

'Señor Scott, I have some bad news.' He passed the note across the desk, and his tone lost its bluntness. 'My sincere condolences, Señor, but your parents were killed in a car accident … er …' He snatched the note back. 'Two days ago.'

Jonathan gaped at him. He picked up the note and studied it for a while, but could not read the Spanish well enough.

'How? Does it say?' He was trying to absorb the news and think what to do at the same time.

'It says the driver lost control and hit a *camion*, a truck, ahead, head-to-head, you understand?' He banged his fists together.

Jonathan nodded, numbed, and stared at the floor. *Why don't I feel anything? There should be a sense of loss or something. Maybe it's too early.*

The captain snapped his fingers at a junior and ordered more tea for him. 'Señor, I'm sorry, but I cannot let you go until this murder is investigated by La Paz. Now you should go back to bed.'

Jonathan followed the advice and walked back to his room. There, he had another fit of vomiting, but it soon passed, and he crawled back into bed and collapsed. He lay awake for a short while, thinking about the accident. *Both Mum and Dad in one go! It's hard to comprehend, but I suppose it's for the best. Mum would never cope if Dad went first.*

For three days life stood still. Jonathan did little else other than sleep, report to the police, try unsuccessfully to see Gudrun and go back to bed. He had a drink every day with the Americans, who had become more friendly and trusting of him. That was good; he did not like being at odds with reasonable people, and he could not blame them for their attitude towards him.

On the fourth afternoon, an insistent tapping on the door woke him. It was light, and he was naked. Wrapping a towel round his waist, he stopped the second round of knocking halfway through. Gudrun towered in the doorway. She had a broad smile on her face.

'Hi,' she said as she hugged him.

He held her head close to his. 'Hello. Your hair is still damp.'

'I did not want to waste time getting it completely dry before I came here. They let me go without my passport. No explanation, I have to report there every day like you do.'

'You want some coffee?' He switched on the room kettle.

'Yes. I've had enough *maté* for a while.'

He told her about his parents.

'Oh Jonathan, I'm so sorry.' Gudrun put her arms around him. 'That's terrible. What happened?'

'He had a heart attack, which doesn't surprise me, and had a head-on collision with a truck,' he said without emotion.

'Oh, how awful.' She paused, studying him. 'Are you upset? You don't show it.'

'No, not in the way most people would be. Dad and I were always at odds with one another, while my mum got distressed on the sidelines. He always provided for us, although there were never any luxuries. He sent me to a good school and to university, so I shouldn't be harsh, but what he did for me was all for his own benefit in the long run. He was never affectionate, a distant man, so I can't summon feelings of loss over him. I wish I could somehow, it feels as if some part of my character is missing. I left home without thinking about him – why should I miss him now?'

'And your mother?'

'I feel sorry about her, yes. *For* her, actually. She never had a satisfactory married life, being bossed around all the time, and he was a selfish man. She loved me and tried to stand up for me, but she couldn't ever change his mind. She tried to comfort me at times, but in the end she sided with him. She couldn't afford not to, I suppose. I don't want to think what my life would have been like without her, though.'

'What are you going to do?'

'The police won't release me yet, not until La Paz have given the okay, but in any case, I don't think it's important for me to be there now. I'll pay my respects to Mum in my own way when I get back.'

Gudrun studied him, concern written across her face. 'I love my parents, I would be on the next plane home. You don't care so much?'

'I'm not cold-hearted, Gudrun. If one of them were ill or injured I would go back straight away, but they are now dead and, as dead people, they don't care. Those attending the funeral or the memorial service are going because it's the done thing; it's conventional, certainly as far as my father's concerned. His business partner will go, of course, but he didn't like my dad, he'll go because it will look bad if he doesn't. Am I very cynical?'

'No, you're right. I can't agree with you, but what you say is true, I suppose. Now, if you are not going home then we are changing our plans.' She wagged a finger at him. 'You must not hike to Machu Picchu, it will not be good for your head. Maybe later, in two weeks. You should stay with me in Cusco as soon as they let us have our passports.'

'What about your friends? I thought you wanted to see them alone.'

A hint of amusement played across her lips. 'Katrin and Kristin won't mind you – only Alexander.'

'Alexander?'

'Are you jealous already?' She laughed at his expression. 'Yes. I think he's in love with me, but I'm sure it's only physical. He will get over it.'

'You don't know me at all, yet you're acting as if we're a well-established couple.'

'Jonathan, you're like an Icelandic horse.'

His eyebrows went up, but he said nothing.

'My father breeds Icelandics, I know a lot about them, I handle them every day. Ninety-nine point five percent of them are lovely creatures. Half of the remainder are not to be trusted, no matter what you do. The other quarter percent communicate with me on a level that is hard for some people to understand. There is one that will come to me without my saying anything or offering him anything. He will push me around with his nose while I try to keep my feet with a bale of feed in my hands until I put it down and stroke him. He will put his hoof on my foot without putting any weight on it. If I run, he runs beside me knocking me around with his head. He plays with me. It's a gesture of togetherness, I think. I have complete trust in him, and I have never taught him to be like this. We just bond. To me, you are like that horse. I feel I can trust you without knowing you. Now we have the wonderful task of finding out about each other without any difficult problems, like, "Will he be upset if I say this?" or "Should I tell him that?" Between us it is easy, no?'

'Wow! You hold nothing back, do you?'

'Is that not good? Is it not better to take the situation head-on? If no, our valuable time is wasted.'

Suddenly I'm hot. It's the sentiment, of course. It may be in my mind, but it's warming me physically. I must stay on top of it, not lose control, not admit the weakness. No. I should follow her example and be open and admit my feelings. 'It's very good,' he said. 'You've won me over, but I think I was there anyway. I didn't believe something like this could happen so fast.'

I'm emerging from the long tunnel of youth where events and people have influenced my life more than I have had influence over theirs. My dad, Castle, the crash, Lisa, Martin and Ginny, Terry, the twins, even Jo, they've all played their part in bringing me to this point. They've confined me, enhanced me, embraced me, played with me, tested me and contributed to what I now am. But a new phase is about to begin, there's brightness ahead, and the light is held by Gudrun.

She lay fully clothed on top of the bed, and Jonathan was in his towel under the covers. There was enough height from the thick pillows for them to appreciate the view. Little boats were coming and going from the wooden jetties which stretched out from the beach.

Gudrun said, 'Tell me about these other women. I don't understand why you think they killed the American, or why you told the police about them.'

Jonathan explained how he had met them and how he believed they were the ones Brad saw going into Carl's room.

'But why were you suspicious of them?'

He hesitated, so she laughed at him, teasing. 'Did you have sex with one of them also?'

How do I tell this woman who could be my future about it? He swallowed. 'Both. They're twins – Germans,' he added, although he had no idea what that had to do with it.

'Both at once?' Gudrun was most amused. 'Quite a man, but so shy. You're funny Jonathan, I do like you.'

'It's not so funny, actually.' He repeated what he had told the police captain.

'Huh. So you think you were almost killed by them? Are they psychopaths, do you think?'

'Maybe. They called themselves Black Widows. I thought it was a joke, but I think they came after me here, partly because I was unfinished business, and also because I could tell the police about them, which I did.'

'So it was one of them that hit you in the toilet while I was talking to the other, I guess.'

'I'm sure of it. We need to be very careful, watchful. The police have not found them, but they cannot be far away. I have this feeling they are not going to stop until they kill me. There's something very determined about them. They were not efficient, and I've escaped. They will come after me, which means you may become a target as well.'

They fell silent. Gudrun digested the information, while Jonathan tried to determine if he was feeling better.

A little later he changed the conversation. 'I've been thinking about what to do with my life. In fact, it was what I was thinking about when you picked me up in the bar.'

'Hah!'

'I used to see my future as an airline pilot. I love flying, and the life appeals to me. But I'm having second thoughts. This backpacking thing is tremendous. The new countries, the different people and their customs; it's fantastic, and I reckon if I could make a living out of travelling to wild places, it would be ideal. The trouble is, right now I'm going through money faster than I anticipated.' Jonathan explained his financial situation in detail, emphasising he had to have a sound business model in order to access the greater portion of his inheritance.

'I have started writing a journal of my travels. Later I'm going to put it into a long article, which I'll sell to some magazines or an agency. It will be the first step on a road to developing and conducting tours for adventurous people in remote parts of the world. It seems like a good life to me. What do you think?'

'Why a journal, why not write a blog and publish it regularly?'

'Because I want a full article, maybe even a book with the whole story, not publish it in parts. What do you think about setting up an adventure-tour company? While we're here and in Peru, we can find tough treks and unusual things to do. There's Inca stuff, the Atacama desert, high mountains ... there's plenty of opportunities to explore.'

'Are you asking me if I want to be part of it?'

'Yes.'

'Yes, of course.' She laughed. 'You will need a woman's help, and one who is strong enough to beat up psychopaths will be a bonus.'

A week later, Jonathan and Gudrun reported to the police station at nine o'clock as they had done every day. The captain walked towards them with a rare amiable expression. He held out their passports.

'You are free to go. The detectives and forensics from La Paz have found no trace of your DNA in Señor Schwitter's room. They found DNA the same as what was recovered from the room of the German women. It is also the same found in a hotel room of another tourist who was killed in Sucre a few weeks ago. They did not find his killer, so now they think is possible these women are responsible for both.'

'You think they are serial killers, Captain?'

'Maybe.' He shrugged his shoulders. 'All the evidence points to them. I am sorry for the trouble, but I hope you understand I had to act as I did.'

24

CUFF'S LIFE

BARRY CASTLE – NOVEMBER

Barry Castle found it hard to follow Cuffy Fucking Cuthbert. The trouble was the man was not a dawdler. Castle could keep up all right, but the person following has to move faster than his quarry. He has to stop to avoid being seen and then move again to catch up. Being large and with his almost-white hair, Castle was easy to see if he charged along the street, so he had to stay well back, even covered in his hooded red jacket. At least he had found out where CFC worked, where he was living and what his car was.

His follow-up call to the hacker was met with a brief response that the boy – Castle could not imagine him as an adult – had not yet tackled the task. Two days later, Castle phoned again as instructed and was told to meet at the same bench that afternoon.

It wasn't raining this time. But he was no less impatient as he watched the river flowing past while he waited for the youthful voice behind him. He was nervous. He had no idea how successful the boy had been, and his plan hinged on the lad's ability. For three years he had dreamed of little else but bringing Cuffy Fucking Cuthbert to his knees. His pretty German cousins would help if he asked them, but injuring or killing CFC was not the best solution, even if it was the most obvious. He wanted the man to feel the pain of his destruction. If his plan failed, Castle would be emotionally destitute; there would be a vacuum in his life, he would have no purpose. He did not have another way to take revenge on CFC and, for his entire time in prison, had dreamed of nothing else. If his plan succeeded, though, it was going to be a triumphant pleasure telling the twins. It was important that they saw he could take effective revenge even if it didn't match their bizarre behaviour.

'I've cracked the accounts. What do you want to do?'

His mind wandering, Castle jumped. 'I want to bring him down, bit by bit until he's in a pit of debt with no way of climbing back. I want you to open an account in his name, but with only me having access using his ID. I want regular payments that he can't afford put into that account.'

The lad sneered. 'That's stupid. If he checks his bank statements at all, he'll soon see there are unauthorised payments, and you won't have taken much money. You're better off draining him in one big transfer and then closing your account and ducking out of sight.'

The impracticality of his scheme hit Castle hard. His plan was shot. He'd been so focused on the one idea, he hadn't thought of alternative options.

'I can't hang about here all day. What d'you want to do?'

'I'll have to think about it, I didn't expect this. How much is in his account?'

'Fuck all really, a bit more than a thousand. Not worth committing a crime for.'

'Shit! I'll call you.'

Pharma-Scott's premises fronted the High Street, which was normally closed to all but pedestrians, although suppliers could bring their vans in past the bollards if necessary. Castle knew there was also an alley at the back which served all the shops in the row for rubbish collection and deliveries.

He pulled up his hood to hide his pale hair and strolled along the street, glancing in every shop window. When he came to Pharma-Scott, he crossed the wide cobbled walkway and ordered a Cornish pasty and a coffee from the little takeaway stall a bit further down the road. Rain fell, and the street cleared of most shoppers. He crept further under the stall's awning, chatted to the woman at the counter and examined the area for security while finishing his pie. There were two CCTV cameras which had a view of the entrance to the pharmacy.

When he had finished eating, he paid and sauntered off along the street on the same side for a few minutes before crossing the road and going back so he would pass the entrance of Pharma-Scott itself. He might pick up something he had missed if he looked at the scene from all angles and gained as much information as possible.

The store door was closed for the weather, giving Castle an opportunity to study the lock without attracting attention. No problem, except there was a fitting for a padlock as well. Again, no problem, although it was in full view of the cameras and would take more time.

He continued down the street and found his way to the service alley at the back. There was a camera there too, but it had been broken off its mounting, hung from its cable and pointed at the ground.

Castle waited a day, then repeated his reconnaissance. He learned nothing new.

He entered the store five minutes before closing. Stooping to stay below the shelf height, he moved to find the most hidden position out of view of the front door. All the other customers had paid and left by ten past six and the quiet was only broken by the cashiers closing up. One by one they left. There was movement somewhere in the back, so he stayed put.

The front door opened again. A voice called, 'I'm off now India. You won't forget the alarm will you?' It was CFC; Castle clenched his jaw.

'No. Goodnight,' a female called from somewhere behind the dispensary.

'Have a good evening.' The front door closed.

Castle waited a few minutes, before creeping towards the back of the store, conscious that as he rounded the end of each row of shelves, he could be seen from the street. Where was this India? A rustle of paper and the sound of key strokes. A book snapped shut, a switch clicked off. He peered round the counter. She was closing her office. She shut the door and put the key to the lock. He had to get to her before she set the alarm.

He was behind her. He clamped a wad of chloroform-soaked cloth across her nose and mouth. She struggled for a few seconds and went limp, but he caught her. Her pretty, cherubic face sent a wave of desire through him. He had not had a woman in well over three years, not since the act which had put him away. He whipped off his glove, lifted her skirt and ran his fingers over her plump, creamy thighs. A few pubic hairs had crept out past the elastic of her knickers. He pulled the flimsy garment aside and clamped his hand over her mound, feeling the coarseness of her down. God, he was tempted; they were out of sight below the counter. *No.* He was breathing hard. The pressure of his erection was incredible. *Zwillings, you two would be laughing at this, urging me on, wouldn't you, you lovely devils?* He stroked her again. *No, stupid. They've got your DNA. They'll have you before the week's out, and you're on licence as a sex offender. You'll go down for years and years and years. No, there are more important things to be done. It's not her you're after.*

He overcame it. He dragged India along the floor to the back entrance, stopped to listen – nothing. Cracking the door ajar, he glanced up and down the alley – nothing, so he lifted in the two jerrycans he had left there. Another quick dose of chloroform for India to ensure she stayed unconscious, and he was ready.

Castle went along each aisle pouring petrol onto the shelves and the floor beneath the racks; he pulled plastic bottles of baby oil down to lie in the fuel, and paper towels and toilet rolls for wicks. With the second can he soaked the offices, the chairs and the carpets, before laying a trail to the back door.

India was groaning and moving. He gave her a little more chloroform and, with a last regretful look, picked her up and carried her outside, dumping her out of harm's way. He stroked her thigh once more, before pulling himself together. She would come round soon enough. Back at the rear door, he grabbed his two cans, put them outside and flicked his lighter.

* * *

Once again in his red jacket with the hood up, Castle studied the aftermath of his previous night's work. The curious crowd was growing. CFC was there too, surveying the devastation. The woman beside him had to be his wife; there was something evident in their body language which told Castle they were a couple. But they weren't a couple united in distress. She was very upset; he was taking it much more calmly. She dropped her hand from her face and reached towards him, but he was standing too far away and didn't notice. She could have moved closer, instead she resigned herself to the gap between them and moved her fingers up to her mouth again. Her eyes were wide with horror, the moisture in them amplified by her awful glasses.

Castle moved closer into the second row of spectators and more to the side of his interest, so they couldn't see him. He barely made out what they were saying.

'I'm going to see India,' CFC said.

'What's she got to do with it?' his wife snapped. 'Why are you running after her? Can't you see what's in front of you? Can't you do something positive instead of seeing that tart?'

'She was attacked last night while working for us. Where's your sense of responsibility and common decency? I want to find out if she's okay, or if there's anything we can do for her. There's nothing to be done here anyway. The fire crews have to finish, the police want to investigate and the insurance company will want to assess the damage.' CFC walked away without waiting for her reply.

Castle found the couple's discord amusing.

25

CUFF'S LIFE

NOVEMBER

For fifteen days after the fire, Cuff, Lisa, her father and the accounts and shop staff had worked flat out to rebuild the Pharma-Scott head office in the other branch, the old Quercus building. Computers were replaced, back-ups restored to the new devices and extra furniture purchased so they could work alongside their Quercus colleagues.

With the trauma of all this behind them and their growing differences put aside, although not forgotten, Lisa was trying hard to be nice. She was cuddling up to Cuff on the sofa while he was sorting his photographs on his computer.

'Cuff, let's go away for a dirty weekend.'

'Sounds good, where?' Cuff hid his caution at the suggestion. She confused him – one moment she was loving, as now, and the next she was emotional, jealous and accusatory. He wasn't sure whether to be suspicious of her motives, or to put it down to some disorder. Whatever the reason, it was difficult for his steady personality to handle.

'On the coast. I fancy seeing the sea and hearing the roar of the waves while we make love in the afternoon.'

'Not at night?'

'Then too. Cuff, I want to get away from this place for a little while. The fire and the last two weeks spent reorganising have been very stressful. We seem to be arguing a lot, too. I want to forget all of it and get back to how we were a few months ago.'

'I can't fault that. What about next weekend if we can find a place in time?'

'Great, I'll do some research. I love you, Cuff.' She jumped up and ran out to get her laptop.

'You too.' His answer sounded like a mechanical response.

It was a good weekend, primarily because it was Lisa's mood that dictated how they got on. She was on a high throughout, so all was well in never-never land. In spite of November temperatures, cloud and occasional rain, they walked and made love and ate themselves silly and walked it off and went back to bed again.

Cuff had dusted off his camera, which seldom got used at home, and spent a good deal of time taking some stunning landscape scenes.

'Look at this one, Lisa. I reckon this is competition material.'

'Oh wow! That's really good. You're so clever, Cuff. I love the orange streak of the sunset on the waves. Those little fishermen's cottages have picked up that colour to balance the picture perfectly. Do you see that? There's another cottage further along, above the adjacent cove. It's almost hidden in the cliffs. Let's go and see it tomorrow.'

'We haven't time, I'm afraid. We'll have to leave first thing in the morning so we can knuckle down to an afternoon's work.'

Lisa's friend Sheila was holding a party. Cuff didn't want to go. He regarded Sheila as part of the problem in his marriage. As Lisa's agony aunt, she issued ongoing advice on babies, of which she had had three. Lisa's cooing and oohing and aahing over the kids was nauseating and way over the top. It was Sheila, Cuff was convinced, who was the fuse to Lisa's frequent eruptions of desire for children, for the subject only came up after the two women had been nattering. As a temporary single mother, Sheila often sought Lisa's attention, because her husband was away on contract in the Gulf on an oil rig, earning unbelievable sums as a diver and stashing it away in an offshore account.

To keep the peace and play his part, Cuff agreed to go. Lisa had mentioned it, but the reason for the party had escaped him by the time the day arrived. It might have been Sheila's birthday, it might have been the dog's birthday, but it was most likely to be the youngest's first word or solid poo. He didn't care; it was an opportunity to get pissed on more alcohol than he contributed, and he wasn't bothered by this abuse of Sheila's hospitality. She, or rather her husband, could afford it.

Lisa was in fine form, he admitted. She was happy to be going to see her friends, she was happy Cuff was with her and, if she were only to admit it to herself, she was happy to be out of their house for an evening. Several beers and a couple of glasses of wine under his belt, he became bored with another husband who was equally bored and went in search of Lisa. She had given up trying to keep Sheila to herself in the face of other young mothers all telling each other of their babies' latest advancements and was wandering around with a glass in one hand and half a bottle of champagne in the other.

'Are you having fun?' Cuff raised his glass to her.

'Lots.' She leant against him, her head on his chest. The pressure of her warm, unsupported breasts aroused him.

She felt it. 'Let's go upstairs.'

'Really? Okay.'

Lisa took his hand and led the way. 'This is Sheila's room,' she said with a giggle as she locked the door and unbuttoned her top.

There was a funny side to using Sheila's bed. It was a little, rather shameful, way to get back at the woman for corrupting his wife's view of life, but he made a silent apology to her husband.

He left the office later than usual, but Cuff had been going over the company's VAT return with India. On their way out, he held the door open for her, laden as she was with shopping bags. He relieved her of three of them, and they walked out to the car park together.

At her little Fiat she put the bags into the boot, closed the lid and gave him a diffident look. 'Thanks, Cuff. Please tell me: are you happy with my performance so far? I mean, I've been here for a while now, but feel I'm only just getting the hang of the way things work.'

'You're doing fine, and you were a great help after the fire.'

Her face lit up. 'Thanks Cuff, you're so sweet.' She flapped her hand in a farewell wave as he headed off to the corner shop to buy some batteries.

Lisa saw them from a distance before she left for home.

Cuff heard the banging from outside the front door. He found Lisa attacking vegetables on the chopping board with vicious, heavy slashes of a large knife. He shook his head. It wasn't as if he was two hours late or had ruined the dinner or something; it was only forty-five minutes. He wasn't going to apologise – why should he? The office sometimes placed calls on him which meant a little extra time was spent there. That was a penalty which came with being the boss.

No greeting. 'What kept you?'

'I've been helping India with the VAT returns.'

'Huh!'

Cuff's hackles rose. This attitude of Lisa's was becoming more common, and he could not understand why. The issue had to be confronted.

'What is the problem? Why are you adopting this tone every time I'm a little late, or doing something out of the ordinary?'

She glared at him, gathering her argument before launching her attack. When it came it was a sneer. 'India! That's not a name – it's a country. Stupid parents giving a child a name like that. Are you having an affair? Are you shagging that tart?'

He laughed. 'God, no. You're being ridiculous. Where did you get that idea?' In a more irritated tone, he added, 'And for your information, India is not a tart. She's a quiet, reserved girl who gets on with her job.'

Lisa kept silent and continued to take out her anger on the vegetables. Cuff shrugged, took a beer from the fridge and went upstairs to change.

Cuff was looking forward to more aerobatics on Saturday afternoon. The boost he had from the last session had long since expired. He had better tell Lisa, prepare her; allow her time to sulk before her post-flight tantrum.

'You can't go flying, I've invited Mum and Dad for tea.'

'Oh for God's sake. Why didn't you tell me earlier? I've booked the aircraft, and if it's changed everyone's got to rearrange their programmes. Why can't you have tea with them alone? I see Michael every day, and I'll see your mum when I'm back. I'm not going to be late.'

'I did tell you, I asked them ages ago.'

'No you didn't.' Cuff stormed out of the kitchen, angry that again she was trying to stop him enjoying himself. He heard her pick up the phone before he stomped up the stairs. Carefully, he lifted the upstairs receiver and put his hand over the mouthpiece.

'Hello Mum.'

'Hello darling, how are you?'

'Fine, Mum. Can you and Dad come to tea on Saturday afternoon?'

'Oh, that's nice. We'd love to.'

Cuff smouldered at this deliberate attempt on her part to control him. He might have capitulated and cancelled his flight to keep the peace, but after that call there was no way he was going to change his plans and join her – to hell with the consequences.

Sheila was late for their weekly meet. You never knew with Sheila, but Lisa guessed the reason she wasn't on time was she'd been entertaining a lover that afternoon. There had been a rather smug and satisfied grin on her face when she walked in.

Because it was late, the tea room had only one scone left for them to share. They did not stint on the cream though, and Sheila used her entire portion on her half of the scone. The result was a thin white smear on the fine hairs of her upper lip. Lisa tapped at her own mouth, and Sheila dabbed her cream-moustache away with a napkin while continuing, uninterrupted, to offer advice.

'I think you have to persist, Lise, darling. You have to remind him what family is all about. It's about having and bringing up children to further our species. He has a duty, it's a natural thing.'

'I don't know what he's going to do. I get the feeling he's so tired of everything, he wants out. He says I led him into marriage under false pretences, that I promised we wouldn't have children in the first three years.'

'I know, darling, you've told me, but you're entitled to change your mind, you're a woman. You should stick to your guns, you're only following the course of nature after all.'

'He's losing interest in me. I'm sure he's having it off with that bloody girl in accounts. I've seen them getting on well.' Lisa paused, staring at her scone, while her friend sipped her tea and watched her. 'Sometimes things are lovely, then if I mention a baby, even in passing, he flies off the handle and we have a row. He doesn't like this and he doesn't like that. I bought a gorgeous mustard-coloured chair for the lounge. He says it's ugly and clashes with everything else, and what's more it's damned uncomfortable. He said I should have asked him first before making a choice. That's all very well, but he won't come shopping with me, so what am I supposed to do? What happens if he gets fed up and wants a divorce because I can't control my emotions?'

'I'd let him go. I'd get a good solicitor and take him for all he's worth and say good riddance. You're an attractive woman, Lise – you can easily find a better husband than Cuff. Do you really want to stay married to someone you're always arguing with?'

Lisa pushed her part-devoured and now unpalatable half-scone away. 'No, but I'm scared of the future – it could be empty.'

'Better empty than ongoing tension, darling. In fact, I think you'd be well advised to go ahead and divorce him anyway. This is not going to come right, not from what you've told me.'

'How's Ginger Ginny?' Cuff asked one evening at The Gargoyle.

The girl herself smiled up at Cuff as he reached them, but said nothing. Martin slipped an arm round her shoulder. 'She's great, she really is. We're always so in tune. How is it possible for a relationship to be so good?'

'Lucky you, I'm glad. You're both so good for each other, I wish I was in the same boat. Phew! It's hot in here,' Cuff shed his winter jacket and folded his sleeves a turn before going up to the bar.

He put their beers on the table and pulled his chair in to get closer.

Ginny was not going to let Cuff's obvious worries be unheard. She touched his arm. 'What's troubling you?'

'My life, in short. A while back, I decided to follow Dad's advice and work towards a prosperous future. I dithered over whether to do this or get out into the big wide world and see where it takes me. I'm now suffering the consequences of making the wrong choice; I'm not happy where I am, and I keep wondering what life would be like if I'd chosen to leave instead of enduring this mundane existence day after day. Would I be crossing the Sahara on foot, or climbing in the Andes, or flying a little aircraft to Australia? Maybe I could help research polar bears in the Arctic – I dunno, but I'm missing out on a hell of a lot of exciting things to experience. To make things worse, Lisa is proving to be a real drag.'

He studied his drink for a moment, watching the bubbles rise. 'She tried to stop me coming to meet you this evening. I invited her to join us, but she refused. But that's only one tiny aspect of the picture. I've told you before of our agreement about having children too soon, and I thought she'd accepted that, but now she won't stop nagging me to have a baby.'

Ginny and Martin said nothing, watching him, knowing more was to come.

'I'm not sure what's happened, but for a number of reasons we're not seeing eye to eye any more. It's as if, having snared herself a husband, she's now trying to bend me to her will. She confuses me. Her mood swings are unpredictable and from one extreme to the other. One moment she's all over me, the next she's crying and accusing me of being selfish and never taking her needs into account, which is simply not true. Then she goes through a period of calm before the cycle repeats itself.'

Martin stroked the condensation off his glass. 'She sounds bipolar?'

Ginny said, 'It sounds more like cyclothymia, which is not as extreme as bipolar disorder. I had an uncle who had regular mood swings from euphoria and incredible optimism to depressive periods when he was quite useless – sad, apathetic and irritable.'

'That strikes a chord,' Cuff said. 'I wouldn't go so far as to call her bipolar, that's quite serious. Anyway, with the relationship going downhill, I wonder if her desperation for a child is her way of holding this marriage together. She's now trying to stop me flying, and that's my one release from the utter boredom of this arrangement. Without the flying, I'll go nuts. She also accuses me of having an affair. She saw me talking to India, our bookkeeper, in the car park after work the other day and assumes the worst. She asked me if I was shagging the woman. She's become insanely jealous, and it's yanking us apart.'

'Are you and India …?' Martin was grinning, unable to hide his curiosity.

'No, but I bloody well will soon if she doesn't shut up. I don't think it would be too difficult with India.'

'So what are you going to do? How can you change things?'

'There are two ways out as I see it. Agree to everything she wants and die inside, or walk away. I'm not going to comply with everything she wants, I did that with my dad for far too long. I'm not prepared to have children too early on and ruin my life, our lives. It'll make me a seriously unpleasant person to live with and be to everyone's detriment. In a few years, kids will be great. I mean that, but not now.'

'So you're going to walk away? I'll help – I reckon Ginny will help too if you like.' Martin gave her a squeeze, but she kept quiet with a serious expression on her face.

Cuff laughed. 'You two! You're so willing. Whatever I decide to do will have to wait until the insurance pays out for the fire. That could be a couple of months yet, so there's plenty of time.'

Ginny put a comforting hand on his arm again. 'It's so sad when relationships fall apart, everyone gets hurt.'

26

CUFF'S LIFE

DECEMBER–JANUARY

It was Friday evening and Lisa was in one of her extra-loving moods. Cuff became suspicious and went on guard when this happened as, if he made the slightest wrong move or facetious comment, her state of mind would change and there would be another row in the making. The easiest solution was to play along and enjoy it.

Lisa's euphoria lasted all of the first weekend in December, though, and Cuff relaxed and shed his misgivings for two days of lovemaking.

On Monday morning he suffered aching joints and muscles, a temperature and a headache. Flu was doing the rounds, and the previous week he had been in contact with a couple of people who had looked like death.

'I feel awful, I'm not going to work this morning, Please make my excuses.'

'Oh dear, I'm so sorry.' She made it sound as if it was her fault he was sick. 'I can ask one of the staff to bring something back for you, if you like.'

'No thanks, we have some headache stuff somewhere, I'll use that.'

'Okay, get some more sleep, and I'll see you tonight. Love you.'

Cuff searched through the medicine cupboard but found nothing to ease his headache. Lisa kept some remedies in her dressing table drawer, so he scratched around, but only came up with her contraceptive pills. He stood up straight and gaped at the blister pack in disbelief.

By the end of the week, Cuff was feeling a lot better. He had not gone into the office at all, but had done some work from home when he was not sleeping off his fever.

Lisa cuddled up to him again on Friday after work, and they retired early. She was in bed first, ready and waiting for him.

She reached across and touched his back. 'What are you doing?'

He was sitting on the edge of the bed facing away from her. His tone was matter of fact. 'Putting on a condom.'

'Wha-a-at?'

'You've stopped taking the pill. You haven't had one since Wednesday last week, so I'll have to be the one to take precautions.'

'Oh God!' Lisa burst into tears and rolled away from him. Her shoulders were shaking under the blanket as he went into the bathroom. He removed the offending rubber and tossed it into the rubbish. Coming back into the bedroom, he reached into the top cupboard and pulled out his sleeping bag. Her sobbing aroused no emotion in him, so he turned off the light and left the room.

Lisa was listless and dispirited, a bit like the miserable weather which was cold and drizzly with not a breath of wind. Trudging along the High Street, she was laden with shopping which felt much heavier and more awkward than it should have done.

The pavement was crowded with early Christmas shoppers. A group was standing chatting and blocking the way. The only way round was off the kerb. She took it and bumped into a big man, stumbled and stepped into the road. He grabbed her arm and pulled her back. A car swerved, its horn blaring.

'Oh, thank you.' Lisa had lost her breath. 'God, that was stupid. I don't know what I'm thinking at the moment.'

One shopping bag had crashed to the pavement and spilled some of its contents off the kerb. She stooped to retrieve it, but his large hands were there first and fished the goods out of the water.

'I'm so sorry,' the man said.

'It's all right. It's as much my fault. It's all these people – why can't they move on?'

'The only thing that's broken is a jar of pesto. I'll get you another from the mini market down the road.'

'No, you don't have to do that. It really doesn't matter.'

'I insist. It won't take long.'

He not only replaced the pesto, but bought her a box of Ferrero Rocher chocolates by way of an apology.

'Oh, thank you. You're very kind. It's not necessary.'

'The least I can do. You're cold. Why don't we go for a quick drink in the Stag's Head? You can warm up there.'

'I ought to get home. It's sweet of you.'

'We won't be long – a nice warming sherry and you can be on your way.'

I've actually got plenty of time, because my difficult husband has gone out to the airfield again. He can't fly in this weather, so what for? He's probably with that fat tart, so why the hell shouldn't I go for a drink with a stranger?

'Okay, let's. But I can't be long.'

Lisa liked Barry straight away. He was charming, good looking in his blazer and tie, and polite, which was exactly what she needed. The stress of her domestic battles melted away with his compliments. They weren't excessive either in nature or quantity, but they made her feel appreciated.

'Can I see you again?' he said as they left the pub.

She held up her left hand. 'I am married, you know.'

'I noticed, but you don't seem happy, and I think we had a fun hour together. It's done me good, for sure.'

'Well … one more time perhaps. Not tomorrow, though – the day after and not on the street. I'll see you in here at four if you can make it.'

'I'll make it.'

Lisa went home elated, her confidence boosted. How long had it been since Cuff had treated her with the appreciation and respect this Barry had?

'Sheila, I can't tell you how this man makes me feel. He's charming, could probably charm the pants off me to be truthful. He treats me as special, which is something Cuff has never done.'

Sheila applied far more make-up than she needed in the belief it made her look younger. Now her face had the smug expression of the more experienced. 'Lise, take it from someone who's been there and done that a few times ...'

'Three, if I recall.'

'Three, yes, but many more men than three marriages can account for, and the odd one with Steve away in the Gulf.' Sheila ladled more cream on her scone and took some time to perch a dollop of jam on top. Before taking a bite, she said, 'Lise darling, live your life. If Cuff is shagging his bookkeeper, you have a licence to fuck this Barry bloke. Enjoy yourself. Life is there to be lived. With all the men I've married and all the lovers in between, I don't regret a moment of it, even if some of them were total twats. Go for it, I say.' She helped herself to more tea and took another bite of her scone, dropping a spot of cream on the table cloth.

'I'm scared – it's wrong, even though I want to. I never thought I'd need attention like this.'

Sheila chortled. 'Eat – you're going to need that energy.'

Six weekly meetings later, with the wind and rain of mid January outside, the tea room was full of hungry shoppers. Sheila had grabbed the last empty table. A private conversation would be difficult; there was not much space between them. Lisa came in to the ting of the door bell. She looked upset and worried.

'Whatever is the matter Lise?' Sheila put her hand on her friend's arm as she draped her coat over the back of the chair. 'I've ordered, so relax.'

Lisa gave a furtive glance around, to see if anyone was listening. 'I've missed my period.'

'Uh-oh. Tell me.'

'I stopped taking the pill to try to get Cuff committed, but he found out and we haven't made love since.'

'So this is your friend Barry, is it? Assuming you are preggy of course.'

'Yes. Oh Sheila, what must I do? Cuff is going to go berserk. He'll never accept another man's child.'

'Will Barry support you?'

'I don't know, I think he might, but he doesn't know yet.'

'First thing, give yourself a test and find out if you really are pregnant. It might be a false alarm. You must have the kit at the pharmacy.'

'Yes, of course we do. Stupid, I'm panicking and not thinking.'

'Let's assume you are, for the sake of this discussion. First, you have to be nice to Barry and sound him out. If he supports you, great. You can tell Cuff with the confidence that you're not alone. If Barry doesn't support you, well, you'll have to hope Cuff will come to accept the fact. You'll have to tell him as soon as you've told Barry. You can't avoid it, it'll come out at some stage anyway. You can pin the blame on him for treating you badly – stand up for yourself, go on the attack. If it comes to divorce, let it happen. It's not the end of the world, and it could be the start of a whole new and good life. Take it from one who knows. Of course, you can always get rid of it.'

'No! I've been wishing for this forever, there's no way I'm going to have an abortion.'

Barry Castle sat in his car looking out at the view through the rain-spattered windscreen and flicked the wipers for a single stroke. He was going to be a father, and that was cause for a celebration. He took a swig of rum from a hip flask and settled lower in his seat, feeling the spirit's warm and soothing flow throughout his body. The news was a shock, to say the least. He was trying to get his head around it and decide what to do.

Was he going soft? A younger Barry would have told the stupid bitch to sort her own problems out and walked away, but this was different, this was a whole new ball game. Something primal had surfaced in him. In itself, the thought of a son sort of pleased him. It proved he was a man, he could procreate, which was more than some poor sods were capable of. Beyond that, though, the baby would be born from the wife of Cuffy Fucking Cuthbert. That was a huge victory. For the rest of his life, the bastard was going to remember Barry Castle had stolen his wife. The son who could have been his was Barry's, and the boy would be told what a shit his mother's first husband was, and maybe he too would find a way to get back at CFC.

What would his pretty cousins say? Marriage and children were not in the Zwillings's future, that was certain. So would they scoff at him? Would they be happy for him? Their opinion mattered; he must try to talk to them.

And Lisa, what about her? Could he live with her for the rest of his days for the sake of his son? She was nice, they were good in bed together, and the mere fact she had the courage to have an affair meant she wasn't a total wimp. And, if they parted later, he'd move on and see the boy without the hassle of looking after him. After all, there were plenty of other wives who weren't too happy, and who'd be open to a fling.

But what if it turned out to be a girl? Would he have the same feelings? Another swig and he was more comfortable with the idea of starting a family. It was going to be bloody great to see that bastard's cuckolded face in the divorce court.

Things were going well, he had to admit. The job might be a second-hand car salesman, but the vehicles were at the luxury end of the market, meaning the commissions were reasonable. Mercedes, Range Rovers, Jags, even a Bentley stood in the showroom ready to provide him a good income. Such vehicles could take a long time to move, so he had some opportunity to do his own stuff, with Bert's grudging permission, of course.

The hacker's words and tone of voice had implied Castle's plan for ID fraud was naive at best. This still rankled with him, mainly because he come to accept it was true, but also because he had not yet thought of a solution. *But now I've got one, and it'll give me and Lisa a really good start.* He would need her cooperation, and for that he had to pretend he already had pots of money, then wheedle some information out of her. The whole thing would come together later in the month after CFC's birthday.

A grey squirrel was frantically digging into the lawn for its cache of winter food. It kept stopping to check whether some other greedy creature had noticed. The scene settled Cuff a little, because he was furious. He was losing control and wasn't sure how he was going to react.

'Who's the father? It sure as hell isn't me!' He could not keep the anger out of his question.

Lisa's voice quavered. 'No one you know. I met him, he was nice to me when you weren't, and we met a few times more and it just happened. This is all your fault anyway. We're married and you won't give me what I want. And you're having an affair, so why shouldn't I?'

His body wasn't cold, but his emotions were. 'For the last time, I am not having an affair and never have done. Who is this man?'

'His name's Barry.'

A black cloud of suspicion crept up and hovered over him. His reply was measured and slow. 'Barry who?'

Her answer was weak and fearful. 'Castle?'

Cuff took a deep breath. The squirrel had taken refuge in the tree. He couldn't see it, but a bough was shaking. Another was on the ground, scrabbling for its goodies.

There was no more indecision to be endured, because there was only one solution. He forced himself to appear calm – difficult when he was so angry. 'Lisa, what happened between us has happened. We cannot undo it. It was a result of pressure from our parents and a lack of understanding on both our parts. We didn't think things through. In truth, we are not sufficiently compatible to make a long-term relationship work. Your efforts to force me into accepting a baby only pushed me further away. What is done is done, and we have to move on. There is no possibility in this life or the next I am going to accept another man's child, let alone one from Barry Castle. Understand that and accept it. There will be no negotiation.'

'You mean you know him?'

'Castle was a year ahead of Martin and me at school—'

'School was ages ago.'

'He was the school bully. While I was at uni, I caught a man raping a girl during a party. That was Barry Castle.'

Lisa gasped. Her hand went to her mouth, and she scrabbled for a tissue.

'He served three years for that and is now out on licence for at least fifteen years. He's supposed to tell the police if he starts a new relationship, and they may inform you of his past if they think it necessary. It was my evidence which put him away. You should think very carefully about this man who is hell-bent on revenge. Before his case was heard, the prosecuting counsel made the point that my accident was sabotage, and it took place immediately before the trial.'

She sniffed and reached for a tissue. 'It can't be the same man, Barry is so nice and gentle.'

'Tall, pale hair, brown eyes, good looking?'

She nodded, a tissue to her cheek.

'Lisa, we are finished. It's over. Don't be sad about that, it's going to save us both a lot of pain. As regards Castle, I've warned you. Better to be a single mother than to be with him. He's likely to be abusive.'

27

JONATHAN'S WORLD

JANUARY

Cusco in Peru.

Jonathan and Gudrun had been together for almost four months, researching their planned future in adventure travel. Enough material under their belts, and they could decide what could be used to entice those who wanted to be off the beaten track and away from the crowds, and who would be willing to pay for the experience. Jonathan had been writing profusely all this while and had received some positive responses from a travel-guide publisher, but they needed more before they would use his information.

They had explored more of Bolivia before entering Peru and making the best of the attractive ancient capital of the Incas. Cusco acted as a hub for their wheel of exploration around the region, and they used it to rest and consolidate their gear in between the most difficult hikes they could find.

One evening, they were sitting in their favourite bar in a narrow side street. It was a pub with a pretension to English or Irish roots which did not fool anyone, but there was a happy atmosphere amongst the backpackers and a few locals, and it was warm. Jonathan was consulting his notebook with a worried frown on his face and using the calculator on his phone.

She laid a hand on his. 'Jonathan, we must talk about this money thing. You have paid for almost everything except my travel up to now. That must not continue, I have to pay my share.'

'This is my venture,' he said. 'I would pay all these costs if I were on my own.'

'This is *our* venture. When I asked if I was included, you said yes. That makes me equally responsible for everything.'

'Well, yes, but I have to ask – do you have the sort of money we are looking at? So far, we have spent a lot and not made a cent. What are cents in Iceland, by the way?'

'We have only króna. It's so small it's not divided. It's equal to one of your pennies, I think. Jonathan, please, I want to be a full partner and contribute as much as you do. If I run low, I will sell an extra horse or two, and if I run low after that I will tell you.'

She was determined. He had come to recognise the subtle change, the hardening in those penetrating eyes when she had made up her mind and wasn't going to be diverted. The force of her will on the American the first night they had met had been very apparent. He was not going to win this argument, and, he admitted to himself as he closed his notebook, he was happy to lose it.

'All right, thanks. I appreciate it. But you must promise to be honest with me.'

'I promise.'

Jonathan went to get two more Paceñas. The barman grinned at him as he flourished the bottles. 'You have good taste, Señor Jon. You one lucky man.'

'It's the best beer here.'

'No señor, I talk about women. How you get them, eh?'

Jonathan shrugged his shoulders. 'What are you talking about?'

Gudrun looked up at him as he put the drinks down. 'What's so serious, *Sæti?*'

'The barman tells me two pretty girls with dark brown hair have been asking about us. He thinks they're twins.'

'Oh. That's not so good.'

'He told them he didn't know us, fortunately. He protects his loyal customers, he says. I gave him a very generous tip.'

'So, we keep our eyes open, now. How did they get here? They should have been stopped at the border.'

'Maybe they didn't used a border post and are in Peru illegally.'

'That's a big risk, *Sæti*. You have to show your passport whenever you check in for a night.'

'I'm sure there are plenty of blind people if you know where to find them. I told you, these girls are very determined – the pair is single-minded.'

Created some six hundred years ago by the Inca, the path climbed a medium slope of cobbled stones. In places, though, it became so steep that larger rocks had been placed to form regular steps – a mountain staircase.

'How many thousands of feet have trodden here?' Jonathan had to shout to be heard over the noise of the stream which cascaded beside the trail and drowned out normal conversation. 'Travellers, pilgrims, priests, lords, peasants, llamas, and now tourists and their porters; thousands heading up to the temple, subservient to their gods.'

'The power of belief.' Gudrun tucked her thumbs under her shoulder straps and shifted her rucksack to a more comfortable position. 'It's so black under the trees ahead, you can't see where the path goes.'

The forest was about to close in on them. Jonathan stopped to look down into the valley. The sky was darkening, and the wind was picking up. Cloud rolled down the mountain and swirled around them. One moment the view was clear, the next was a grey, misty wall before it cleared again. The first few drops of rain pattered on his jacket.

'Poncho time,' he said and dug Gudrun's out of her rucksack pocket. He helped her into it and pulled it over her pack. She did the same for him before the rain fell in earnest.

'I think we're alone on this trail. I haven't seen or heard anyone at all today.'

'Sensible people.'

They broke out of the patch of forest, leaving the shelter of the trees. A freezing wind hit them with vicious gusts and drove the rain in near-horizontal sheets.

'Look.' Jonathan pointed as the cloud cleared for a moment. 'There's a ruin up there. That'll give us some cover from the wind at least.'

Rain lashed at them as they approached the building, and Jonathan shivered at a trickle of water which ran down his neck.

'What is this place?' Gudrun asked.

'It was a guard post. Must have been roofed in its day.'

Thick stone walls about two metres high were set on a promontory which commanded any approach from below. They shaped a room which might have been a community area. Where the structure oversaw the valley, the walls dropped to waist height. No enemy was going to be able to climb past the guard post without detection.

Jonathan pointed. 'See how the entrance is blocked by this interleaving wall. You can't see directly in or out.'

'Why? It's like the entrance to a public toilet which has no door.'

'Much easier to defend. The enemy can't rush you or attack with more than one man at a time, they have to work around the end of this obstructing wall. Come, let's get inside, there must be a corner out of the wind. Hopefully, this storm won't last long.'

The wind whipped and howled down the mountainside, but it took most of the rain and blew it to the far side of the room and over the top of the walls.

'Come close *Sæti*. Conserve our warmth.'

They huddled together and waited, heads down to avoid the icy rain.

'If this lasts, we can always spend the night here,' Gudrun said.

'True, but we ought to get higher if we can. The pass isn't much further.'

A head peered round the entrance wall. Red hood of its poncho up, a black scarf covering the nose and mouth, the figure came in, raising a gloved hand in greeting. Gudrun nodded in return and nudged Jonathan. He looked up as a second person entered.

Something wasn't right. *Both of them have very small rucksacks under their ponchos; must only be daypacks. Are they mad? They're woefully ill-equipped for this altitude, 4,000 metres or more, in freezing temperatures and driving rain with what little they've stuffed in those tiny bags.*

Identical clothes, identical packs – they can't help themselves, these two.

He stood. It was difficult with the weight of his cumbersome rucksack. He tugged at Gudrun. She glanced up and clambered to her feet, pulling on the stone wall for support. One of the figures moved towards them. A knife appeared.

'Whoa! Anna, Hannah – let's talk about this. Let's talk about what you want in a civilised fashion.'

The woman pulled her scarf down and gave him that same sweet and innocent smile he now knew to be evil. She looked at Gudrun. 'I'm Hannah, we met at the lake. Jonathan. So nice to see you again. We missed you.'

Anna said calmly. 'We are going to kill you, actually. You know this already, we think.'

The twins ignored the rain which pelted them where they stood. Jonathan and Gudrun were on the sheltered side of the room. There was no point in moving towards the narrow entrance, a knife was blocking it.

'But why?'

'We told you at the start what we call ourselves, actually,' said the one in front.

'You knew what Black Widows do to their mates, also,' said the other by the entrance. Her blade was at least nine inches long and pointed at the ground. 'And ...' She paused. Was it for effect?

'And,' the first continued for her sister, 'Rolf asked us to!'

'Who the fuck is Rolf?'

'Oh – he is Barry to you.'

'What? Barry who – Castle?'

'Yes, of course. Barry Rolf is our cousin, and he knows us very well. He loves us, actually.'

'Bloody hell!' For a moment, Jonathan was dumbstruck. The twins waited, confident, their sweet expressions belying their intent.

'Why didn't you kill me much earlier?'

'We liked you. We had good fun, no?'

'You killed another man in Sucre didn't you?'

They glanced at each other. 'Ah, so the police worked that out, finally.'

He had to keep them talking while he tried to think. Both he and Gudrun were hampered by their heavy packs which were difficult to shed from under their ponchos. 'You won't survive up here with what little gear you have in those day packs.'

'Oh Anna, Jonathan cares about us. So sweet.'

'Jonathan, we are not staying here. When you are dead, we will run down the mountain. In two hours we will be warm and dry. And you will be wet – and very cold.'

Jonathan had the twins' attention. Surreptitiously, Gudrun managed to worm her arms out of the voluminous sleeves and into the body of her poncho. Under its cover, she eased the right rucksack strap off her shoulder. Then the left one. The pack sagged back against the poncho, pulling it tight around her chest. Only the waist belt held it to her.

'Enough of the nice conversation, now.' Hannah advanced a step. 'Rolf's wish is our command – he taught us that phrase. He is not so clever, but he loves us, and we are family. So, Jonathan, are you ready? It will be quicker if you don't fight. We don't want you to suffer.'

'Jesus, you're twisted.'

A sheet of rain blasted across the room. Anna took a step forward and wiped her face clear.

'Sorry, big girl, but you have to go with your man. You can see is not possible for you to stay alive, no?'

Gudrun released her belt clip. The rucksack thumped to the ground behind her. Her eyes locked to the twin's, she felt for it, grabbed it, whipped the heavy load up in front of her and charged. Anna stabbed. The knife sank into the pack. Gudrun kept going. Anna fell flat on her back, Gudrun on top, the rucksack between them.

Anna fought under the weight, trying to free her knife. Gudrun smashed her farm girl's fist into the pretty face: once, twice, three times. Anna was out cold and bloodied.

Hannah leapt forward to protect her sister. Jonathan hit her from the side. She slashed at him: cut his poncho. But her twin was more important. Her focus was on Gudrun. Jonathan threw himself at her, knocked her sideways. She slashed again. A sting in his side. He winced, ignored the pain and punched with everything he had.

Hannah fell back on the wall. Her head smacked into the rock, her face sagged, and she crumpled to the floor.

'You all right?' Jonathan reached down to help Gudrun.

'I'm good.' She noticed his pained expression. 'Are you hurt?'

'She cut me.'

'Let me see.' Gudrun pulled up his poncho. His jacket was slashed at the side, his belt severed, and blood was oozing down over his trousers.

'It's only a surface cut, I think, but we must dress it.'

'First we must secure these two. I've some spare straps in the top pocket of my pack. We'll have to take them down. They'll die up here overnight.'

'Do you see the concern in my face, Jonathan? We should leave them here.'

He gaped at her. 'Are you serious? You don't mean that.'

'I mean Every. Bloody. Word. These psychopaths tried to kill us Jonathan! We, you and I, need to go down, and we need to go now. You must see a doctor as soon as possible. Our kit is damaged and wet, and we also would have a very bad night.'

Jonathan was staggered. Her ruthlessness was real; that familiar look in her pale eyes told him so. He would never have dreamed such an attitude existed. It was ugly. His love for her was not diminished, but this needed watching.

'Yes, we must go down, but we take them with us. To leave them here would be to let them die, and we are not killers. We are better than them.'

'How is your cut?'

'Uncomfortable, but okay. The stitches pull a bit. You think I'm weak, don't you?'

'No, *Sæti,* you are not weak.' Gudrun put her arm round his shoulders and pulled him close. 'You are a man of principles, a good man, a sensible man. You are better than me. In my temper, I would have left them to find their own way down. I don't think they would have died. They would have come round and made a difficult trip down the mountain after us. They might have escaped. You saved them and handed them over to the police. So you were right. If we had followed my impetuous way, they might have tried again to kill us.'

'Yes. I didn't think of that at the time. I thought we shouldn't leave them to die.'

They were sitting in a bistro, enjoying the warmth and hot food. Jonathan could not get over how quickly the afternoon's excitement had faded into the background with the return to Cusco.

'So, since tonight is going to be spent in comfort in a nice bed, warm and dry, are you going to pin me down and punish me for having bad thoughts?'

Jonathan laughed. 'You like to test me at every opportunity. I'm not sure I'll manage it.'

'I have no doubts, *Sæti,* none at all.'

28

CUFF'S LIFE

JANUARY

Cuff was relieved there was no other choice. This marriage to Lisa was ill-conceived, and the result was stillborn. There was no love left after such a short time. He'd been a fool to let her overcome his scepticism about marriage. And there was her unfounded jealousy. *Is there a quicker way to lose someone than to let your jealousy take control?*

Cuff met Martin and Ginger Ginny at The Gargoyle to discuss his future. The pub had become a strategic centre for all his plans. It was the place where schemes for Cuff were devised and torn apart, beer was consumed, other schemes evolved from fresh ideas, and more beer was downed.

Martin and Ginny sat across the table from him, a large bowl of potato chips between them. He had complete trust in these two, Martin because they were close and had always been there for each other, and GG because Martin had no hesitation in telling her anything and everything. She was wonderful; she was quiet, seldom said a word to anyone other than Martin, but when she did speak it was always sensible, often clever and sometimes humorous. She had more common sense in her than a whole school of teachers. Cuff was certain he could rely on her.

'I want you to understand that from my perspective this is not a battle between Lisa and me. At the root of it, we made a mistake, we're not compatible, and we don't have the same goals in life. I told you long before Christmas this marriage has to end, and I should have killed it then, before it became so uncomfortable for us both. It's worse now, because a child is involved – and it's not mine. If I were a good-hearted soul, I'd accept the kid, overcome whatever difficulties stand in the way and mend the marriage. But with some spawn of Castle's? I would resent that child from the start. I would be impossible to live with, and the whole thing would be ruinous for all concerned. All I can think of at the moment is how to take revenge on the man.'

'That's not a sensible way forward, Cuff.'

'I know, Ginny, but think: Castle's intent on his own revenge, so he comes up with a sick plan to ruin my family life. Of course, what he doesn't realise is the marriage is already on the rocks, and he's doing me a favour. He impresses Lisa with oodles of charm while I'm being unpleasant, so I suppose I'm a bit to blame. But he brings a child into the world purely to satisfy his hate. What kind of future does the poor kid have with a provenance of hatred?'

Martin said, 'So you want to avenge yourself because of his revenge? It sounds senseless to me. Rather direct your energy into getting out of the mess as cleanly as possible.'

Ginny took a chip and nibbled at the end. 'What effect will a divorce have on Lisa?'

'I wish I were a hard-hearted son of a bitch, because it would be so much less complicated if I didn't care about what happens to Lisa. I don't think she'll be devastated because she loves me, but she will agonise over her and her child's future and security.'

Rain drew their attention and caused a lull in the conversation while they watched the downpour and listened to the patter of drops on the window.

Still staring outside, Cuff broke the silence. 'Lisa isn't a bad person. But she is weak and confused, and I don't want to see the child suffer from her mistakes. I honestly don't wish to see her hurt any more than through her self-inflicted torment. I want to part amicably, and the most valuable thing I can do for her is to steer her away from a life with that bully.'

'How?'

'I'm going to delay any union between Lisa and Castle for as long as possible. That'll stick a finger in Castle's eye, but it'll also give Lisa a better chance to see the man for what he really is before she goes with him. She's going to go through a lot of pain, but it's for her own good in the long run.'

'So?'

'We can either divorce, or I can vanish. The trouble is, divorce is not permitted for a marriage which is less than a year old. And the process is so ugly. Waiting for our year of marriage to pass while we run the company together will make life impossible.'

'So you're going to disappear?'

'It's the more attractive option for a number of reasons. I can leave as soon as I'm ready, which I have an overriding urge to do, to rid myself of this whole ghastly situation. Lisa will try to trace me, which'll take at least six months. There's bound to be delays, with her giving birth in September. When she can't find me, she can apply for a Presumption of Death Order. A few weeks later, the court will declare our marriage to be over. With a bit of luck, this wait will be sufficient time for Castle to show his true colours, especially if he has to cope with a crying baby.

'She'll be free of me then, but she won't be able to claim on my estate for seven years, thus denying my assets to Castle. Not that it makes much difference, because I've written my will on similar terms as our prenuptial agreement, granting her all the marital assets, not that there are many. He won't be able to touch my non-marital ones which consist of my house – Dad settled the mortgage a long time ago – and my inheritance. If Lisa wants to share her assets with Castle, that'll be her choice. She'll have her own income, car and the use of my house. She'll be self-sufficient.'

'You're going to let her stay in the house? Why don't you sell it?' Martin asked.

'I don't want to force her out of the house after I've left, nor am I allowed to. She can stay there as long as she wants, provided she doesn't marry again. Her future spouse, Castle or another, will have to provide for her. The downside, of course, is Castle will probably take advantage, move in with Lisa and share the possessions I'll have left behind, but that's a small loss to bear and might even accelerate a breakdown in their relationship.'

Ginny shook her head. 'This is a truly bizarre conversation. You two are discussing what to do with Cuff's assets after he's presumed dead, or maybe really dead. And it's all about denying Barry Castle any benefit. This is supposed to be to Lisa's advantage, but will actually be to her greater unhappiness.'

'Put that way, you're right – it is weird. Even so, it's what I believe is best.'

'What are you going to do about the company?' Practical Ginny again.

'I wondered about leaving Lisa my share of Pharma-Scott. The Hineses would then have full control.' Cuff laughed. 'Dad would be scratching at the lid of his coffin in rage at the mere hint of it. But I thought gifting Lisa my share might allow Castle to profit, so I dumped that idea.

'All this preparation for my death might be wasted, of course. I'll always have the option of being found alive in up to six years and 364 days' time, depending on the situation.'

'I wish you'd stop hinting at things and tell us what you're going to do.'

'I will do, of course, but I haven't thought it through yet. When I have, I could do with you guys' support and help. If you don't want to, or think I'm wrong, please say so. Don't help me out of loyalty. If one of you is willing and the other not, put your own concerns first – I certainly don't want to come between you.'

Martin shook his head. 'Don't be daft. Whatever you've done has been huge entertainment for me and, until I met Ginny, my only source of excitement. This looks like the start of a long journey, and I'll be proud to play a part.'

Cuff looked at Ginny.

'I'll be frank, Cuff. I normally keep my feelings to myself, but I have to say I don't have anything in common with Lisa. I've nothing definite against her, but she's not a person I would trust. From something she said once, a casual remark, I think she used you. Her ruse has not worked, and now she's sulking and might do anything. However, you are man and wife, and she is going to suffer when you leave. Are you certain you've considered every avenue to make your marriage work? Are you one hundred percent confident there is nothing else you can do? She is going to go through a lot of pain, you know.'

'Ginny, are you saying that as a woman supporting her own gender, or as a person supporting a person?'

'As a person. I'm not supporting Lisa, I've given you my view of her, so it's not about her being a downtrodden female. I only want you to be sure you know what you're doing, and you're not just being selfish.'

'I admit I'm being selfish, but I know this situation is only going to get worse, and it's better to kill it now than both of us having to endure even more pain in the future.'

Ginny nodded. Cuff reached out and gripped her arm for a few seconds.

'Thanks, you two,' he said, 'you're the best of friends.'

Cuff contrived two linked plans. It took him a while to get them right because, having lost all interest in the company, he had to appear to be working hard while actually plotting and scheming his future amid constant interruptions. Everything had to be done under the pretext of something innocent. If Lisa suspected what he was planning, the whole scheme would collapse. He listed all the things he had to do, and set them in the order they should be done before deciding on a date to commence the countdown to the decisive moment.

The first plan covered the practicalities of how he was going to disappear. Driving him on his theoretical journey were his thoughts of Jo back at school. His sneaking into her room in the night had won her over, convinced her he was a man. Their puppy-love affair went on throughout their final year, stepping up through the gears to the heavy-petting phase. It would have gone further, but for lack of opportunity; there was no doubt about that. Cuff chuckled when he remembered a few wet dreams over her. If he found Jo again, could they pick up where they left off? She was much more his type than Lisa, more a drifting hippie, a Bobby McGee, a symbol of freedom. But things wouldn't be the same, they never are.

Second, the hated subject of money. It had to be addressed, it was so important to get it right. His father's nagging that one couldn't be too cautious lay deep in his psyche, and there was no doubt it had an impact on every decision and every move, how each related to the others and what risks each incurred. His inheritance would be sorted without a problem, but the company might be a difficult matter.

A week before his birthday, Cuff asked Michael Hines and Lisa for a board meeting in his office. Michael, and Lisa, who had come armed with a notepad and pen, took chairs facing the desk. Cuff stood behind his own chair, his sleeves pulled up and his tie loose as he addressed them.

'I'm resigning my position as director,' he said, and waited for their reaction.

Michael's mouth sagged open for a few seconds. Lisa dropped her pen as her hand went up to her mouth and tears welled, but she stayed silent.

Her father said, 'You what? You can't do that!'

'Yes I can. Under the shareholders' agreement my dad set up, I can. So I'll transfer my shares to you both after we've had the company valued. Because I realise you're going to be inconvenienced, I have no intention of asking for my full due. In fact, I'll settle for fifty percent of the company's worth rather than the sixty-five. You can pay me when the insurance money is through.'

'We can't use that, it's company money, not for the directors.'

'You can take a director's loan from it. You'll have enough left over to rebuild or relocate the premises.'

'But ... but why?'

'Please understand, Michael, this is nothing to do with personalities. You've been a pleasure to work with, but I'm not suited to a life like this. I'm bored out of my skull with the tedium of this existence, so I want to be rid of it. I'm going to find something more stimulating to do.'

'For God's sake, Cuff, we don't have enough money to carry on the business without you.'

Lisa's notebook flopped to the floor to join her pen. She made no effort to retrieve it, but fished for a tissue instead.

'Michael, you ran a successful pharmacy prior to the merger. You've made a good profit from the joint company, and you'll soon have the insurance money from the fire. You can do it again easily.

I'm making you a very generous offer. If you don't accept it, I'll be forced to sell to a third party, who will then have a controlling interest; I'm sure you don't want that.'

Lisa was sobbing. 'Cuff, I don't understand you. You have responsibilities to us, to all the employees and to our customers. You're giving that up, giving everything up, including *me*.' She picked her notebook off the floor and slammed it on the desk. It made a loud slap. 'You're selfish and cruel.'

Michael put a gentle hand on her arm.

'Lisa, please,' Cuff continued, 'This has nothing to do with our relationship and the course it's taking. You must continue working here, but I want to be alone in whatever it is I'm going to do – I don't enjoy partnerships.'

'What are you going to do?'

Cuff shook his head, but didn't answer.

Lisa's tissue was sodden, but she continued to mop her tears.

Michael Hines yanked open the office door and stormed out, muttering to himself.

Castle gazed out into the night from the parking area above the town. He could see no detail through the raindrops on the windscreen. Below, a traffic light went through two full cycles of green to amber to red and back again while Lisa talked. She had reclined her seat until she disappeared below the window line – her way of hiding from the world. She had told him she wanted to talk, and now she was sharing her misery, unburdening herself after CFC had dropped his bombshell and ruined everything. She was moaning how awful things were, and how Cuff was being selfish and unreasonable.

'Don't you usually tell these sort of things to your mate, Sheila, first?'

She was looking up at the car headlining. 'Yes, but she's gone off for the weekend with some man. Besides, you're my closest friend as well, Barry. I can talk to you, can't I?' Her hand searched for his thigh and rested there.

'Of course you can.'

'I don't know what to do.' She explained the business offer Cuff had made. 'The trouble is, he's about to get a massive inheritance from his grandad which will allow him to go off on his own with no thought for the rest of us. He wants rid of the company, but we need him to help. Do you think we should buy him out? Dad is resisting, but I don't see what else we can do. We can't compel him to stay, and if we don't do what he says, he'll find someone else to sell to, and then they'll have control.'

Castle looked away from Lisa and out of the window so he could hide his excitement. Things were falling into place. There was one easy and simple answer, but he pretended to consider the problem for a minute.

'You're right,' he said eventually. 'Raise a loan if necessary to buy him out. There's no point in having further contact with him if he's not interested. The sooner you have total control of the company, the sooner you can get on with your life. Cuff hasn't changed in the years I've known him – he's selfish and will just mess things up if you keep him around. When does he get this inheritance?'

'Thanks, Barry, I knew I was right.'

'Let me know how it's going. If you need extra money to pay him, I might be able to help.'

'I didn't realise you had that sort of money?'

He hesitated. He was digging a hole for himself in very dangerous ground by pretending to be rich, but if the gamble paid off, it would be worth it. 'I don't broadcast it.'

'You're so sweet. I'm sure we'll be all right, though. Dad moans a lot, but he's quite clever with financial things.'

She had not answered him on the date for the inheritance; he had to press her. 'What's Cuff going to do? When does he get his money so that he can go and do what he wants?'

'I don't know what he's going to do, he hasn't said, but I'll bet it has something to do with his bloody flying. He's been acting strangely recently. I'm sure he's up to something. He gets the main part of his inheritance when he turns twenty-three next week. I'm not sure how much it is, but it's something like a quarter of a million.'

Castle's brows shot up. *Next week? It's time to put the hacker on alert to monitor the account. I'd give my right arm to know what the bastard is going to do.*

Aloud, he said, 'I don't know much about the law or divorce or anything like that, but you must be entitled to half his assets. You need to get a solicitor onside as soon as possible. Cuff has money he's not going to share with you, and that has to be contested.'

If Lisa was successful in claiming half of Cuff's legacy, that would qualify as a great second prize. First prize, though, would be to clean out Cuff's account as soon as the sod had the money from his share of the company as well as his inheritance. He had to ensure Lisa kept him abreast of her progress in settling with Cuff so the hacker could act immediately.

If he did get hold of it all, he could keep up his recent pretence that he'd always had money, they could have a great start for their family, and the fortune would be his to control, especially if he ever wanted to walk away.

29

CUFF'S LIFE

FEBRUARY

Cuff had never been abroad, although he did have a passport; Kevin Scott had insisted travel to the Continent, let alone more distant destinations, was unnecessary, cost too much, and you didn't know what bug you were going to catch.

All subsequent actions would depend on whether he was going to stay in England or begin afresh across the Channel. Staying put would be the safest option for a while. Although he was more likely to be found in a country like Britain with its sophisticated systems, it wasn't as high a risk as when crossing international borders. On the other hand, a quiet crossing to France avoiding passport controls would open a range of opportunities. Passports weren't stamped as you moved around Europe, and sometimes they were only subject to a glance, he was told.

He needed a disguise. He had first thought about this in January, but could not change his appearance until he had left. Growing a mature beard would take weeks. Letting his hair grow so he would have a ponytail or shaggy locks would take even longer. While waiting he could have a wig, or he could dye his hair or become an elderly gentleman with a hat and a walking stick. Whatever he decided on, the change had to be quick and realistic. There was plenty to think about, and he needed to buy the materials.

He also needed two iPads, rather than laptops – they were more portable – as well as two inexpensive smart-phones. None of these purchases should be made locally; he would have to go to a city, even London, to maintain some anonymity.

Time away from the office here and there to avoid suspicion was required.

The forty-year-old, sixteen-foot day sailing boat was resting on its trailer in the boatyard. Cuff walked round the little vessel, inspecting it for damage and examining the fittings for strength and security. She had a hull of deep blue and a small white cabin. The owner padded around behind him, offering helpful comments. He was selling, he said, because of ill health, but was very sad to see his pride and joy go. He had had lots of fun in her.

'May I see the sails, please?'

'Of course. They're inside, it's too windy to have them out today.' The man laughed, but there was a touch of sadness in his voice.

It was obvious that the boat was a treasured possession. It was maintained well enough, although it had several unimportant flaws and needed some work to bring it back to a pristine condition. It was good enough for Cuff's purpose, of a size he could manage on his own, and was inexpensive at under a thousand pounds. The only downside was the name: *Wave Rider*. Such a name conjured images of a force-eight gale, with the tiny vessel happily bobbing about on the crests while the crew either got drunk or were violently ill, or both.

'Did you want the outboard motor? I'm selling it separately.'

'No thanks, I already have one.'

He'd made a good deal. It didn't matter if there were any hidden faults, and it didn't matter if the little yacht couldn't ride the waves as well as it claimed.

* * *

Cuff's will was complete, done and out of the way.

He bled his account down by withdrawing the daily cash limit. He would have to arrange with the bank for distribution of the final amount. There was one more debit order to go through before they were all cancelled.

He was becoming impatient and irritable with the slow pace of events. *I need to be off, to be free of all this clutter in my life.*

Cuff decided the 1st of March was to be his disappearance, his 'D-Day'. With eight days to go, he transferred all the relevant and important information from his computer to a special hard drive, which was compatible with the iPads he had bought.

Cuff was on his way to The Gargoyle for another strategy meeting, when he collided with a woman. A strong and familiar perfume alerted him before he recognised her. 'Oh, hello Sheila.'

When she saw who it was, her expression turned cold. 'Cuff. I want a word with you. Lisa is hurting, and you're being a right selfish bastard.'

'There are two sides to every story, Sheila. For example, I'm sure she's told you I'm having an affair. I promise you I'm not. It's all in her head. I don't want her hurt, I'm not cruel, and I'm not being selfish. You are looking after her, aren't you?'

'Yes, as best I'm able. Are you trying to interfere between her and Barry by telling her he's a rapist?'

'Yes I am, and it's true. It's for her own good. He's dangerous, Sheila. Maybe not now, but I guarantee he'll be abusive. You should try to stop that relationship going any further for her sake. She won't listen to me.'

'Are you surprised?'

Cuff stifled his thoughts, instead saying, 'Please try.'

That cold discussion made him late.

'I'm concerned about Lisa,' he announced to Martin and Ginny when he reached the pub. 'She's watching me. She's trying not to appear nosey, but I catch her peering into the room where I am and checking her watch when I go out. I'm sure she suspects something, although she can't have a clue what it is. In case she rifles through my things, I'd like you to hold all my new purchases until I need them.'

'Of course, no problem.'

'I'm also worried about when Michael Hines is going to pay me for the share transfer. He keeps trying to wriggle out of it, but I didn't give him much option, and I'm not going to back down. He's waiting for the insurance money, of course, but I bet he'll try to keep up the argument even after that's through. Now, important stuff.'

His tone was serious. Martin and Ginny both leaned forward. 'What?'

'I've left my house and any money I won't have used to you.'

'Christ! You're mad, Cuff. Thanks for the thought, thanks a million, but that's far too much to leave me.'

'What about Lisa?' asked Ginny.

'If I leave it to her, Castle will get his bloody paws on it. There's also all my physical possessions for you to dispose of as you wish to your own benefit. Most important: as I'm going to vanish off the planet and therefore can't have an active bank account, please open a separate account in your own name. I'm going to transfer a substantial amount into it, because there'll be the payment from Michael, all my cashed-in policies and the second part of my inheritance which I haven't yet claimed.'

'Oh, you managed to persuade the executors you deserve it, did you?'

'Yup. They thought the idea of an aviation career was sound, which is great. Anyway, when I contact you from wherever I am and ask you for a specific sum, you withdraw it from that account and give it to me in a manner we can decide upon depending on the circumstances at the time. This will probably be through a money transfer company like Western Union to an agent. Using a credit card will make it much easier to trace me. For your pains, you can withdraw a hundred quid a month from that account.'

'Don't be daft. I'll do it for nothing. I don't need to be paid for it.'

'Please, Martin, I want to pay you, it'll make me feel better. Also, there's an element of danger in this, as from the beginning of March you'll be aiding and abetting the walking dead!'

'*What?*'

'I hope you know what you're doing, Cuff. Have you got a back-up engine?' Ginny stepped down into the *Wave Rider* from the jetty.

Cuff handed her a life jacket. 'I learned to sail at school with

Martin. It was only dinghies, but this isn't much bigger, and it's more stable with a fixed keel. No engine, though.'

'I gave up on sailing, I much prefer to have an outboard,' Martin said.

Ginny looked lost. 'What do I have to do? I'm au fait with power boats, but the lack of an engine is a bit worrying.'

'Move your weight when I ask you to, otherwise relax and enjoy yourself. Martin will help to begin with, but I want to be able to sail her alone, which I'll do when I'm used to her. There's only a light wind today, so it won't get too exciting.'

Martin was on the jetty and had released the mooring lines. He was holding the rope in his hand, ready to climb aboard. At a call from Cuff, he did so and pushed off. The bow moved out from the jetty, and the jib caught the breeze and pulled the little vessel out into the estuary. Martin raised the mainsail and secured it. Cuff adjusted the sheets to set the sails as he wanted and sat next to the tiller. They were off.

After a while, Ginny, who had been letting her long red hair blow unchecked in the wind, capped it in place with a beanie. 'This is great. It's so peaceful.'

'Right,' Cuff commanded after a few manoeuvres with the wind in different directions, 'Martin, your job is over. You can keep Ginny warm while I handle this ship of the realm on my own. If I shout for help, you'll have to drop her to save us all.'

Two hours later, Cuff brought the little boat around into the wind so it glided up to the jetty.

'Thanks, Martin, I feel good about that. Pub lunch – I'm buying.'

Cuff had done his homework and found he was doing nothing illegal in the act of disappearing. But if he committed fraud in the process or took some other action which crossed the law, it might indirectly involve his friend, which was something he was never going to do.

It was D minus four. His credit card had been cancelled, he had no debt and he was about to have loads of cash. From now on he would be a cash shopper. He would not use the iPad for the Internet until he was well clear, and he would do without email for as long as Martin could keep him in touch.

Martin's future involvement was worrying. His friend was

exposed to a huge secret and was about to be the source of Cuff's information, money, communication and more. The trouble was, Martin, with his usual enthusiasm, was treating this as a great escapade. Like those pranks at school, Cuff's disappearance was something Martin could not participate in, yet was desperate to be a party to. So Cuff had to take measures to protect his friend from himself, hence the need for a second phone. If Martin used his normal one to call Cuff, that could be investigated and questions might be asked. With an unknown, unregistered phone for the sole use of communicating with Cuff, Martin should be out of danger.

The most difficult thing was Cuff had to tell Lisa he was going away for a week. He found her in the kitchen preparing her supper of a simple sandwich and a glass of milk. For the first time he noticed she had the beginnings of a bump in her trim figure. He put his slight flush of anger aside.

'Oh,' she said, without the hostility he was expecting, 'where are you going?'

'France, to meet an old school friend of mine who now lives in the States and is on a business trip to Paris. I'll be back within the week.'

'Oh. Well, I hope you enjoy it.' She sounded as if she could not care less, as if everything between them was lost and there was nothing left to fight for, as if she had given up. He was solely to blame in her eyes. It was not true, and only increased the certainty that what he was doing was right, and the sooner he got out and let her get on with her life, the better it would be. While that was true, he was still concerned about the pain she was feeling. Surely, with him out of the way, she could move on.

Four more things needed to be done. The first was to move the money as soon as it was in, but the other three could wait until the final morning: stop all Internet activity, cancel his email account and destroy his computer.

30

MARTIN BEALE

FEBRUARY

Martin did not fly often and had to admit he wasn't any better than average as a pilot. Terry knew he enjoyed it enormously, though, and encouraged him to carry on while monitoring what his son did to ensure he stayed within his capabilities.

On a cloudy day in February, he was preparing his dad's replacement Cessna for flight, his mind flitting to the accident as it did every time he inspected the machine.

A young voice behind him said, 'Hi, sir.'

Martin twisted in his bent-over position to see. A youth of about fifteen or sixteen was standing there. He was skinny and dressed in jeans which were crumpled at the ankle and frayed at the heel. They barely clung to his narrow hips, inviting a tug to yank them down. His hair was dark and greasy, and he was afflicted with terrible acne.

Martin smiled up at him. 'Hello?'

'Sir, I gotta speak to you, I can't keep quiet any longer.'

'What about? What's the matter?'

'I know who it was what sabotaged your other plane.'

Martin stood and banged his head on the tail. He made a pained expression and tittered at his own stupidity. 'Really? Who?'

'Well, I don't know his name exactly, but I know what he looks like. I saw him do it, I reckon.'

'But that happened over three years ago. Why didn't you say something then?'

'I wanted to, I did. Every time I saw you or your dad or your friend go flying, I wanted to say something. But I was only thirteen, and me mum made me keep quiet. She said it wasn't our business, and we shouldn't get involved. She said there'd be trouble from that bloke if he knew I'd seen him. But it's been worrying me, and I want to make it right. I mean, he nearly killed your friend, and it's not right he gets away with that.'

'Could you identify him? Does he come here often? Have you seen him since then?'

'I come here a lot, I just love the planes and the noise and watching 'em fly. I've done it since I was a kid, but I only saw him twice: the day when he did it, and again in the early morning before the accident. I was standing over there at the corner of the hangar.' He pointed. 'I'd recognise him again, for sure. He was in a red hoodie, but I did see his face for a mo', and he was big.'

'My name's Martin Beale, what's yours?'

'Jake Jones.'

The boy was still a kid. 'Will your mum let you go for a flight with us?'

Martin had switched on a floodlight. The change in the worried, scruffy teenager with an inferiority complex and spotty features was immediate. A huge grin split his gaunt face. All those years of enthusing over aeroplanes and watching them from the ground, seeing them being refuelled and maintained, being envious of the students and scornful of their obvious nerves when they were about to go solo while he was itching, dying to just get into an aircraft, even if it didn't move. Suddenly, out of the blue, he was being offered a flight. He had won the lotto.

'My mum? No way! But I won't tell her. D'you mean that?'

'I'll need to check with my dad, it's his aircraft, but he'll want to hear what you've got to say about this man.'

Martin and CJ had always had their suspicions the saboteur had been Barry Castle, but that was purely based on the timing of the accident being immediately prior to Castle's trial. Jake Jones' description of the man could fit, though, so Martin needed to take him to identify Castle. It would be easy to find Jake at the airfield, but he had no idea where Castle lived. Newspaper reports and court records would have his address at the time of the trial, and he could trace him from there.

Barry Castle of 39 Upton Street ... the record read. Got it! It was early in the day and there was no time to waste. Upton Street was not far from the route Martin always took to get to the motorway.

He waited on Castle's road short of number 39 until seven that evening. He was bored, tired, hungry and getting cold. How long he should keep this up? After all, Castle might not even live there any more. A woman in her fifties had left the house and returned a couple of hours later with shopping. She was the right age to be Mrs Castle, but the only time Martin had seen her before had been at her son's trial. That was a long time ago, and he had no idea what she looked like now.

As he was about to give up, the big man ambled along the road with his distinctive short steps and turned in through the front gate. Once Castle had inserted his key in the door, Martin left for home.

It wasn't difficult to persuade Jake Jones to sit in the car and watch for Castle. Martin's promise to take him flying was enough bait. Not that bait was needed – the kid was keen to become involved; it relieved the boredom of his life and gave him something positive to aim for.

Castle closed his front door for his daily walk to work. Jake leaned forward in his seat, studying the man's back.

'I dunno, it's been a long time, and I only saw him twice, like I said. But he's about the same size.' As Castle turned away from the door and presented a side view, Jake's tone dropped again. 'I'm not sure. I'm sorry.'

'Run after him and get a closer look, will you? You're quite safe – he doesn't know you. Remember, you've got to be sure, he could be innocent.'

'Right!' Jake's face lit up with the prospect of meeting the eye of a murderer while remaining hidden behind his anonymity.

Martin watched Jake walk casually towards Castle, then, as soon as he was safely past him, run back to the car.

Before he got in, he said, 'It's him all right, I'm sure of it.'

'Good. Well done, Jake. Have you got time for us to report this to the police?'

'Let's go!'

They sat side by side at a desk while a police sergeant took their statements.

'You can look up the crash; it was determined to be sabotage,' Martin suggested.

The sergeant went away and returned with a file. 'It says here that only one suspect was identified, but he had an alibi.'

'But I saw him do it. I'm sure of it. I know it was him,' said Jake.

'All right. These are serious allegations, so I'm going to pass this information over to the inspector. Wait here, please. I don't think he'll be long.'

Castle sat in the police interview room alone. From his past experience and watching TV crime dramas it was a pretty safe bet he was being watched, so he refrained from picking his nose and blew it instead. There were terms to his licence as a sex offender, so his relationship with Lisa and not having told the police about it must be the reason he was here. The trouble was they might tell Lisa, and that could destroy everything. She would support him, wouldn't she? She wanted a father for her child, their child. His worry caused him to fidget and scratch himself.

The door opened. He struggled to conquer his nerves.

'Mr Castle, my name's Detective Inspector Wright. May I call you Barry?' The accent was heavy and from up north somewhere. He had a military bearing, upright and proud, his suit a uniform.

There was no point in answering him; this type was going to do exactly as he wanted, whatever Castle replied. The man looked solid and tough with a broken nose and hard grey eyes. He was old school. He was still an inspector despite his age. Why had he been passed over for promotion? Was it because he was a little unorthodox in his methods, whatever they might be? Did he adopt unacceptable practices like 'leaning on' his suspects? Were those concrete fists now resting on the table right in front of him ever used to further the man's investigations?

Wright sat on the opposite side of the table while a young, fresh-faced plain-clothes officer called Jackson took notes beside his boss.

Wright's first question came out in a pleasant and non-confrontational manner. 'Barry, can you account for your whereabouts and actions on the 10th of October 2003?'

Castle stared at him. His jaw dropped. What the hell was he on about? It couldn't be Lisa, which was good. 'How the bloody hell do you expect me to remember what happened on a date well over three years ago?'

'Let me help you out. On the 11th of October 2003, the day afterwards, there was an accident involving a light aircraft.'

Castle swallowed and licked his lips. That was history. He had provided an alibi, his mates had verified it, and there'd been no repercussions. Nothing had led to him, and it was pretty certain he had got away with it.

Wright put his finger on a document in the file he had brought in with him. The thick digit ran along the line he was reading. 'A Cessna 172, I believe, crashed into a wood after an engine failure. A smoke grenade was activated in the cockpit, curbing visibility to the extent the pilot was unable to see to land the aircraft. The smoke grenade and a flash grenade, which had caused the engine to be starved of fuel, had been placed in the cockpit and engine compartment respectively by a person or persons unknown. Unknown until now, that is.'

'You're not looking at me?'

'We've been looking at a number of leads for some time, but you have recently been identified by someone who saw you working on that aircraft on the day before the accident. You're not a qualified aircraft engineer, are you?'

'No. Why would I do such a thing? This is ridiculous. I told your lot then that I was with friends.'

'The inspector who investigated the case at the time has since retired, but we don't let things slide under the rug round here, and you're now dealing with me.' DI Wright gave Castle a grin which did not stretch to his eyes. 'The pilot of the aircraft that crashed was due to testify against you in your rape trial on the 15th. His evidence: an eyewitness account of your actions during the assault that was crucial to your conviction.'

Castle watched the inspector close the file, patting the papers to make sure they were tucked inside. 'That was a pack of lies. The bitch was lying and Scott lied. He had a score to settle with me.'

'Nevertheless, you were convicted for rape and have served your time. Now, can you explain what your actions were on the day before the crash?' The file rose off the table and smacked back down with a crack, which made Castle jump.

'I already told you, I was with friends, for fuck's sake.' He swallowed to bring the rising pitch in his voice under control.

'That's a pretty broad excuse, Barry. What were you doing with your friends? Nothing in your diary?'

'I don't keep a fucking diary, and they backed me up.'

'There's no need to swear, lad, Jackson here is a sensitive soul. You shouldn't get so stressed about things, no need – not yet, anyway. I presume you'd have no problem with participating in an identity parade? You know, similar individuals to your good self all in a line to see if the witness can pick out the guilty one? Good man.' His humourless grin switched on again. 'It'll eliminate you, of course. Whoever did sabotage this aircraft faces a whole range of charges like attempted murder, wilful damage to property and several under the Aviation Act such as endangering the safety of an aircraft. Heavy stuff.

'Thank you for your cooperation, Barry. I advise you to see if you can remember what you and your mates were doing on the 10th of October. And if you can find anyone else to verify your story, so much the better. Off you go. We'll be in touch.'

Castle missed the step and stumbled as he left the police station. *What the hell is going on? Who the fuck saw me tampering with that plane?* He had better reinforce his alibi with both his mates.

31

CUFF'S LIFE

BARRY CASTLE – FEBRUARY

'Yup?' The youthful voice on the phone once again had a background of keyboard noises.

'This is critical. From now on you need to monitor Cuffy's account, like every hour. As soon as the money is in, you need to transfer it to the other account.'

'I'm doing nothing until you pay me. Another thousand. When you're ready to do that let me know.'

'A thousand! I don't have a thousand, but I will when you transfer it.'

'It doesn't work like that. I take a helluva risk doing this, and I want the money up front.'

'Look, can't you accept five hundred and take the rest from the sum you transfer?'

'I only work with cash, it's safest.'

It rankled Castle to have to beg from weeds; the reverse was normal. He forced the words out: 'Please, I can't afford to let this go for the lack of cash. Take five hundred now and fifteen hundred from the transfer.'

There was a long silence.

'Hello?'

'All right. We'll do it your way, but it'll be two thousand from the transfer. Let me know when the five hundred is ready for pickup.' *Click.*

Castle smashed his fist onto the tabletop. The little nerd had the better of him, and there was sod all he could do about it.

Castle left the money in the bin beside the bench as before. This time, though, he waited.

'Why are you still here?' came the high-pitched voice behind him.

'I've been told that the sum is about to be paid, so it should be in his account any time soon.'

'Depends how it's going to be done. It can take up to three days. I'm on it, I'm watching it all the time, but it wasn't there when I left.'

'How do I know that you won't steal more from me?'

'You don't, but I'll only take the two thousand. It's not good to insult your business partner, it makes for bad relations.'

'I'm on edge over this,' Castle grumbled. He got to his feet and walked away without looking back.

D minus two, and there was still a lot to be done.

Michael Hines had made his payment a few days earlier. As soon as it was in Cuff had moved the money into Martin's account, together with the refunds and what capital there was from his personal insurances. Only his inheritance was outstanding, and that was booked to come through that very night. Cuff stayed up, too excited to concentrate on a late-night movie, and tried to keep calm with whisky.

He accessed his account at one o'clock and kept the site open by fiddling around on the page. As soon as the transaction was showing he planned to move the maximum amount permitted online to Martin's account, then visit the branch when they opened in the morning to transfer the balance.

Cuff was waiting at the bank's door when it opened at nine. Unlike with an Internet transaction, he was able to transfer an unlimited sum from the branch. But nothing is straightforward. The cashier had to call a superior to ask questions about such a large amount. The man was satisfied with Cuff's truthful answer. Well, it was truthful up to a point. He said he was paying Martin for a debt over an aircraft that he flew, but the origin of the money was accepted because, with some clever forethought on their part, he had a letter from the executors confirming it.

'Yup?'

'What's happening? Is the money there? How long will it take you to transfer it?'

The sound of computer keys being tapped at a frantic speed came down the line. 'I'm getting into the account right now. Be patient.'

Castle was fidgeting and scratching his groin again. The kitchen clock showed 9.23 in the morning, but his mother liked to set it a few minutes ahead.

'Uh, oh!'

'What?'

'He's been withdrawing the maximum daily amount from the account every day for the past week. It looks like he's going to empty it.'

'Shit! Is the big money there, though?'

'Yes.'

'Well, transfer it quickly.'

'I'll do that, but stop shouting at me.'

The clatter of the keyboard continued.

'Fuck!'

'What?'

'Damn, fuck, damn!'

'What, for Christ's sake? What's the matter?'

'It's been withdrawn. The money's been moved – now. That's tough, he got there before us.'

It began in his neck; the temperature rose until his cheeks were hot to touch. His head was going to burst. 'You could have done this early this morning! The money would have been there by two. I want my money back. You little fuck, you've failed.'

'Fuck off. I've lost too, remember.' *Click.*

Castle cried. He hammered his fists onto the table until they hurt. CFC had the better of him yet again. *Well, it will only make the revenge sweeter when I do catch him. But what is he doing? Why is he withdrawing all his money and closing the account?*

192

32

MARTIN BEALE

FEBRUARY–MARCH

'Mr Beale, DI Wright here. I'm letting you know Mr Barry Castle's alibi checks out. That's according to his two friends Mr Larry Mayhew and Mr Jeff Bennett, anyway. They both have identical stories – down to the very last letter, as it were.'

'Thanks for letting me know, Inspector. It leaves us with a puzzle, though.'

'It does indeed. But rest assured, this case is not closed, and we'll keep looking into it.'

Martin put the phone down with a satisfied nod: the DI was thinking the same as he was, Larry and Jeff were lying. He couldn't say where his hunch came from, there was no rational reason for it, but he followed it anyway.

The two gutless wonders who had hung around with Castle at school, his self-appointed gang members who would do nothing without their big leader telling them, were avid football fans. They would spend every weekend in front of the TV or at a live match within reach. Martin didn't know what team they supported, but he had a distant memory of someone telling him they had often been involved in football violence.

He looked up matches which had been played on the 11th of October that year and found England played Turkey in Istanbul. The interesting thing was, to avoid hooliganism, English fans had been warned not to travel to Turkey as they might be refused entry to the stadium.

Larry and Jeff drank in The White Hart, their local. It was one of those pubs that tried to appeal to a new generation by installing contemporary furniture, a pool table, darts, TVs which could be seen from any corner and a jukebox.

The first night Martin went there, he had no luck. The next night he found the pair playing darts. Nearby was a table with two pints on it but no drinkers, so Martin bought himself a beer and sat next to it, and waited. Their game over, Larry and Jeff left the board to some would-be players and took up their glasses. With their arrival came the acrid stench of stale cigarette smoke. Martin kept quiet; these two had had a few by the looks of them, and he worried they'd become violent if he annoyed them.

It was Larry that realised first. 'If it isn't little Ginger Beale, how's that?'

Jeff squinted at Martin. 'So it is. How's little Ginger? How come you're slumming it in here instead of wallowing in an expensive country pub, eh?'

'Your beers are low,' Martin said. 'Want another?'

The two glanced at each other in surprise. 'Why not?'

Martin went to the bar from where he watched the two men with their heads together. Were they plotting a little fun with him, or trying to work out what he was doing there?

'I was having a discussion with a friend the other day about the England-Turkey match in Istanbul,' Martin said as he set the drinks down. 'I said it was Rooney that missed the penalty, but he said it was Beckham. I said I thought you guys were there so you'd back me up, no?'

Jeff laughed. 'No way. You're wrong, Carrot Top. Rooney nearly scored, and it were Beckham that missed the penalty. The score were nil-nil. We went there, but were turned back. The bloody

Turks wouldn't let us in, would they, mate?'

Larry grumbled at the memory. 'They warned us not to go 'cause we might not be let in, but we reckoned we'd give it a try. Spent the bloody night squeezed in a room with others and then put on a plane back 'ere on the Sunday. Bloody waste of time.'

'Barry too?' Martin held his breath. *Are they too drunk to realise what I'm asking?*

'Oh, Barry weren't there.'

Martin stood. 'I've got to go for a piss.' He headed for the toilet and glanced back as he got to the door. Barry's acolytes had their heads together again, and they looked serious, too serious. Martin ducked behind the crowd and made it to the pub door without being seen, thanking heaven he was small.

It was the 1st of March and a day after he had effectively destroyed Barry Castle's alibi. Martin was cycling home from the airfield as it was getting dark. There was a chill in the air that gave him a shiver as he left, but he knew he would be warm by the time he reached home. If not, and he smiled at the thought, Ginny would heat him up one way or another.

Cycling was not Martin's favourite pastime, but it did give him exercise and he was pretty useless at anything else. Walking took too long to get anywhere, and running was too exhausting and left him sweaty.

Ginny said it was dangerous on the road for cyclists and he should buy a bike for trail use rather than chance his life with the traffic. She had a point. After all he'd had a few scares when aggressive drivers had missed him by mere inches, and once a pressure wave from a truck had sent him wobbling and almost into the ditch. But he accepted these things, telling Ginny, 'You can't dodge all the risks all of the time' – *hadn't CJ said that at some point?*

A few cars passed him on the road; he heard the engines well before they reached him. His flashing rear light gave them ample warning of his presence, and they all kept well clear. He pedalled on, breathing in the cool air, knowing he was doing himself some good, except for exhaust fumes, of course. The next corner was sharp and cars needed to slow down to take it. He was wary of that corner because of the high hedges and the fact that drivers could not see him until they were almost on top of him. He rounded it without incident, though, and set off down the long straight which followed. Trees on both sides had been trimmed into an unnatural, sharp-cornered tunnel of branches by the constant passage of big trucks. If there had been a moon, it would have only shone narrow slivers of light onto the road, but the moon was hidden by cloud. He was not concerned; home was not far away.

Another engine was approaching from behind, and an oncoming car had its lights on high beam, dazzling him. He struggled to see ahead, so kept his eyes down and focused on his own meagre pool of light. The driver did not dim his lights even though the car behind him was getting close. *Careless bugger!*

Blinded by the high beams, or using his mobile phone, or drinking coffee, or munching a pie, or lighting a cigarette, or deliberately, the driver behind Martin took no evasive action whatsoever.

The strike hit the back wheel first. The bike shot forward and out from under him. Wrenched from his pedals, Martin spun up over the bonnet, thumped into the windscreen, slid up and over the roof and dropped like a sack of potatoes to the road. He rolled twice, his limbs flailing. Excruciating pains shot through legs he could not control. His left arm screamed at him. Sharp pangs stabbed his chest with every breath. Overwhelmed by agony, his face twisted into an ugly grimace.

Tyres screeched and the car swerved, rolled almost to a stop, then accelerated away into the night.

His bike was crushed, but somehow, Martin's rear light survived and continued to flash upwards at the overcast sky.

33

CUFF'S LIFE

MARCH

Panic threatened to swamp Ginny. If she let it, it would seize control of her mind and leave her incapable of a decision. Broken legs and an arm, cracked ribs and internal injuries, they'd said. Internal injuries could be life-threatening, couldn't they? *Oh, Martin! Sweetheart, I asked you not to cycle on the roads after dark. Why didn't you listen, why did you have to do it?* She could do nothing to help him, he was in the operating theatre, but Cuff? Cuff was going to do something idiotic, and without Martin there how would she ever be able to help him? He had to call it off, do it another time, change his plan, whatever, but he had to be stopped. He would be heading to his grave if she didn't act.

She went out of the hospital so no one could hear her on the call. It rang and rang and rang, while she paced the car park, before it went to voicemail. She left a desperate message and tried again.

* * *

The weather forecast for the English Channel was ideal. A front was on the way and should hit the area around two in the morning. It was heralded by a quarter moon, which became less and less visible as clouds scudded through its silvery light until it was obscured. The wind was forecast to reach force five, which meant about nineteen knots with an eventual wave height of around two metres. In a little boat with a lone sailor in open water this was more than pushing the limits of Cuff's capability; his experience was dinghies in sheltered conditions, not the open sea. He was going to reef the sails to reduce their area and make the boat more manageable. And, Cuff reasoned flippantly, without any logic whatsoever, she was called the *Wave Rider* and would have to prove she was well-named.

Something was fluttering about in his stomach and his mouth was dry. This was probably a very foolhardy thing to do. No, there was no 'probably' about it: it was foolhardy. But everything was slotting together, and that bode well, didn't it?

A little before midnight, Cuff walked out onto the jetty dressed in a wetsuit and carrying a huge rucksack. Conscious of the CCTV camera on the pole behind him, he imagined how those who would be searching for him would look at the recording and shake their heads at the stupidity of taking such a little boat out into a brewing storm in the middle of the night.

The wind whistled around the rigging of all the boats, and halyards slapped against aluminium masts in a ringing agitation of his nerves. It was a fraction of what it was going to become. He dumped his pack into the boat and opened the sail bag. Rigging the vessel with the sails flapping unrestrained in the stiff breeze was both stimulating and stomach churning. Instead of a burgee, the little flag which would normally be hoisted to the masthead to show the relative wind, Cuff raised a single white light and secured its power lead to the mast.

He cast off the *Wave Rider* and let the wind carry the vessel away from the jetty before he adjusted the sheets and pulled the sails in. As soon as he did, the little boat shot off, eager to meet the sea when it left the estuary.

'*Bon courage!*' he muttered to himself with an eye to France, and dropped his phone over the side as he had planned. It wasn't going to be of any further use, traceable as it was.

Leaving the shelter of land, the waves were monstrous. They came at him in unending succession, each one a regular repetition of the last. They loomed out of the darkness, visible only through their breaking white caps and glistening spume, to heave the little vessel upwards before dropping it in a stomach-lifting fall.

Cuff had his hands full. On the wave crests the wind hit with its maximum force – lean outboard to balance it. The troughs were sheltered – move inward. Over and over again. It was wearing his body, and the darkness, the howl of the wind and the sharp slap-slapping of loose canvas were taxing his mind.

He spoke aloud to keep a hold on himself. 'This is a nightmare. This is bloody madness. It's far worse than I thought. Should I go back? No, I can't risk turning the boat around in this sea. It's tough, but I've got the hang of it now. As long as it doesn't get any worse. I hope Martin will be all right; he's pretty competent with boats. But in these conditions? Christ, what have I got him into?'

After an hour, with the wind now almost at its maximum forecast level and the sea still rising, Cuff checked the GPS; he was still short of his chosen position, but not far. He searched for the arrangement of lights he was expecting on the headland; his back-up marker in case the GPS failed. He could only see them when the little boat lived up to its name, because in the troughs, with the wave height being halfway up the mast, nothing was visible but the next wall of water bearing down on him. A little further, just a little, and the pattern would be perfect, the lights lined exactly as he wanted them. He switched on his masthead light, checked the GPS again and sailed on.

Am I imagining it, or is the wind getting stronger – surely this is more than force five?

A violent gust slammed into the *Wave Rider*, knocking her over into a dangerous heel. Cuff was already leaning out to balance her. He let out the main sheet to spill some wind. It wasn't enough; the boat heeled further. He was almost standing upright. He let the sail go, but his feet slipped on the wet surface. He fell across the cockpit and into the sea on the far side. Without his weight, the tiny vessel followed him over. The mast slapped into the water, sails dunked, unable to rise. Cuff scrabbled to get back on board, but his safety line caught on something and held him back. Trapped, his head was pulled underwater with every wave. Fighting to keep his wits and take a breath whenever possible, he traced the line to the end, unclipped it and swam free.

Bobbing in his lifejacket, he took some desperate strokes to get back to the boat. But the *Wave Rider* was already yards away, slewing beam onto the sea.

The wind forced itself under the sail at a crest, lifting.

She sprang upright and drifted rapidly out of reach. *My God! That boat was my life support. What the hell happens now? Don't panic, whatever you do, don't panic.*

Massive waves loomed out of the dark. Each threatened to engulf him, but instead swept him upwards in a great surge of energy. At the crest he was hit full in the face with spray. The first two times he swallowed water. *It's easy to see how men drown like this.* He forced himself to stay calm; there was nothing else he could do.

The automatic light on his lifejacket had activated. *This is useless. No one will see it. Half the time I'm in the troughs.*

He scrabbled for the more powerful torch clipped to his belt and switched it on.

34

JONATHAN'S WORLD

MARCH

Jonathan decided to hook up to the Internet for the first time in a month. 'God knows what my inbox is going to be like,' he moaned as he tapped at his phone. He ran his eye down the list, singling out the messages he ought to do something about. A recent one from Terry stood out as important. That was unusual. Terry didn't normally need to communicate, and if he did he would get Martin to pass the message.

'Oh God!'

'What is it?' Gudrun sat down and put her hand on his thigh. 'What's the matter?'

'It's my friend. He's been in a hit-and-run accident. He's in hospital in a critical condition. When was this? Two days ago.'

'What are you going to do?'

'Hang on, there's more.' He read on for a minute. 'Martin has a witness who saw who sabotaged his dad's aeroplane and caused me to crash three years ago. I must go home to see him.'

'Oh yes, you must.'

'Will you come with me?'

'Yes,' she said with her sharp nod. 'Of course.'

On the flight home, Jonathan dozed as a weak alternative to full sleep. This partnership with Gudrun was so comfortable: their travels together, their cooperation and mutual reliance, the trust which had been instant and thereafter taken for granted.

The night he had met You had been the turning point. *God, I'm glad I didn't choose to succumb to my father's will. I can't imagine what my life would be like if I'd stuck with Lisa.*

Since then, he'd drifted along, ready for any eventuality, but not actively looking for a partner. When the ideal woman turned up, he'd know. She'd be someone who thought the same way as he did, who enjoyed the same things he did, whose view of the future was the same as his, and who was prepared to put everything she had into that relationship. Someone like that would never give cause for a serious disagreement. Ten years might pass before she appeared; no matter, until then his life could remain uncomplicated.

Then along came Gudrun.

Did that mean he was ready to settle down? No, not in the usual sense, not marriage and kids and a home and Sunday lunches and an annual holiday with the rest of the country – no. But to have a relationship which allowed them to travel, to explore, to have reason to be curious, to share their excitement on a daily basis even if only through little things – yes. And was this giant of a woman, this powerful goddess, this kind and caring person the one he wanted to share his adventures with, the one he wanted to be alongside him through his explorations? *I feel pretty comfortable with that scenario. Our relationship is sound, it provides us with stability, and the solid foundation we need as a springboard to launch our adventurous and interesting life.*

He was looking forward to showing Gudrun off to his friends.

35

JONATHAN'S WORLD

BARRY CASTLE – MARCH

Barry Castle had been reading the paper every day since he learned of Jonny Fucking Jonathan's arrest for murder in October. The very short Skype he had with his cousins at the time had left him confused. The twins must be escaping. Why else would they dye their hair?

Since then, he had made several attempts to Skype with the girls, but they were not responding to his messages. He called his aunt in Germany. She was equally in the dark and upset, because she wanted to wish her daughters a lovely Christmas. Then in January she called Eva in tears. Hannah and Anna had been arrested in Peru for murder, she said. The Federal Foreign Office were supporting her, and the German press were pestering her.

Castle had mixed feelings. He had a deep love for his cousins and was upset they'd been caught. Who was their victim? Had they managed to nail JFJ?

He learned nothing from the British press; they were not interested in Germans in South America. It was significant, though, that there were no reports of JFJ being killed, so maybe he was still in jail.

Castle thirsted for bad news, even though he would have preferred to be the agent who delivered the fatal blow. Did they have capital punishment in Bolivia? He would have to look that up. What about Peru, where the girls were?

He ambled into the newsagent one Saturday morning to find a dark-haired woman with ridiculous glasses absorbed in the paper. Over her shoulder he saw the headline: *BRIT MURDER SUSPECT DUE HOME.*

He grabbed his own copy off the shelf and stood beside the woman. 'I know this bloke. He was at school with me, the little shit.'

'I know him too,' she said, 'and you're right. He is a shit. We were going to get married, start a family, and he walked out. No warning, nothing. He just packed up and left.'

'Fancy a cup of coffee?' Castle seized on the opportunity. 'I think we have something to talk about.'

Castle decided he could add to the news-rag's knowledge of the suspect murderer for a big fee. After all, it was his duty to see the British public knew what kind of man had been arrested and had been receiving consular support at their expense, wasn't it? It deserved a trip to London.

'Hello. I want to talk to whoever wrote the article on the Brit arrested in Bolivia for murder. I've some background information he might want.'

The receptionist pointed to a phone on the counter. 'I'll put you through to the desk.'

'Mike Spence.' It sounded as if he was typing feverishly and holding the phone between his ear and shoulder.

'Would you like some background on the Jonathan Scott story? I know him well, I was at school with him.'

'Were you now?' The typing stopped. 'Depends what you got. I'll be downstairs in five. We'll grab a coffee in Costa on the corner.'

Mike Spence was a thirty-year-old junior reporter. He was an obese man who had difficulty moving. Castle could not put him in the shoes of an active journalist chasing stories, no matter how hard he tried.

'Well?' said Spence, putting his coffee on the table and taking out a small recorder.

'What's it worth?'

'Depends what you got, but not much, the story'll go cold after he gets back here.'

'I can tell you he's a heavy drinker.'

'Aren't we all?' The reporter laughed. 'But we might use that.'

'He gets out of control when he's drunk, likes fighting, parties a lot and does stupid, risky, illegal things. He also walked out on his fiancée to go to Bolivia. He was going to take over the company from his dad, but he walked out on that too, leaving his fiancée to mop up. The employees had no boss and their jobs were in danger. He's a selfish bastard. Obviously I can go into detail, but what's it worth?'

'I'll have to run it past my editor. As I said, the story will go cold. What you have might prolong it, but it depends on what else is in the news. I'll tell you now it's not going to be more than thirty quid.'

'What? I thought you paid in the hundreds, if not thousands?'

Spence stirred three lumps of sugar into his coffee. 'Look, I can tell from the way you're talking, your main interest is to put some dirt out there on Scott. I'm not interested in your motives as long as the information is basically true. We can't afford to be sued over a very unimportant story, though.'

'You're going to meet him off the flight, aren't you? Give him the third degree?'

'Oh yeah.'

'Will you let me know the flight when you have it?'

'Sure. Gimme your number.'

All that were unusual in the crowd in the arrivals hall at Heathrow were the reporters and cameramen from the only two newspapers which took an interest in the story. They were scanning the arriving passengers and edging around the crowd for a better look and a good shot. There were a large number of flights arriving in the late afternoon, and the flow of arrivals was constant and heavy.

Jonathan and Gudrun retrieved their backpacks and passed through customs without being challenged. Emerging through the automatic doors into the arrivals hall, they faced a sea of faces.

Someone shouted, 'Jonathan, over here.'

He ignored the call as he was not expecting anyone to meet him, but it was repeated and he turned to face the flash of a camera, then another and another.

'Jonathan, tell our readers about your arrest. We'll give you an exclusive.'

'What was jail like?'

'Why did you fight that American? Did you beat him to a pulp?'

'Jonathan! Everyone knows you have a reputation for fighting, tell us about it, tell us why. Exclusive rates, mate!'

'Were you drunk, Jonathan? Our readers have a right to know.'

The crowd took notice and gravitated towards the couple. Jonathan had no idea his police interview, not even an arrest, was news at home.

'Hey, darling, what's your name? Are you Jonathan's partner?'

Jonathan was now annoyed. He gripped Gudrun's hand and led her away without giving any answers. A reporter clutched at her sleeve, but she let go of Jonathan's hand, clamped her farm-bred fingers around the reporter's and squeezed. He yelped and let go. A photographer was in front of them getting a shot from a low angle. Jonathan resisted the urge to kick him out of the way. A story might not be there, but the press could always make one up. They did have some good photos, though.

Lisa and Castle watched this circus from a distance. She rather liked Barry's name for him, JFJ, and had adopted it herself. If expanded to the full title it expressed precisely what she felt about him. She could use it knowing its meaning, yet sound polite. Now, she found JFJ's discomfort amusing. *I hope they tear you to pieces, you bastard.*

In his new girlfriend, her jealousy raised its ugly head again. The woman was impressive with her height, she had to admit, but Lisa searched for as many faults as she could find. *Those pale eyes are horrible, cold and untrustworthy, her hair is a mess, her mouth too thin, and she needs some make-up; I don't like that light tan.*

Lisa followed the couple to the Heathrow Central Bus Station where they joined the queue for tickets. As soon as she realised where they were heading, Castle broke off and went to fetch the car. Lisa continued to watch while, loaded down with backpacks, JFJ and his giant girlfriend waited at the bay for the Reading bus.

Castle responded to Lisa's call by driving round to pick her up. The bus had still not left, but was loading, she told him. They knew it was going to Reading Station and there were no stops en route, so it was a simple matter to go straight there and wait to see what JFJ would do next.

Earlier, over their first coffee, they had explored their individual ideas about how each would like to deal with Jonathan, but neither divulged their full intentions. They did not know each other, and Lisa was not going to trust Barry straight away. But now they had worked together, even for that limited time following Jonathan and cooperating with phone calls and lifts, Lisa told him a bit more of what she could contribute to their joint revenge.

'I like your idea of stealing his ID,' she said as they sped along the motorway to get well ahead of the bus, 'and I think I can help you there.'

'Oh yeah?'

'Jonathan left his laptop behind when he ran out on me. I don't know what's on it, though, I haven't opened it.'

'Bloody brilliant! That's awesome.' Castle banged both fists onto the steering wheel. 'Does it need a password? It's got to have some useful information on it, if not lots.'

'I don't know about a password, I don't think so. He emptied his accounts, he told me, so you won't be able to get any of his money.'

'Pity. Still, there's got to be something on it that we can use to get back at him.'

Lisa waited across the street outside Reading Station while Castle drove into the only place nearby where the car would be ready to move – the underground short-term parking.

The tall woman left the bus ahead of Jonathan. They were hidden behind the vehicle as they collected their bags, and Lisa had to move to see where they were going to go next – the taxi rank.

Castle picked up Lisa in time to see which cab they had taken. As long as the taxi did not use privileged bus lanes, they would be able to keep up with it, which they did until it dropped the couple off at an ordinary semi-detached house in Pangbourne.

Lisa watched Jonathan ring the doorbell and wait. He made some comment to the female, and they laughed. The door opened, and a redheaded girl came out and gave Jonathan a tight hug.

'That's that creep Martin Beale's girlfriend,' Lisa said. 'I wondered the other day where he lived. I should have guessed JFJ would stay with Beale, at least initially, since he has tenants in his parents' house.'

36

JONATHAN'S WORLD

BARRY CASTLE – MARCH

Lisa and Castle pored over Jonathan's laptop. They were sitting side by side at a table in Starbucks and getting in each other's way. Tempers were short. He was irritated with her, as she kept sticking her finger on the screen to point at something and hiding what he was looking at as she did so.

'Barry, please stop scratching yourself. It's rude, and your jeans are losing colour in that spot. It looks, um, odd.'

His jaw clenched briefly. 'Huh? What? Oh, right.' He put his hand back on the table. 'Look, you know him better than I do,' he said harshly. 'You do this on your own and I'll do my bit later. You say there's no money in his account, but he must have put it somewhere. Maybe there's a clue on there.' He stabbed a finger at the screen. 'We want something to blackmail him with, or some scandal to tell the papers about. Maybe he's got some porn. Maybe there's some dirt we can show his Viking tart and stuff up their relationship.'

'All right. What are you going to do?'

'It's too hot in here. I'm going to get another pay-as-you-go card from the corner shop. I'll be back shortly.'

Castle took a few deep breaths of the cool air outside the café. He turned to go and bumped into a boulder.

'Watch it!' His immediate aggression fizzled. 'Oh.'

DI Wright's hard grey eyes pierced Castle's shell of innocence. They mined his brain for lies and sought his criminal intent. The detective's broken nose and solid jaw line created a certain impression; the officer was not a man to be treated lightly. He was smart, like an off-duty sergeant-major, in a tweed jacket and tie with well-polished heavy brogue shoes. He was carrying a litre of milk.

'Hello Barry, nice-looking lady you're with in there.' He inclined his head in the direction of Lisa who was bent over the laptop. 'Respectable type, I'd say. Business acquaintance? New girlfriend? May I remind you that, as a convicted rapist, you're being watched, so you make sure you keep your nose clean. All right?'

'You can't go around harassing people like that. I've paid my debt.'

Wright's mouth took on an ugly twist. 'Your sort are never able to repay that kind of debt, Barry. You leave a young woman traumatised for the rest of her life, and you think you can repay your debt? Have you told that lady what you did? Have you notified us that you want to start a new relationship?'

'She's not a girlfriend; we're talking business.'

'You're being watched, Barry. Make sure you behave.'

The DI marched away, leaving Castle stripped bare. *Fuck you, you bloody copper. I'm not going to be put off, and I'm getting closer to JFJ and his giant Viking bitch all the time.* There was another option for revenge, one for which he didn't need Lisa.

'I've found a list of passwords!' Lisa exclaimed when he rejoined her. 'At least I think they're passwords, but I don't understand what they refer to, it seems to be coded.' She adjusted her glasses and pointed. 'Look, Barry.'

'We're going to have to work on that lot. There's got to be a website in there which is useful to us. Anyway, what we're going to find on that computer is for the long term. I've a plan for now, and

I'll need you to drive a car for me, if that's okay?'

Lisa was in the local shop glancing through the paper to see if it had dragged up any further dirt on JFJ and his woman. Mrs Singh, the owner's wife, tugged at her sleeve.

'Ma'am, I see you talking to that big man many times. Please excuse me if I minding you business. You know he was in jail for rape, and they have him on some list for rapists? You know this? I'm sorry if I mind you business, but I know you not married. This man may be danger to you.' Shaking her head at the state of affairs, she added, 'So many bad men are danger to women.' The old lady wandered off to the counter.

Lisa caught her breath. 'Thank you for telling me. Thank you, I'll be careful,' she called when she recovered. *Oh my God! What am I going to do?*

The second half of Lisa's weekly scone, laden with cream and strawberry jam, took up most of her plate. She had told Sheila what Mrs Singh had reported while she ate the first half and, instead of starting on the second, was nibbling at her bottom lip while she waited for her friend's advice.

Sheila took her time answering. Her opinions were normally given in a light-hearted manner based on her own experience, which was all about enjoyment and nothing to be proud of, but this was another matter.

'Rape is supposed to be about control, Lise. As I understand it, sex is rarely the motive. If you want to risk associating with Barry, you need to make sure you don't upstage him, be as subservient as you need to, to avoid his wanting to dominate you. Don't be around him if he's been drinking and, whatever you do, don't drink with him.'

Lisa put her scone down after taking one bite out of it. 'I understand. The trouble is, Barry's the only hope I've got of getting back at Jonathan. He's left me feeling so bitter, I need revenge for my own sanity.'

'If you have to, you have to,' Sheila replied. 'I understand, I've been there too. But, Lise, darling, be careful, be meek and not too attractive when you're around him. And keep reporting back to me.'

Lisa had been hoping for something more optimistic from Sheila, but the woman's uncharacteristic concern at the mention of rape only added to her nervousness.

212

37

JONATHAN'S WORLD

MARCH

'A quick freshen up after that flight,' Jonathan said to Ginny over a cup of coffee, 'and we can go and see the man. How is he?'

'He's in a sorry state, but as chirpy as always. He's well on the mend, don't worry.'

Gudrun had finished her drink. 'I'll go and shower. You chat.'

Ginny grinned at Jonathan. 'Wow. After all this time in a partnership desert, and you turn up with a prize like Gudrun. Is it serious?'

Jonathan squeezed her shoulder. 'I believe so. I hope so.'

Martin tried to grin at his visitors without hurting himself. It was a tight-lipped effort because his grazes and cuts threatened to open up if his face stretched too much. Both of his legs were in casts and elevated. His left arm was also in a cast, but he could use his fingers. His breathing was shallow, as his ribs hurt with every intake of air. His invisible internal injuries had been repaired on the operating table and were healing, and he was off the critical list. Ginny perched on the bed and held his hand in both of hers.

Jonathan introduced Gudrun. 'This wreck lying here is Martin. Don't be put off by that damaged exterior. Underneath the shambles on the outside beats a brave heart.'

'Hello, Martin.' Gudrun greeted him warmly and held his hand without squeezing it, as if with all the other damage that too must hurt.

'You all have to sign every cast,' Martin said. 'I've never had a broken bone before, so three at once is good going. I need a record of them; Ginny will take pictures.'

He told them of Jake Jones' story while they added their signatures to his legs and arm. 'We told the police. It's time that sod was put away for good.'

'It wouldn't surprise me if he did it,' said Jonathan, 'although I'd never have guessed he'd stoop to murder. When the prosecutor inferred he might have done it to prevent me from testifying at his rape trial, I rejected the idea as I didn't believe he had the courage.'

'It's easier, I guess, if the accident is remote from you when it happens – not like stabbing someone, where it's right up close and personal.'

'Would he have known Jake had told you what he'd seen?'

'I don't see how.'

'It's odd that as soon as you know something which might implicate him, you're run over. It reminds me that I was set up for a crash.'

'Oh no, that wasn't because of Jake.' Martin told them of his meeting with Larry and Jeff and the destruction of Castle's alibi. 'If it was deliberate, it was because of them.'

Jonathan was working on developing their adventure-tour company. Some of this time meant meeting publishers in Oxford, London and Bristol who might use his articles and travelogues.

Apart from researching wild areas for possible tours, Gudrun was desperate to take some exercise. She could not serve any purpose being with Jonathan all the time, so she decided to walk. Ginny, who had many things of her own to attend to, including visiting Martin in hospital, took time to explain the system of footpaths and bridleways which run throughout Britain. She showed Gudrun a map of the area, and the tall Icelander plotted a route for herself across fields and through the nearby woods for about six miles. She planned to walk every day and hoped Jonathan would sometimes be able to come with her.

The first day she set out it was raining, but that was no hindrance. She took no notice of the cars parked along the street, and she didn't see one of them was occupied.

An hour and a half later she passed the car again before opening Ginny's gate. Because she didn't know Barry Castle, she couldn't recognise him.

Gudrun set off on her walk the next evening. The weather was foul, but she was used to strong winds and rain, and her jacket was waterproof. It was mild here in England and, in any case, being wet and cold was a temporary state. She was already used to this walk and had wanted to vary her route, but the distance she needed could only be achieved on these paths. For variety she would have to drive to another area, and she didn't want to take Martin's car. It was about time Jonathan took some time to find a good car, so they could be independent.

With the low cloud and rain, it was dark much earlier that evening, and she strained to see ahead to where the path entered the forest. It was going to be as black as a cave in there, but short of returning the way she had come, there was no other route back.

Once inside the wood, above the canopy, the cloud had taken on a faint orange glow from the town lights. This failed to penetrate through to the ground, however, and she had to resort to feeling much of her way. Every now and then she strayed off the path and was stopped with a branch in her face or across her chest.

Actually, this is stupid. The trouble is, I like the forest – after all, we don't have too many in Iceland – and it's a nice experience being inside one; if it's light, that is.

The dark and the unknown caused a little girl's beliefs to surface. Are there *Huldufólk* in the woods? Although he never claimed they existed, her father would not deny the presence of elves – hidden folk – but her mother was vocal about them; they had been an important part of Iceland's isolated culture for over a thousand years and many more before that in the settlers' original lands.

There were even four little houses for the elves in their back garden. Each was about thirty centimetres high and had tiny windows and doors outlined in white paint. Her mother kept them spotless.

But Gudrun was of a younger generation, subject to a more advanced education. To others, she would never admit to believing in elves. But her deep-rooted childhood superstition, instilled through primary-school games and bedtime stories, prevented her from denying their existence to herself and, in this haunting situation with her heightened senses, she sought to befriend the little people as a means of self-comfort.

Why worry? They live in rocks and lava fields, and there is no lava in these woods. But maybe, here in England, the Huldufólk come in a different form and live in forests? There was no reason for the elves to harm her if she showed respect and did not offend them; in fact they might protect a believer. *Stop it, you're being ridiculous.*

So focused on finding her way and appealing to her elves was she, that Gudrun ignored the crack of a twig behind her. She heard it, but it was a natural sound, and the trees were making noises all the time as they swayed in the wind.

38

CUFF'S LIFE

MARCH

The lone fisherman's hut was set on a narrow plateau about halfway up the cliffs. The first time Cuff had visited, during one of those days taken off work to reconnoitre, he had to descend a cleft in the rock, a mere split only as wide as his outstretched arms, which continued past the hovel and on to a narrow beach which shared the cove with a jumble of rocks. The sides of the passage were a mixture of stone and tufted grass and were so steep he could not be seen by anyone above. In fact, the hut itself was not visible except from the sea and the headland which jutted out to the west, the position from where he had taken that memorable photo on Lisa's 'dirty weekend'.

The orange glow of the setting sun in the picture had been reflected off the hamlet of white cottages situated above the adjacent cove to the hovel. He explored the whole area. The two paths, one to the cottages, the other to the hut, met on the clifftop near a track and a narrow circle where he had parked his car.

The cottages had all been empty. They were available for summer visitors to rent, but no one wanted to be there over the winter; they were far too primitive and spartan with outside toilets and a single room for sleeping, washing and cooking. To hide in one of them would be relatively comfortable, but they were too accessible, and he might be disturbed by an early holiday arrival. They were from an era when the fishermen rowed out to sea in boats they kept on the beach below and walked to their destinations. Nowadays those hardy men lived in the village two miles away, had motor vehicles of some description and went to sea in diesel-powered vessels.

The flat area on which the lone hut was built was set about a hundred feet above the sea. It was part natural and part hewn from the surrounding cliff face. The building was in too poor a condition to ever be rented out, and only two yards separated the front door from the cliff edge. Cuff knew it was going to be draughty and bitterly cold, but it was an ideal hideout.

He was there now and had settled in, but saw no positives to his existence for the foreseeable future: he could not make a fire in the daytime if the wind was light for fear the smoke would be seen; strip-washes had to be in cold water, which he collected from a fissure in the rock behind; and other miserable discomforts were hardships to be endured while he left his beard and hair to grow, but it was little worse than for the folk who had lived there a century before. From wood he had gathered and some cord Ginny had brought him, he made a rudimentary table and a seat.

He was sat there one evening, warming his hands while his food heated. Was there, he asked the soot-blackened walls, someone he should thank for surviving after his capsize? Other than Ginny, of course.

Everything had gone according to plan – except for the weather, which had grown far worse than expected. He had always intended to reach the rendezvous point as entered in his GPS and indicated by the arrangement of lights on the shore. Martin, in his motor boat and guided by the GPS, would be there to meet him. Once they made contact, Cuff would jump overboard and leave the *Wave Rider* to drift away with a duplicate set of all his possessions for the future, including a rucksack and even another iPad. In case Martin had difficulty finding him, Cuff was to shine his torch upwards onto the sail as a beacon. No one on shore was likely to see the torch at two in the morning in the inclement weather, so they reckoned it was quite a secure plan.

But the capsize had been accidental and premature and left him short of the selected spot, and in such conditions, fifty yards' separation might as well be a mile. He couldn't see the lights, and had to fight off despair as the *Wave Rider* vanished into the heaving sea, its little masthead light waving a final goodbye.

Cuff took a grip on his feelings. *Do something positive.* He shone his torch upwards into the rain, hoping there would be enough reflection off the drops for Martin to spot him. It was a long shot, but there was sod all else he could do.

How much time had passed? He had been getting very tired and very cold, even in his wetsuit, and the constant heaving up and down was nauseating. The little yacht was never to be seen again. But even as she left him to die, another glimpse of hope made a brief appearance. As he reached a peak, he saw a boat. He flashed his torch in its direction before he sank out of sight into a trough. Then it was closer – recognisable. *Martin, you're bloody wonderful!*

Another wave passed, Martin vanished. Hope died again; it was an illusion. *No, he's here, he's here.*

Cuff was so cold his muscles refused to work. He could not pull himself aboard. Hands reached down and found him, gripped his arms and pulled. He managed to get an elbow up and over the side, then another. The hands found his belt and heaved, but with little strength. His wetsuit caught on the gunwale, and the waves tried to drag him back. It was an exhausting struggle, but somehow their combined efforts got him into the boat. For a while, he lay on the bottom boards like a great landed fish, moving sporadically in its final struggle to stay alive.

He sat up and crept forward on all fours to the wheel.

'Ginny! What ...?' He held her hard in a hug and landed a cold, wet kiss on her cheek. 'Ginny, I owe you my life. But where's Martin?'

Ginny told him, shouting over the wind. 'You mustn't try to see him, Cuff. There's nothing you can do. He's in good hands and will be out of danger soon. You must not expose yourself now.'

'I knew you could handle a boat, but this is a helluva sea.'

'I reached the spot, but you weren't there. I checked and checked, the lights on the shore, the GPS, over and over again. I was petrified I was in the wrong place and had let you down.'

'Never.'

'It's like being on some gigantic violent roller coaster. I searched around at each crest. The flashes of lightning helped, but I could see nothing but spume and spray. I was trying to come to terms with you being dead. You were over an hour late. I didn't know how long to wait, if I should call the rescue services. If I did, your plan would be ruined, but better exposed than dead. I had just picked up the microphone when I saw your torch. Then it disappeared, and I thought I was hallucinating.'

'Thank you for waiting, for risking so much for me.'

The excitement of the rescue sank out of Ginny, and she turned to anger. 'Why are you men such bloody idiots? What are you always trying to prove? Martin's as much of a clown as you are, and a lot of that's your fault.'

Two days later, someone found the *Wave Rider* on the rocks and reported it to the coastguard. The police identified its owner from the contents of the boat. After an extensive search which found only a discarded lifejacket, Cuff was declared missing.

39

JONATHAN'S WORLD

MARCH

Gudrun weaved her way by feel through a clump of holly bushes. The path was not straight over that stretch, and she held her hands up to protect her face and eyes from the prickly leaves at every bend. She could not remember how far it was to the road from this thicket. It could not be much further, but time and distance were distorted in the dark, and her normal stride had been reduced to slow, short tentative steps.

Huldufólk, my friends, I believe in you. I'm intruding in your territory, but I mean you no harm. There's something sinister in here tonight. I can feel it. Guide me out of here, please.

With her nerves stretched taut in the darkness, she jumped as her neck was clamped by a heavy arm and a knife made a sharp prick in the skin of her throat.

The wool of a balaclava was coarse against her cheek as a voice hissed, 'This knife is very sharp. Walk on down the path, and don't try to be clever or I'll open you up.'

He must have had a head torch. The knife relaxed for a second and a beam struck out ahead of her. He was close; his arm was fast around her neck, and his chest rubbed against her back. Now and again his feet clashed with hers, and once his shoe ripped hers off her foot. The damp earth was cold through her sock.

He forced her forward, and the blade sliced the surface of her skin with every jolting step. A trickle of blood oozed down her neck.

Before they cleared the trees another balaclava-clad figure stepped forward with a roll of tape. They were clumsy but quick. The knife to her throat the whole time, her wrists and ankles were strapped, a tape was stuck across her mouth and a blindfold tightened over her eyes.

Some failure on the track towards Reading meant many services out of Paddington Station were delayed. Jonathan phoned Gudrun, but the call went straight to voicemail. He tried again, but this time left a message.

It was well after dark when he reached Martin's house. He let himself in the front door and found Ginny in the kitchen.

'Hello, GG. Where's Gudrun? I've been trying to call her.'

Ginny stretched up to kiss his cheek. 'I'm getting worried. She hasn't come home from her walk. She should have been back by six. I hope she's all right and hasn't got lost or fallen, or something. I haven't done anything, as I thought you'd be back by now.' She crossed the kitchen and picked up a phone. 'I was going to call her, but saw she left this here on charge. Silly of her – it's on silent, so I didn't hear it ring.'

He frowned. 'Do you know the route she took? I never asked.'

'Yes.' Ginny showed him on the map. 'It's the only route she could take from here.'

'Which way round did she go?'

'She always came back through the wood. She said she found it fascinating, and she went that way this afternoon.'

'I don't like this. Something must have happened for her not to be back. She's so capable. What made her daft enough to walk through the woods in the dark? She's probably lost and wandering around without a torch. I'm going to go back along the path; the opposite direction to which she took. May I use your car, please?'

'Of course.'

Jonathan first drove around all the roads Gudrun could have reached. *Surely, once she found a road she would have stayed on it, even if it led in the wrong direction – wouldn't she?* The car squelched to a stop at the parking spot. He struggled into his jacket while in the car and put on a head torch. The rain switched from light to heavy and back again, but did not let up. Whenever the trees swayed in a gust, they dumped their water in buckets onto the path, which was already squishy with mud.

He called out to her over and over again. Hurrying along and sliding in patches of ooze, he shone his light left and right while the wind howled and whistled through the trees, which groaned and creaked in response.

Her shoe lay there in front of him. He stooped to pick it up, but hesitated. Something told him to leave it where it was. Instead, he phoned the police.

The dog handler greeted Jonathan cheerfully. The weather was not going to damp his spirits, nor those of the dog who was completely undeterred. 'Zoggy will find anything if the evidence is there.'

'A Malinois – fabulous animals.' Normally, Jonathan would have paid the dog more attention, but tonight he could not be interested. The officer showed Gudrun's shoe to Zoggy, who tore off down the path back towards the parking area. There he cast about for short while, before looking up at his handler.

'He's done, Mr Scott, the trail's cold. The lady must have gone off in a car. Sorry I can't help you more – it'll be up to the regulars now.'

'I'm worried about her,' said Lisa.

'Well, don't be. We're not going to hurt her. We're only going to make her bastard boyfriend suffer. It's one of many harmless things that will get at him and break him down. And I'm going to go on doing them for the rest of his fucking life.'

They were sitting on wooden boxes in a dim and draughty room. Litter was strewn all over the floor, with the lightest material concentrated in one corner where eddies of wind had carried it. The walls, originally blue, were blackened with soot. Charred beams above them had once held an upper floor. That was gone along with the roof, leaving a clear view of the clouds which raced past above.

'When are we going to release her?' Lisa asked as she watched Castle twist his boot in a vicious destruction of one of the many cigarette butts which were scattered around him.

'After a while. While he sweats it out, we'll demand a ransom for her, twice, maybe even three times to keep him on the hook. We'll wait until he thinks she's dead or run away and he gives up, before we let her go.'

'You don't know him, he won't give up until he has an answer.'

'Then she stays a long time.'

Lisa was complicit in a real crime, and it was too late to get out of it. She had been so focused on hurting Jonathan, she hadn't appreciated what they were doing.

'This is kidnapping! Do you realise that? It's not her you need to get at.'

'What's the difference to what we've already done? Don't worry, we won't hurt her.'

Mrs Singh's words had shaken Lisa, and she couldn't forget them. Barry was scaring her. There was an underlying element of violence to his callous talk and angry movements.

'She needs food and water, a toilet and some blankets. She'll die without them.'

Castle thought about that for a moment. 'All right. I'll get a bucket she can use, and you can get the blankets. We'll take it in turns to provide food and water, one day each. We'll bring it here, but when we go in, we'll do it together. I must come with you, because she'll have you for breakfast if she's loose. Don't you go in there alone.'

'And you?'

'I can handle her. She might be a bit taller, but I'm much heavier and much stronger. She'll be weak and easy to overpower if she tries anything.'

Lisa was the first to arrive at the ruin the next morning. Their captive would be hungry, as they had not fed her the previous night, so Lisa had put together a simple breakfast: a hard-boiled egg, some cold meat and cheese and a couple of slices of buttered bread. When Barry arrived ten minutes later than they arranged, they unlocked the door and went through.

The electricity long since disconnected, the only light in the cellar was a sliver which found its way through a slit of a window set at the outside ground level, but brambles and nettles almost covered it, reducing what illumination might have been available to a narrow pattern which crept around the room with the passage of the sun. Lisa held an electric lantern, and Barry had a powerful torch which picked out their captive shivering in the rickety chair where they had left her the night before. Her blindfold had been removed, but her hands were still taped to the chair, and her mouth was still sealed.

'If looks could kill …' Barry shone his torch into the girl's face and laughed through his balaclava as she shied away from the glare. 'Listen carefully, bitch. We're kind.'

Lisa winced at his words. Why was it necessary to be angry and rude to this woman? Whatever had happened between Barry and Jonathan, had nothing to do with her. *You could at least be civil, Barry.*

'We've brought you some breakfast,' Barry was saying. 'My friend here is going to take the tape off your wrists and mouth so you can eat. We'll bring you food once a day and take your shit out when the bucket's full. Don't even think of escape, because I'll be here with the knife. This place is the only part of this ruin that survived the fire. The fire brigade never came, because no one knew there was a fire. It's isolated, far from anywhere. No one will hear you if you scream, and you can't get out of this room. It's a cellar. One door, one way out, and that'll be locked. So you might as well relax.'

Lisa put the food on the floor in front of the chair. When Castle was behind the prisoner with his knife, she ripped the tape off the girl's right hand. When it was free she met a pair of pale, penetrating eyes, as cold as their colour. They never blinked and never wavered, and Lisa wilted under the retribution which threatened from their depths.

With a quick rip and a short gasp of pain, the woman tore the tape from her mouth, leaving her skin red and inflamed. She unwound the strapping from her left wrist with more care.

In spite of his threatening words, Lisa sensed Barry was on edge. He was taking no chances. Lisa watched as he laid the knife against the girl's throat, and a thin rivulet of blood dribbled down her neck to moisten that from the previous night. No sign of pain was given.

Lisa stepped back to a safe distance to watch the woman eat. Barry joined her.

Between mouthfuls their captive asked in an unnatural but steady voice, 'Why am I here? What do you want?'

Lisa could not answer, she wasn't sure herself. Barry kept quiet.

'What do you want with me?' the girl repeated, more forcefully this time.

'You'll find out.'

Lisa kept her voice soft, as if she didn't want Barry to hear. 'What's your name?'

The cold eyes flicked from Castle to her. They captured her, studied her. Lisa was drawn into them and unable to look away. Moments passed.

'Gudrun.'

Her food finished, Gudrun stood, the plate dangling from her right hand. Her head almost touched the low ceiling and was bowed. Barry's torch had never left her, the narrow beam focused on her face. Unnoticed below the beam, her arm swung, and her wrist flicked in a backhanded movement. Lisa caught the flash of a deadly white Frisbee rising towards Barry's head. He ducked, his arm raised in self-defence. The plate shattered on his torch. A glint of anger flashed across his face for a moment, before he laughed.

Lisa called an emergency tea with her agony aunt three days earlier than usual. She told Sheila how they had abducted this Nordic woman and were holding her in a ruin.

'You did what? Good bloody grief, Lise darling, what the hell have you got yourself into?'

Lisa nodded her confirmation. Horror had replaced Sheila's normal half-amused expression, which reinforced Lisa's own shame at what she'd done.

'Lise, I'm no saint, as you well know. I've always treated my men as if they lived life as I do, to get the maximum enjoyment without too much concern for feelings – but cruel I've never been. Your Barry is violent. First rape and now kidnap. You're too close to him. As I said last time, you've got to keep your distance.

'We've got to do something to prevent him harming this woman who you say is not to blame in any way. You've got to tell Jonathan what Barry is up to. Let him deal with it. These two men are equal shits and you should get them to destroy each other.'

'I can't, I'm scared of what Jonathan will do to me if he finds out.'

Sheila didn't reply at first. She sipped her tea, regarding Lisa over the rim of her cup. 'I know what to do, and I'll do it for you.'

Sleep evaded Jonathan. He paced around the house, tidied up by replacing a few things he knew were out of place, sat down and switched on the TV, gave up in disgust after a few seconds, switched it off again and resumed pacing.

Gudrun had left her shoe in the mud, and the scent from that shoe had vanished at the parking area. She left in a car. She did not have one, so someone else was involved. Had that someone made her leave her shoe? Where had he taken her? Jonathan assumed it was a he, but it could be a she, couldn't it? And how had he/she done it? Gudrun was very strong; it would take a big person to overpower her, unless …

These thoughts and others tore around in his head until he went to bed at last, where they resumed, keeping him awake for hours.

He woke groggy and was still going over the possibilities as he made a pot of coffee. Food was out of the question. Ginny usually slept until late, so he did not expect to see her at that time. She came into the kitchen in her dressing gown, dishevelled and tired, her red hair tousled and unbrushed.

'Look.' She held out a sheet of paper. 'It was pushed through the letter box.'

Jonathan took the note. 'What is it?' He studied it for a minute. 'It's a postcode.'

'Oh, stupid of me – he hasn't left a gap between the two parts, so it looks like gibberish. It's too early for me.'

'Ginny, please fire up your computer, this could be where Gudrun is. Who sent this, I wonder?'

'Do you think it's a trap to lure you there?'

'Maybe, but how can I ignore it?'

40

JONATHAN'S WORLD

MARCH

'Ginny, open up Google Maps please and type in the postcode.'

'Jonathan, I'm quite competent with computers, I know what to do.'

'Sorry, sorry. Of course you do, I'm on edge at the moment.'

It didn't take long for Ginny to identify the area covered by the postcode. They found eleven houses once maximum zoom had been reached. Eight of them were in a development which Jonathan remembered being built while he was at university. The other three were on the fringe of the area and it was hard to tell if they were even covered by that postcode at all.

'I'm going over there now.'

'Where are you going to start? In the estate? I think there should be two of us for safety. I'll come with you, and we'll do it much quicker.'

'No, it won't be quicker, because I'm not letting you knock on doors on your own. We don't know who or what to expect and it might be dangerous. Thanks, Ginny, but you stay here. Phone the police, that inspector Martin saw, and give him the postcode.'

'Wright, DI Wright.' She sounded disappointed.

Jonathan decided to cover the development first. The houses were all in a small community which wouldn't take long to eliminate from his list.

What should he look for? Might it be someone he would recognise? He would have to rely on his instincts, on what struck him as suspicious.

The first house in the estate had a child's scooter lying on the front lawn as well as a toddler's plastic push-car with a pony-shaped head on it. Most unlikely, but they might have seen something if Mummy was at home with the kids all day.

A young woman answered the door. Her hair was messed, there were egg stains near her shoulder, and she had a toddler's red shoe in her hand. She glanced back for her child as she answered his question. 'No, I haven't seen any strangers here, sorry.' The toddler appeared behind her leg and squinted up at him. The woman made to close the door.

'Sorry, but do you know the other people in this community?'

She made an impatient gesture with her lips. 'The people next door are in their seventies, but all the others are young. Good bunch really.'

'Thank you. I can see you're busy.'

She gave a resigned look to heaven and pushed the door closed.

The septuagenarians did not answer his knock so he moved on to a fruitless result from the other houses. Back in the car, desperation threatened to grip him. Was the gift of a postcode a red herring? Calm down, there are other places yet to be visited.

Ginny phoned, interrupting his uneasy thoughts. 'DI Wright said his team will be leaving for the area soon. He said you should leave it to him, as you could make the situation worse.'

'What situation?'

'He said there were various possibilities, but it's best not to speculate. I gave him your number, he'll phone you.'

Jonathan hung up and unfolded his map. As he spread it out the paper quivered, and he flexed his fingers to still them. His phone rang again, an unknown number. *I'll bet that's Wright to tell me to back off.* He let the call go to voicemail and switched on the ignition.

The next house on his list was a farm. He bumped along the rough dirt track through muddy puddles, mentally apologising to Martin for abusing his car. The place was isolated and perfect for hiding someone with all the barns and sheds around. A grizzled old man answered Jonathan's knock with an enquiring look and no words.

'Good morning. I'm sorry to disturb you, but I'm searching for a very tall blonde woman who has gone missing round here.'

The old man shook his head without answering. A short, dumpy, middle-aged woman came up behind him, and Jonathan repeated his question.

She was rosy-cheeked and wearing a flowered apron. 'Sorry, love, we ain't seen no one strange around here in a while. The dogs would 'ave barked, for sure, at a stranger, and they ain't barked in two days, eh, Grandad?'

The old man shook his head. Jonathan asked them to phone the police if they saw her and said his thanks. 'She's not dangerous, just lost and a foreigner.'

It took a long time to drive to the last house, because there was no direct route. He fretted at the narrow lanes where it was impossible to drive at any speed, and almost hooted when he came across a flock of sheep being driven into a nearby field. He stopped and got out while he waited, taking the opportunity to talk to the farmer. No, the man had seen nothing unusual around there since that escaped prisoner two years ago.

The imposing gateway to what appeared to be a country mansion introduced him to a long avenue of a driveway lined with huge beech and chestnut trees. As soon as he caught a glimpse of the place, he knew this was it. Where better to hide than in a ruin far from curious eyes? He left the car off the drive and under the trees out of sight.

Barry Castle refused to rush. He dragged out the delicious anticipation of his lone encounter with the Viking as he drove to the ruin. Rape, he argued, had been used to subdue peoples since humans had existed. So this was not to be an alcohol-fuelled assault on a helpless victim; she was to be a spoil of his war. Her degradation would humiliate JFJ; proof he could not defend his woman against the victor. The Viking would suffer in the process too, of course, but that was not Castle's concern.

He had parked his car out of sight at the back of the house as usual. Clutching a plastic bag of food, he clambered over debris and took a key from his pocket.

Before he had captured Gudrun, he had fitted a bolt to the cellar door. Why the door had survived, Castle had no idea; maybe the roof was different on that end of the house, or maybe the fire ran out of combustible material. He did not care, was not interested. The cellar was good enough to hold his prize for as long as he needed it to.

The new padlock opened with a soft click. He removed it and, before drawing back the bolt, unsheathed his long, very sharp knife.

The click of the lock being released alerted Gudrun. She had not slept well; the floor was filthy and hard, and the blankets the woman had brought were not enough to fight off the cold. At least they hadn't tied her up again. She was as much thirsty as hungry, but whatever breakfast they brought would give her strength.

Whenever they had come before this, there had been two of them – one too many for her to win a fight. If she had known only one would come this morning, she would have planned an attack.

A torch was switched on and followed down the few steps by the tall, muscular man with a balaclava and sadistic eyes, and that awful knife.

It might have been wishful thinking, but it had seemed the woman sympathised with her, that she did not want to be a part of this kidnap. The man, however – he was enjoying whatever he was doing. And why had she been kidnapped? She was of no financial value through her parents, although Jonathan had all that money; not that he had tried to access it yet. If she was to be ransomed, it had to be by someone who knew of Jonathan's inheritance. If not, what did he want? It couldn't be sex if the sympathetic woman was complicit in her capture, could it?

The man closed the door behind him and walked towards Gudrun. She retreated. He put the plastic bag he was carrying on the floor and stepped back. Without speaking he indicated the packet with his torch, and she came forward to get her food. She sat on the floor beside the bag. The smell was not appetising, but suddenly she was ravenous. He stood above her, staring down in silence as she tucked into some cold, greasy sausage and soft white bread. In the torchlight she saw a dirty thumb impression in the slice and almost gagged. The food was disgusting, but it was food.

She finished and wiped her fingers on her jeans, put her hands on the floor to support herself in getting up, and leaned forward. The speed of the knife to her neck frustrated her idea of fighting him. The nick stung.

His foot was in her back, pushing her to the floor. A brief relief of pressure, then it was his knee with his full weight on her, and the knife still there. She knew what was going to happen. Flight was not possible, but fight was.

Her lungs were squeezed. 'Wait,' she gasped, 'wouldn't it be better if we had good sex? This way you get bad sex, but if you take the knife away I can give you good sex. I like big men.'

Castle laughed. 'Nice try. No chance I'm going to put this knife down; besides, you're missing the point. Very carefully, darling, move your hands down and undo your jeans. One smart move and I'll slit you.'

She was on her stomach, her face in the dust, his knee in her back. The knife was at the right side of her neck and had again drawn blood. He meant what he said. She had to obey, but she was not going to submit without a fight. Her hands trembled, but she pushed her right one under her tummy towards her belt buckle. His weight would not allow her to raise her hips to give herself room to release it. She moved her left hand too, but did not trap it underneath.

'Come on, be quick.'

He had withdrawn his knee and was now sitting on her back, crushing the air out of her.

'You're too heavy. I can't get my hands down there.'

He rose a fraction, taking his weight on his thighs. As he went up, even by that infinitesimal amount, with all her strength she bucked her body. He was off balance. She lashed back with her left arm and knocked Castle to the side. The knife slid across her neck and round to the back. The slash stung, but she was upright. Castle was in a crouch and rising. Gudrun kicked him in the face. He swore and clambered to his feet. He ignored her next blow. His punch hit the centre of her chest, thumping her back against the wall. Her head whiplashed on the brick. She slithered down and collapsed in a heap in the dust, her legs folded under her.

The house had once been a magnificent Georgian mansion with three floors, the upper with dormer windows in the roof. It was isolated and hidden from prying eyes by huge and ancient trees. The fire had taken its toll without anyone's knowledge in the middle of a winter night when all good citizens were fast asleep, and when the house was unoccupied. The roof had collapsed, the floors had burned through and the debris had tumbled down into the bottom floor space. Over the years, the outer walls had crumbled in places, and collapsed masonry lay in heaps. The ground-floor rooms were still contained. Without their doors and ceilings, they formed a simple maze.

Jonathan circled the house. An unknown car was at the back straddling a path which used to take the cooks from the kitchen to the vegetable garden. Now, there were no vegetables, only weeds. The ashes of the wooden door had washed away, leaving a heap of rubble from the collapsed wall above and some charred pieces of timber which made an ineffective barrier to entry.

He prowled through the ruin room by room, carefully navigating the piles of brick and stone while trying to keep his head up and look around. The only intact door had a bolt on the outside, and a new padlock hanging from the barrel eye. The bolt was not slid to.

He took a step towards it and kicked something loose. A large stone chocked the bottom end of a roof beam which was leaning high on a wall. With his contact, the foot of the beam pushed the stone aside and slid across the floor with a slight scraping sound until the full weight of the heavy timber crashed onto the rubble with a noise which reverberated through the building.

41

JONATHAN'S WORLD

MARCH

A heavy thump came from above. A tremor rippled through the cellar roof, and dust fell from the ceiling.

'Fuck!' The Viking bitch would have to wait. Castle picked his knife off the floor and strode to the stairs. Was the crash part of the natural decline of the place, or was someone waiting outside the door?

He reached the top of the short flight of steps and glanced back. The torch lay in the dust shining a bright circle on the opposite wall, but the dim reflection was enough to see the woman was still immobile.

Castle eased open the door, an inch at a time. Thank fuck he had oiled the hinges and freed the thing before setting it up as a cell. Nothing moved outside. With the door open wide enough to allow his body through, Castle peered round it – nothing. Not a sound, not a movement, nothing. This wasn't right; something had moved in here, and where was the someone who made the something move?

Following the wall, he came to the next doorway. He knew it was a room which led to two others. A length of timber, like a fence post, lay at his feet – ideal. It might not be a good idea to show a deadly weapon if he met a perfectly innocent person, or some kids who could tell mummy what they saw. The post was damp and slippery with mould, but it would do. He crept on, trying not to make a sound. The first room was empty. The second opened to a passage on its opposite side, and there were some rooms off the passage: a pantry, a larder, a general store perhaps. Whoever was here wouldn't spend time searching these little rooms; a glance inside would be sufficient, so where was he?

A head peered around the doorway. It was looking down the passage. The head was turning. Castle was quick. He raised the post, smashed it down. But it was slippery and twisted from his grip. The pole only caught the head a glancing blow, but the head still went down.

Castle lifted the head by its hair. 'Jonny Fucking Jonathan! What a nice surprise, just who I want. This gets better and better. You're coming with me to watch, but first …'

He landed a hefty kick into Jonathan's ribs. He picked up the timber again and with both hands swung it down from over his shoulder onto the prone body, and again. His anger, no longer subdued and calculating, came boiling to the surface to relieve his frustration at years of mistreatment. He could not stop himself; he flung the wood aside and kicked the man who had put him in jail, made him suffer, humiliated him, destined him to a life as an outcast, a criminal, a sex offender and a man who would be monitored for the rest of his existence. With each accusation came a vicious boot to the unconscious body.

'Hey!'

Castle was consumed by revenge – focused on one thing alone. It took a second for the call to sink in. He whirled round, presenting his front, and got a massive kick in the groin.

He dropped like a wet cloth, clutching himself and screaming. From the floor he turned his head and met the cold glare of a merciless warrior, inviting a series of Viking clichés. Was this how they looked twelve hundred years ago? Unkempt, unforgiving, dirty giants with tousled hair and fierce eyes? Was this how they looked before the axe came down to split your skull? Was this how they looked before they cleaved your ribs apart with that axe, ripped out your lungs and flung them up over your shoulders in what they called the Rite of the Blood Eagle? As Gudrun swung her leg back for the second time, his imagination overwhelmed him, and he wet himself.

'All right, that's enough.'

Castle was moaning, curled up in the foetal position. The owner of that familiar north country voice appeared, his hand clamping down on the woman's shoulder. She whirled around, ready for her next opponent, but the voice stopped her.

'Detective Inspector Wright, Thames Valley Police. Relax, miss, we'll take over.'

'She assaulted me,' snivelled Castle through his pain.

'Is that so?' The inspector inclined his head to align it with Castle's. He had a quizzical look on his face. 'I didn't see anything. Did you see anything, lads?'

'No, sir.'

'No, Inspector.'

'I didn't see anything either,' said the one female constable, who was pointing a finger. 'But she's bleeding from her neck, sir.'

The Viking crouched by JFJ, who was groaning. 'He's been hit on the head,' she said. 'He's had a head injury before.'

Wright snapped, 'Ambulance, Michaels, now.'

Castle whimpered as he struggled into a sitting position, warily eyeing Wright who bent to put his face a few inches away and give him the benefit of his hard look.

'There you are, Barry, no one saw anything untoward. We came out here to this house because it was a lead in finding Miss Einarsdóttir. Why am I not surprised to find you here as well and mixed up in something nefarious? You and I are going to have a nice little chat, quite a long chat, I think. Barry, you remember I said the person who sabotaged that aeroplane would face a number of charges, including attempted murder as well as some under the Aviation Act? Well, I think we might add to that list with abduction, attempted rape, assault … and what about leaving the scene of an accident? There might be more, but in fairness to your good self, we need to have a nice little heart-to-heart to make things quite clear, don't you?'

'What accident? I haven't had an accident.'
'Oh, so you don't deny the other charges then, Barry?'

42

CUFF'S LIFE

BARRY CASTLE – APRIL

When he was alone, Castle let loose his anger and frustration in bad-tempered pacing, swearing and rough handling of anything he touched. He had so far broken two cups, a vase and a door handle, none of which went unnoticed by his mother, who was becoming very concerned for him. Almost every attempt he had made to bring Cuffy Fucking Cuthbert down had failed. Only shagging the man's wife and giving her a child had been a success, but it held little satisfaction in terms of revenge, because he learned the outcome had benefited the sod. CFC had almost walked away from the aircraft crash, and even setting fire to the pharmacy had ended up in the man's favour. Castle had failed to rob him of his fortune, thanks to the incompetence of the hacker. *I'd get that little shit too, if I could only find him.*

There was still a way to go before he could get his hands on that money, though.

CFC had to be proven dead, or, if he were hiding somewhere, found. If he were dead, which Castle doubted, Lisa could inherit his estate straight away. Otherwise she was going to have to wait for seven years. If he were to be found alive, Castle could think what to do about it – seven years is a long time to wait.

He had no evidence CFC was hiding, but it would be typical of the man to do that: take a risky, adventurous path and do something out of the ordinary.

Which was why he became so curious about an apparently ordinary event.

On a Sunday afternoon while locking his car, Castle looked across the narrow piece of park which faced his house and saw Martin Beale and his girlfriend coming back from a day away. Their car was spattered with mud, as if they had been on a gravel road. He knew they'd gone out early in the morning in a nice clean car. What was odd was that the same thing had happened two weekends earlier. Most people would have thought nothing of it. Beale had a perfect right to go wherever he wanted and to get his car dirty in the process if it turned him on.

Castle kept a close watch on them. Beale and his carrot-topped tart went out the following Sunday, and Castle tailed them to a pub where they met some other friends for lunch. She was driving, because the weed was still on crutches after his accident, which gave Castle cause to smirk a little. The next Sunday proved more fruitful, however, as they went out early, returning shortly before dark with the car covered in mud again. *So, they do this every two weeks. Zwillings, my pretty cousins, we'll follow them next time and find out what's going on. I bet you we'll find C bloody F bloody C.*

Castle was up and ready to leave on the next likely Sunday morning. He had a quick breakfast and made a couple of ham-and-cheese sandwiches to take with him. With the car's engine warming for a few minutes, he squeegeed the windows clean and loaded it for the day. Back inside, he drank his coffee and kept a watch out the front.

Sure enough, soon after seven Beale's car drove past on the far side of the park. Castle jumped up, shot out of the front door and set off in pursuit.

The woman was not an impatient driver, she was cautious, which allowed Castle to keep them in sight and follow at a careful distance without difficulty. They were heading for the motorway. Castle switched on the radio, which was tuned to a rock station, and hummed along to some of the music, tapping his hands on the wheel in time to the beat. They were heading west on the M4. There was a surprising amount of traffic for that time on a Sunday, but it wasn't difficult to keep Beale in sight. *Where are the little creeps going?*

After an hour and a half and near Bristol, they took the services exit and parked. Castle watched Beale limping beside his redheaded girlfriend as, like a couple of walking carrots, they went into the restaurant area. Carrot-bloke sat at a table while carrot-tart joined the queue for coffee. Castle took the opportunity to go to the toilet and made sure they were still there when he came out. He bought a packet of sweets from WH Smith and went back to his car to wait.

Three more hours, now on the M5 beyond Bristol and they were well into Cornwall. *Where is this little weed going?* They at last turned off the main road and headed for the southern coast. Half an hour more and they were on a narrow lane with earth banks or stone walls on either side, which, according to Castle's GPS, dead-ended at a tiny fishing village.

He kept well back, as they were the only two cars on the road. As he crested a rise, he had a good view across the rolling countryside, divided in a rough patchwork of fields by drystone walls and hedges. The girl turned off onto a dirt track and headed towards the cliffs. This was getting very interesting.

They were about a quarter of a mile ahead. Castle could not drive any closer without being obvious. He swore his frustration, parked in a field gateway, put on his jacket and a beanie in the face of a strong wind and continued on foot.

The surface was wet and soggy, and horses had churned the mud into ankle-deep wallows in parts. He cursed as he stumbled along, unused to anything other than a pavement.

Bloody muck, how do people live and move around in this soggy, useless place? His trainers were covered in mud, horse manure, slime and water, his feet were soaked and cold, and it was raining hard. Reaching the top of a small rise, he looked down onto Beale's car in time to see a leg disappear inside and the back door close.

I'll bet a pound to a pinch of shit that was CFC! I knew the bastard was alive. Now I have the option of finding and exposing him so Lisa can drag him into the divorce court. That option will only get her half of his assets at best, but the alternative will bring twice the reward. I'll have to ditch the idea of long-term pain for him in favour of a quick and final solution – one which will produce a body. And there's a bloody good reason for speed – there'll not be another chance before long.

Where had he come from? Where was he hiding out? Through the rain, Castle made out a path leading from the little turning circle to the edge of the cliffs. That needed to be explored, but he was ill prepared at the moment. His body was wet, his feet were soaked, the wind was howling in his ears, and he was as cold as a corpse. He couldn't endure this for much longer while he waited for CFC to go back into hiding. *Is he living in a bloody cave?*

43

CUFF'S LIFE

APRIL

Cuff strode up the cliff path, enjoying the effort in spite of the slippery wet stones and being buffeted by the wind. The gusts whistled and flowed around the rocks and threatened to rip the tufts of grass from their shallow soil. The rain was sometimes horizontal, sometimes coming from another direction and sometimes even blowing uphill in its attempt to soak him to the skin.

He reached Martin's car and pushed his nose against the driver's window at Ginny. They laughed and motioned him into the back. Shedding his rucksack and jacket, he shook them off and jumped in.

'Whew, it's coming down.'

'How are you?'

'I'm fine, getting a bit bored stuck here, but feeling good about it. How about you two? How are the legs? I don't get a signal down there, I have to come almost to the top here to talk to you.'

'Then you'll keep fit! We're good as always, thanks, although

I'm fed up with hopping around on these crutches. We have news, though,' Martin announced. 'I told Inspector Wright that Larry and Jeff admitted to being in Turkey for the football and therefore they couldn't have been with Castle. He checked the records – which took some time, I don't know why – confirmed it, and then interviewed Castle again and, to cut a long story down a bit, he's been charged and is out on bail for the second time.'

'I hope that convinces Lisa he's not a suitable dad. In spite of everything, I can't help feeling sorry for her – nothing has turned out her way.'

'She came to see me, which was a surprise,' Martin said.

'Oh yes?'

'She asked me whether I thought you were dead. I told her how you had planned to escape and disappear and must have died in the storm. She seemed to accept it, but was no more unhappy than when she came in. I told her you gave me power of attorney with respect to the house, and I should sell it in the event of your death or on your instruction, with the proceeds to be added to your estate. I also told her why – you wanted to ensure Castle gets the least benefit.'

'What did she say to that?'

'Nothing. Shook her head. She can't understand this enmity when he's so nice to her.'

'While it suits him.'

'She looked hopeful when I explained how she could get a divorce in about six months through a Presumption of Death Decree.'

'I hope that'll be enough time for Castle to show her what a bastard he is. The trouble is I think Lisa is one of those women who will stick with a violent man in spite of everything he does.'

Ginny passed two new phone batteries to Cuff. She poured coffee from a flask and handed the cup back over the seat.

'Thanks, Ginny.' Cuff took the drink in two hands, cupping them around the mug. Steam built up on the windows. 'When was this?'

'The bail was last Friday.'

'Castle has a way of getting off lightly or remaining undiscovered. He sabotaged the Cessna for certain, I'm pretty sure he set the fire in the pharmacy, and he may well have been involved in your hit-and-run.'

'We could set a trap for him.'

Suspicion marked Ginny's face.

'We could use Jake as bait,' said Cuff.

'*No.* You can't put that kid in danger,' Ginny said, 'that's neither fair nor responsible.'

Cuff put a hand on her shoulder. 'We can keep this under control. Don't worry, Ginny.'

'No, I said. I won't have you taking risks with the boy. Let the police handle it.'

The men knew she was right, and they fell silent for a while. Cuff pulled his rubbish bag out of his rucksack and left it on the floor for Martin to dump in his own bin. Ginny was scratching through her belongings. 'I've a present for you,' she said over her shoulder, and held up something which resembled a squashed, eyeless, dead cat.

Cuff laughed and put the wig on. Ginny turned around in her seat and straightened the thing.

'There,' she said, 'it makes you look like a lesser-known poet.'

'Lesser-known is *in* with me.'

The wig was Cuff's hair colour and long enough to sport an infant ponytail secured with a simple hair band. 'Thanks. I'll be able to go into the village like this. And it matches my beard – perfect. You're very thoughtful, Ginny.'

His beard had grown to a reasonable length and thickness, and he had left it unkempt. His hair was not long enough to sport even a two-inch ponytail, so he wore the 'dead cat' on his head. He checked his appearance in his tiny mirror. *This is no good. Anyone will see through this disguise, or am I being too subjective?* He made a few adjustments and decided to risk it. It was more effective than nothing at all.

Before heading out, Cuff packed all his kit away and cleared his rubbish. There was no telling when he might have to leave in a hurry, so he wanted to always be prepared.

The walk into the village took almost forty minutes from the car park. He used the time by questioning whether it would ever be possible to pass himself off as someone totally different and avoid suspicion. Would a shopkeeper say he looked odd and out of place? Would another spot the wig was not his natural hair? All sorts of people lived on the fringes of civilisation in this part of the world:

artists of various descriptions who sought the prevailing peace for inspiration, naturist and faith cults, tree-huggers, environmentalists and peaceniks – anyone seeking to evade the rush of modern life. Could he fool people into believing he belonged on the fringe, or would they see through his scruffy pretence?

There wasn't much available in the tiny cluster of houses, boat sheds and the couple of minute shops, but he bought some basic supplies: milk and eggs, bread, butter and a bottle of whisky. It was approaching lunchtime, so he sought out the single pub, put his pack down in a corner and ordered himself a pint of bitter. The barman gave him a polite acknowledgement, thanked him for the cash and went back to drying glasses without another look.

So far – so good; Cuff was a little more comfortable. Two middle-aged, weather-beaten and tough-looking men in heavy, oil- and dirt-stained jackets came in, gave the barman a cheery greeting and came over to sit at the next table with their pints. They acknowledged him, one giving an almost imperceptible grin, before carrying on their conversation. Cuff had been worried that, in this tiny little fishing village where tourists were probably tolerated only for their money, he would stand out as a foreigner and be subject to cool greetings. But up to now, nobody had taken any undue notice of him.

He was halfway through his pint when the bloke next to him struck up a conversation. 'Passing through?'

Cuff nodded. 'I saw your village on the map and thought I'd come and have a look out of season. I imagine you see too many visitors in the summer?'

'Right enough, but they help support the economy. Where you stayin'? Most places are still closed after the winter.'

'I'm camping up there, off the coastal path.' He waved an arm in the opposite direction to his hovel.

'Rather you than me in a tent. They say there's a storm comin' in later this week. You'd be better off finding more solid shelter for a day or two.'

Cuff downed the last of his pint. 'Thanks for the advice. I'd best be off to sort things out.'

The two men gave him friendly looks, and he thanked the barman. *Being noticed had to happen at some stage, but I'll be better off shopping further afield in future.*

* * *

The next day the sun was out, and its warmth held any chill from the light breeze at bay. Cuff stood outside the cottage and looked out across the English Channel. The visibility was unlimited, and he counted the number of ships he saw. Time was marching on, so, before going for a whole day's walk, he packed his gear into a huge rubbish bag as usual and tucked it out of sight behind a dilapidated seat which was too rotten to sit on. He put on a jacket and his empty pack, which he used to bring back fuel and kindling from the woods he passed.

Once on the coastal path, he became another hiker, but he only met one seasoned couple when he overtook them as they ate their lunch. It was still too early in the year for most people to be visiting, but in a few weeks' time they would come in their droves. He would have to move on before then.

As the day progressed, the breeze picked up to reach about ten knots in the afternoon, which negated the sun's warmth and chilled him when he stopped moving. It was even colder as he entered the cutting of the cliff path, for it was in shadow. Halfway down the cleft, the cottage beckoned. It might be cold and draughty, but it was out of the wind and more of his warm clothing was in there.

Reaching the level ground on which the cottage sat, Cuff looked around to confirm no one else was about before going to his water source and taking a long, cold drink.

The door gave its customary creak, threatening to fall off as it did every time he opened it.

On the far side of the dingy little room stood a man. Cuff started in surprise, but put on an angry face – a waste as he was unrecognisable, a silhouette in the doorway. The man looked alarmed. Behind him, at first unseen in the gloom, was a woman.

'What do you want?'

'Oh, sorry,' said the man. 'We thought this place was unoccupied. I'm very sorry, we didn't realise …'

Cuff didn't reply. The couple were quite young, younger than him and less confident. His wild, unkempt appearance was frightening them. Let it stay that way.

'You can make it to the next village before dark,' he said.

'Yes, yes, of course. We'll get out of your way. Very sorry, but there's no sign it's occupied.' The man packed away what little they had taken from their rucksacks. The woman – more a girl, she must have been nineteen or twenty – hadn't spoken; she was huddled on Cuff's rudimentary seat and shivering violently.

Cuff stood watching her for a moment. 'You're cold.'

She did not answer, but began to struggle up. He put out a gentle restraining hand and reached for his sleeping bag. He draped it round her shoulders, and she murmured a grateful acknowledgement through chattering teeth.

'You'd better wait until she's warm,' Cuff said.

'Thanks.' The man looked young and inexperienced, unable to deal with such a simple situation.

Half an hour passed without conversation. The girl had stopped shivering and was able to talk without her teeth chattering. 'Thank you, we'll leave now. I'll warm up on the climb.'

Cuff watched as she picked up her pack and carried it outside as if it would take too long to put on in the hovel. The man followed her out with a sideways glance at Cuff. He watched them as they moved out of sight on the path to the clifftop before firmly closing the door.

44

CUFF'S LIFE

APRIL

There was one street in the fishing village. It descended the steep hill between the cliffs, straight down to the harbour, along the harbour front, which was the only level stretch, and back up a short slope before rejoining itself two buildings up from the waterfront. It was narrow and Castle had to squeeze his car up against the stone wall with two inches to spare to leave room for another to pass. He parked it there and got out to walk around. The pub would be the best place to enquire, and it was almost lunchtime anyway.

He ordered a pint of bitter and a pie and took his drink to a vacant seat by the window. There were three other customers having a high-spirited conversation at a single table, and a young couple seated side by side on the bench next to him.

When the barman brought his pie, Castle said, 'Have you had any strangers in here in the past few weeks?'

'A few. There ain't many at this time o' year.'

'Recently?'

'One fellow.'

'Could you describe him for me?'

The barman half turned his body back to the bar and took a step in that direction. ''Ard to tell his age 'cause of the beard and long 'air. Spoke well, educated. One of 'em what comes down 'ere to escape London and 'ug a tree, bit of an 'ippie sort, if you ask me.' He took another step away.

'Oh, we saw him!' said the young woman next to Castle. 'Well, it sounds like him.'

'Yes, he shooed us out of that ruin quite rudely,' said her boyfriend.

'He was a bit scary, although he was kind to me.'

The barman turned back to them. 'What ruin is that?'

Castle had taken the Wednesday off to ensure he did not meet Ginger Beale in Cornwall. He parked his car where Beale had done and stepped out. First, he threaded his belt through the loop of his knife-sheath, before ramming a beanie on his head and donning his jacket to fight the chilling wind. The path he had seen from the rise the last time he was there led off to the east.

It was obvious where it left the car park, wide and used, but what he had not seen from the rise was how it was overgrown with bracken and brambles about five yards in. He kept up a steady stream of profanity about the bloody countryside and nature as he delicately picked the brambles aside. The vegetation receded as he moved forward, though, and he was able to make good progress.

After a few minutes of descent, he came round a corner of the rocks to a white cottage. He stopped and surveyed the scene. Nothing moved, so he went forward taking care to keep out of sight of the two windows which flanked the single door. There was no sign of life at all. He reached the corner of the cottage and listened, but all he heard was the wind. Ready for anything, he raised his head to the little window.

Inside, the cottage looked neat but barren, with no hint of occupation. He moved forward to the window on the other side of the door and peered in there. Nothing. Round the back, there was still nothing. He saw the next cottage and frowned. They hadn't talked about that in the pub.

Castle found five cottages in all, and all were devoid of life. They weren't as run-down as the young couple had described, either. He must be in the wrong place. *Bloody hell, I've wasted an hour on this and got nowhere. Where is the bastard hiding out?*

Back at his car, fuming and frustrated, he downed a cup of lukewarm coffee from his flask and looked blankly out the window in search of a solution. The beginning of another less well-worn path led away from the track's end. Staring at it, his optimism rose again.

This path was much steeper than the other, and several times he almost lost his footing on the loose stones. He tried to keep calm while enveloped in the rage this induced. He needed to save his anger for CFC.

Cuff was budgeting using a pencil, a little notebook and the calculator on his phone. He was, yet again, working out how much he was spending and how long his funds were going to last before he broke into his self-imposed reserve. At that point he would have to find a job to avoid using his flying funds, as he called them. He needed something to do anyway; he was achieving nothing and wasting time as he waited for his hair to grow so he could blend into society incognito.

The job would have to be manual and under the radar; something that was taken by immigrants from Eastern Europe whose boss didn't pay the minimum wage, and who might well be illegal. They might even be slave labour – that would be interesting.

Back in June, he had chosen to settle down, marry and further the family business. The consequences of that decision were far from what he'd envisaged: the death of his parents, a broken relationship, a dangerous mission to escape and vanish, a brush with death and now a long miserable wait to live a life as another person. So what had been the point of trying to be conventional over the last six months, when he had faced situations that could have resulted while enjoying himself had he chosen another life?

He had made his choice under pressure from others, but Cuff couldn't blame them for trying to have him in the business or be a member of the family. Of course they tried, it was their vision of an ideal life as they knew it.

No, it was entirely his own fault for listening to them. He was to blame, because he was responsible for his own actions. He should have followed his instincts and said no from the beginning. That would have avoided all this unpleasantness, and would have at least saved Lisa much of her pain.

Why do we humans go to such great lengths to change others into reproductions of ourselves? An organised religion seeks to accumulate more followers by instructing them in its way, the only true way, and decreeing that all others are blasphemy. Husbands and wives argue their spouses should think as they do and like the things they like. Mothers anchored by children encourage childless wives to procreate. People trying to change others into copies of themselves causes rifts in friendships, ruination of business partnerships, marriage breakdowns and even divorce and, in the case of organised religion, cruelty and wars, the very things every god stands against. Is it merely a human desire to have others share our values, or is it really about power?

The lesson was people should do what they are best equipped to do, make the choices they feel are right for them and do what is natural for their character. And other people should not force them to do something which is contrary to their nature – advise, yes; force, no. So Cuff made a vow to himself that he would never try to change another person. If he could not accept them for what they were, then their ways should part, or at least not come together.

Rock struck rock outside. Cuff grabbed his stuff and retreated to a position against the wall and beside the window. He scanned the room. *Damn!* He had left his camping stove on the makeshift table. The window was so dirty the stove might not be seen, with a bit of luck. He strained to hear, but only the sound of the wind over the hole in the roof was audible. The light from the window dimmed. Someone had blocked it; someone was looking in.

It was time he left this place. Two intrusions on his privacy in as many days, and more would follow as the weather warmed. Cuff waited until the light increased again. Where had they gone? Round the back? He had left nothing out there but boot-marks. Should he go out, or stay put and hope they went away? He waited.

After ten minutes, Cuff reckoned they had gone, but where? If they'd gone back up the path that was it, but if they'd continued on down to the cove, they would be back. He pulled on his jacket and inched the door open.

Sunlight from a break in the clouds glinted off the sea ahead of him. Seagulls screamed at each other as they rode the updraught while they scanned for food. The wind never stopped; it made a kind of music as it flowed around and between the cliffs, and in and out of his hovel.

'Thought you'd get away, did you?'

Cuff whipped round in surprise. Barry Castle stood at the corner of the building with a very large knife in his right hand. He was fingering the blade with his left. Cuff said nothing. He'd rehearsed this. Not a scene with Castle specifically, but in case he was ever challenged by someone. If he played dumb, they might think he was homeless and disabled somehow.

'You don't fool me. It's still Cuffy under all that hair and beard and filth. You're not so clever. It was easy to find you by following your little carrot-topped friend.'

Cuff continued to play dumb.

'You must wonder what I'm going to do now. Shall I spill the beans to the police? You must be guilty of some crime in this botched deception. Shall I taunt you by telling you exactly how I fucked your wife? Shall I ruin your plans by telling Lisa you're alive so that she can take you to the cleaners in a divorce? I'll marry her and live off your money.' Castle laughed at that. 'Or, shall I toss you off the cliff? Lisa will inherit your entire estate, and I will get to share it and have you out of my life forever.' He stopped fingering the blade and let his right arm fall so the knife pointed at the ground; it was almost a foot long. He moved forward two steps.

Cuff was wild-eyed; he stepped back, mouthing nonsense. 'Unh … unh …' He shook his head and raised his hands in defence.

'You can't fool me, Cuffy. I've known you too long. Underneath all that homeless shit hides the turd that put me away. I can see your eyes, and your sleeves are up like they always were.' He advanced another two steps, spinning out the uncertainty of what was going to happen.

Cuff continued to retreat. There were only another two paces left before he would be blocked by the rock face. To his left was a short, steep and slippery grass slope before the cliff fell away in a sheer drop to where the waves battered themselves to death on the rocks below.

Castle brought the knife up. He held it underhand, the tip

pointing at Cuff. 'I don't want to use this, Cuffy – I'd prefer it if you jumped off the edge, then it would be a natural death, no knife wounds, you see? But if you won't oblige, I'll be forced to use it and you'll still go over.' He grinned in the comfort of his power and success.

Laughing, Castle made a playful lunge. Cuff backed away the last two steps. His shoulder touched the rock. Castle advanced one more step. If he stretched he could cut Cuff with the knife tip. He held it forward towards his prey, wiggling it, teasing, enticing Cuff to be stabbed if he wanted to fight. Castle was enjoying his triumph. Anger overcame Cuff's fear.

There was no more sense in pretending to be dumb, but Cuff was not inclined to speak. He wasn't going to beg; it wouldn't do any good if he did. There was only one option. He sprang, swinging his left arm up and knocking Castle's knife hand to one side. He smashed his fist into the big man's belly, forcing him back and towards the drop.

Castle's right foot missed the edge of the flat terrace and slipped onto the grassy slope. He went down on one knee, his back foot sliding. He panicked and drove his knife into the turf. It stopped his fall, but his legs below the knees were over the void, his body bent forward over the curve of the slope. He raised a leg and tried to get a boot to grip on the grass. It wouldn't. One hand was clinging to the knife handle; the other grabbed a tuft of grass. He hung there, unable to pull himself up the convex surface.

'Help me!'

Cuff did nothing. He made no move to help, merely stared at the man. 'Why should I? You're scum, Castle, bullying, cruel scum, and you were going to kill me.'

'Help, for Chrissake!' A shrill voice from trembling lips. 'For God's sake! It was a joke to scare you. Help me.'

Cuff lay full-length on the flat surface, his shoulders level with the edge, and reached down to Castle's left hand, the one without the knife. He gripped the man's arm. Castle let go of the tuft and made a wild grab; he caught Cuff below the elbow.

'All right, I've got you, but I can't pull you up.' He had to drive some sense into Castle's panicked brain. 'You'll have to get your feet up higher.'

Castle struggled to raise his boots to grip, but they kept sliding and digging out clumps of turf, which disappeared over the void. As he fought, he slipped downwards bit by bit. Each slip dragged Cuff outwards. The rock edge was across his breast line. His right foot felt a tiny ridge in the ledge as he slid. He forced his boot down to hook onto it, to add a modicum of grip to his efforts.

'Stop struggling, you're making it worse,' Cuff shouted.

Their faces were an arm's length apart. Castle was crying, his eyes wide and desperate, the hope in them fading. The bully was tiring. Their combined sweat weakened their grips. Already their hands had slid down each other. Castle tried a big heave, pulling up on Cuff and his embedded knife. Cuff's foot lost its scrap of purchase. He slid out another inch. The point of no return, the point where he would be powerless to stop tipping over, was near.

A choice: let Castle go or be dragged to death with him.

Another heave. The knife loosened. Castle screamed. He let go of the handle and clutched at Cuff's other arm. His panicked grip was a vice. His nails dug in, gouging bloody tracks in Cuff's skin as they slid downward. Cuff was slipping outwards. It was now or never.

High on the headland which faced the cottage, the only place from where the hovel could be seen, sat a man studying the cliffs and looking for Cornish choughs, which were quite rare. His binoculars tracked along the face nearby without success. There were plenty of gulls and shags, but no red-billed choughs. He adjusted the focus and looked further afield. The lone cottage came into view, his eye drawn to an object of human creation.

Abruptly his attention was caught by the desperate plight of two men at the cliff edge. They were far away, but not so far he could not see the perilous situation. It would take him at least half an hour to reach them; there was nothing he could do but phone 999. He watched, captivated yet horrified as he made the call.

He was still on the phone, trying to give the location when he gasped, 'Oh my God!'

By the time the faint traces of a scream reached him, the situation was over – concluded.

45

JONATHAN'S WORLD

APRIL

'These swans don't give up, do they?' Martin said.

He, Gudrun, Ginny and Jonathan sat at a table by the river watching the birds keeping station next to them with the everlasting hope that food would appear. The table and benches were damp from an earlier shower of rain, leaving the four as the only customers sitting outside at The Gargoyle.

'Anyway, what progress, adventurers?' asked Martin, taking a large gulp of beer.

'I've managed to persuade the executors I've spent my first instalment wisely and am well on the way to setting up a viable business. That means they'll release the rest of the money next week, and we can get to work.'

Ginny was toying with her glass, rolling it around the rim of its base. 'That's wonderful. And work means what exactly? I'm still a bit confused.'

'Travelling to remote parts of the world and researching exciting, adventurous expeditions for people who are prepared to be brave and experience something out of the ordinary, to accept some hardship and go where others have not.'

'Where?'

Jonathan sipped his beer as he prepared to answer Ginny's question. Decisions – there were always decisions to be made. A lifetime ago, as it seemed, he had chosen to leave home and travel. Instead of continuing to exist – not live, merely exist – in a mundane life with a wife he was not suited to, he had experienced danger and overcome it, revelled in wonderful scenery, learned much from foreign cultures and found the person with whom he wanted to spend the rest of his life. Without doubt, he had made the best possible choice. Now – his glance switched from Ginny to Gudrun – another decision had to be made. Should they go back to South America, or take on some place new, say in Africa. Which path would grant them the greatest rewards? Where would life-changing experiences be found? And, where could they make a difference, for that too would bring its own rewards?

Whatever choices they made would open gates to an uncertain future and slam shut doors on other possibilities. No clues as to which was best were obvious at this stage.

'We've a few ideas for South America, but we need to go back and make arrangements with local people and organisations. There's all sorts of things to think about: special insurance, search and rescue options, medical evacuation, local travel, guides, equipment for extreme conditions, good rates for group air travel, accommodation and so on. We've made a list, but I'm sure it will grow with experience. Next on the agenda might be somewhere in Africa – perhaps Mozambique or Namibia. More research is needed.'

'When will this kick off?'

'We're going to Iceland first,' Gudrun said. 'I want my parents to meet Jonathan.'

'Are you going to get married?' Ginny's face lit up with the happy excitement that comes with news of a wedding.

'No.' Gudrun laughed. 'I want my parents to know their daughter has found a wonderful man. Someone they can have confidence in. But also, we will look around the country for the best tours there.

Maybe combine one with Greenland to make it different, because Icelanders have the whole tour thing sewn up already.'

Jonathan regarded his friends. 'You two look like a pair of smileys.'

'If you go and get married without us there will be big trouble,' said Martin.

'I promise you, we won't do that,' Jonathan said. 'I don't know how you can even think it. Marriage is a long way off, anyway. You two will come on every one of our expeditions for free, forever. I'm calling them expeditions rather than tours, because it sounds – and will be – more basic, hard and adventurous than a tour, which has echoes of a bus trip. We're going to call ourselves GJ Expeditions.'

'We are? And you're putting my initial first? Isn't he gallant?' said Gudrun, clambering to her feet and towering over the table. 'Who wants another beer?'

* * *

Before You Go

Thank you for reading ***Scott's Choice***. If you enjoyed the book and have a moment to spare, writing a short review on Amazon, Goodreads or your favourite site would be greatly appreciated. Authors depend on reader opinions in order to produce enjoyable works. Reviews help authors to further their careers.

To find out more about the author and his works please visit: https://www.helifish.co.uk where you have the option to subscribe to his mailing list.

You can also find him on Facebook:
http://www.facebook.com/casole75
and on Twitter: @helifish74

I look forward to hearing from you.

Also by CA Sole:

The Scott Series:

Nature's Justice is the first sequel to *Scott's Choice*. It traces Jonathan's life as he and Gudrun experience a horrific event in Southern Africa. Witnesses to the killing of a rhino and the sighting of the person responsible for the trade in horns, they are chased and hounded over a thousand kilometres from the Kruger Park through South Africa and Botswana to the Victoria Falls.

The Pilot is the second sequel to *Scott's Choice*. Cuff Scott tries to follow a career to become an airline pilot, but his attempts to lead a stable and prosperous life are ruined by events.

At the flying school where he instructs, he becomes aware of someone smuggling illegal immigrants into the country by night. That's not his only problem. His student is being stalked by an increasingly dangerous man, and she thinks it's him.

It seems that trouble seeks him out and brings his

inherent instinct for adventure to the fore. He is forced to question if he's really the persona he's trying to be.

#

A Fitting Revenge is a thriller about extraordinary events that happen to ordinary people.

Your friends are in deep trouble. What if you take a step too far to avenge them?

In England's southern farmlands, Alastair is helping his close friend to avoid a punishing divorce from Sandra. But Sandra is merciless and determined to win in her way.

As Alastair is drawn into a situation which he battles to control, the love binding him and Juliet is ripped apart. With the common goal of rescuing their friend, they strive to work together, but the tension between them only widens the rift as Alastair faces the ruination of his life.

Fighting his way out of the turmoil, Alastair stretches reason to exact a terrible revenge for the extortion and assault that has affected his friends. In doing so, he discovers a side to himself which he never knew existed.

Revenge must be taken, but is Alastair's 'eye for an eye' concept too extreme? Will Juliet remain a love lost?

The Author

CA Sole began writing in 1990 with a thriller titled Zahak's Breath. An agent took it on and, after a few not insignificant changes, submitted it to a publisher. The first rejection dented his ego and left its mark! Colin took the extraordinary and foolish step of giving up his full-time job to write in 1995. His confidence took another hit, and he had to return to work for enough money to buy beer. He persevered, wrote a couple of short stories and about half a novel. That short manuscript has been incorporated into one of the sequels of the Scott series.

Colin's first published novel, *A Fitting Revenge*, came out in 2016 and quickly received 4- and 5-star reviews on Amazon and Goodreads. His second book, CJ, was done through a small publisher and also received a small number of 4- and 5-star reviews. However, Colin's lack of enthusiasm (and plain laziness) over marketing resulted in poor sales. CJ has been rewritten and published in the summer of 2019 as *Scott's Choice*. It has two sequels: *Nature's Justice* and *The Pilot*.

* * *

Having been in the British Army, a professional helicopter pilot and an aviation consultant, his work has taken him all over the world to some 66 countries. He lived and worked in Africa – North, South, East and West – for 43 years before returning to England for good. It's therefore not surprising that the background to Colin's books is travel.

There is far too much of the less trodden world left to see.

To find out more about CA Sole's works and future projects, please visit: https://www.helifish.co.uk